HERODOTUS

THE GNOME OF SOFIA

AGAINST A BACKDROP OF POLITICAL CHANGE IN
SOUTH EASTERN EUROPE, LIES, DISGRUNTLED COMMUNISTS,
COLD WAR WARRIORS, INTRIGUE, DECEPTION & MURDER

PATRICK BRIGHAM

HERODOTUS

THE GNOME OF SOFIA

MEMOIRS
Cirencester

Published by Memoirs

MEMOIRS
PUBLISHING

25 Market Place, Cirencester, Gloucestershire, GL7 2NX
info@memoirsbooks.co.uk www.memoirspublishing.com

HERODOTUS: The Gnome of Sofia

ISBN: 978-1-909544-19-2

'TO MADI'

FOR ALL YOUR PATIENCE

"Oh what a tangled web we weave,
When first we practice to deceive."

Sir Walter Scott, 'Marmion', Canto vi. Stanza 17.

PART ONE

THE BEGINNING 1975–1999

CHAPTER ONE

1996 SOFIA

SIR ARTHUR CUMBERPOT hardly noticed the grey vista of Moskovska Street. If he looked out of his first floor office window at all he knew what to expect. There would be a dreary line of Ladas and Moskovitch; Trabants and Wartburg, puffing out the same acrid blue smoke which had been poisoning the atmosphere of this little Eastern European capital for years.

Sofia in 1996 had hardly improved, despite the alleged political changes. The local newspapers liked to refer to these changes as 'The Silk Revolution,' but this was a sham. The same people still pulled the strings in Bulgaria much as before, and for the most part the wool over Sir Arthur's eyes.

Sir Arthur was far more preoccupied with the routine of embassy life. It was incumbent upon him as the British Ambassador to oil the wheels of diplomacy, something he did with consummate ease, but with little effect. His favourite catchphrase was 'Constructive

Inertia,' since it was clear to him that the British Government's policy towards ex-communist countries was largely infallible, especially if one didn't do anything at all. He was once moved to remark to his wife Lady Annabel, 'Did you know Annabel, if you actually do nothing at all, you can't do anything wrong!'

To this end his appearance as a leading light within the Bulgarian diplomatic community was sensibly reserved for occasional visits to cocktail parties and diplomatic receptions. With Ned Macintosh his Foreign Office advisor at his side—known fondly at the embassy as Dirty Macintosh—he would occasionally make rousing although quite futile speeches, denying his ability to assist almost any needy cause through the famous British Know How Fund. Leaving his audience without a glimmer of hope, it was clear that knowing how and actually doing something were a very long way apart. In order not to seem totally ineffectual he would usually end his address by assuring his audience that Great Britain would support them through thick and through thin and would never let them down.

Gordon Brown had once suggested in a speech in the House of Commons, that most British Embassies could be replaced with a room in a three-star hotel and a laptop for all the good they served! But the Foreign Office had greatly scorned his views on Value for Money in order to pursue a policy of progressively increased spending, especially on embassies abroad. This meant that the ambassador's residence in Sofia had only recently reopened, after a Two Million Pound renovation and facelift.

Sir Arthur mused that it was only right that a Foreign Office mandarin such as himself should end his illustrious diplomatic career in a luxury mansion surrounded by servants. Despite his humble beginnings, Sir Arthur now enjoyed the remnants of a colonial life and its trappings; often taken for granted by aristocrats and plutocrats, that he had so often envied in the past. Regarded as a hardship posting by the Foreign Office, his extra pay was squirreled away each month in its entirety, into the Watlington branch of the Halifax Building Society.

Sir Arthur could still remember the semi-detached house where he was born in the suburbs of London. Croydon was all that he knew then, a place where he too rarely looked out of the window, knowing full well that his suburban street was no more than a predictable line of Morris Minors and the occasional Ford Anglia.

In order to support his doting family his father Norris Cumberpot had willingly surrendered his budding artistic career as a potter, by taking a job at the local Gas Board where he had been the District Manager for a number of years. Any clay pots he made in recent times were either kept in their integral garage, if they were passably good, or—if they were dreadfully misshapen—in the garden shed.

Many of his father's better creations were given as Christmas presents—to friends and relatives—who took out these ashtrays and wobbly nut bowls on the rare occasions that they were visited by the Cumberpots.

This also went for his wife's knitted pullovers and jumpers. Christmas was often festooned by woolly wasp-like people who wore her lovingly knitted creations secretly indoors, and absolutely never in the street for prying eyes to see.

Norris and Myrtle Cumberpot devoted their lives to young Arthur, and in the modest post-war surroundings of suburban Croydon, they had very little choice but to send him to the local grammar school to complete his studies. His sister Pricilla—according to the standards of the time—was groomed and destined for motherhood in the vain hope of her marrying a doctor of medicine, or at the very least an estate agent.

Sir Arthur never talked about his humble beginnings, and remained in denial of all things south of the river Thames—except MI6 that is! These days his talk was about his retirement in Oxfordshire with perhaps a little studio flat in Ebury Street. This was to be close—as he put it—to his relatives, by which statement he tried gamely to elevate himself but to ignore his cousin Ted who had a fish and chip shop in Wandsworth High Street. What was unclear about him was why he was in Sofia in the first place. But whatever diplomatic sin Sir Arthur might have committed in the past would have to remain a mystery for some time to come.

In common with many in the seventies and eighties, Croydon Grammar did not necessarily send its star pupils to a red brick university. Education was free then, and many gifted scholars found themselves walking amongst the dreaming spires of Oxford, or through the hallowed cloisters of Cambridge.

Kicking a football around the back garden of his home, or bouncing the ball off the garden shed—which made his father's pottery rejects rattle on the shelves inside—his future successes remained just a distant hope in the hearts of Myrtle and Norris.

When Arthurs 'A' level results were finally declared, everyone was astonished. Four good A Level passes would take him to Oxford! And he accordingly found himself amongst the elite of English academia and the study of History—Ancient and Modern. Thanks also to his 'O' Level Latin and a battered copy of *The Histories by Herodotus*, he made his way to Beaumont College and three years of bliss. That is except for the one thing that his parents did not predict. The problem was that Arthur's diction rather let him down!

Many young people at the time—or baby boomers as they are now generically referred to—had developed a kind of Essex boy accent rather like Mick Jagger or Terrence Stamp and that was also true of some at Oxford, but it was still the norm for the elitists to have a posh accent if they were to progress into the City of London or the Civil Service, although today this is not as important.

So Arthur started to change his ways and speech, to try to fit more easily into the chattering classes, student clubs and political associations, together with amateur theatrics and the famous alternative comedy.

First he bought a pair of tightly fitting cavalry twill trousers with slanted pockets and turn-ups, which he wore with a Harris Tweed jacket—a silk handkerchief in the top pocket—and suede shoes. This was de rigueur student attire at the time together with a college tie, scarf and student's gown. Astride a battered bicycle, he now believed that he had finally discovered a world in which he could dwell for eternity. But what about his father Norris and mother Myrtle? They of course went from being a part of the solution, to being a part of the problem.

The problem was that no matter how proud they were of young Arthur's achievements he was no longer very proud of them. All his newly acquired friends had big houses and he found himself preferring to visit other people's posh abodes rather than visiting his own loving and doting family in South London. Had he become a snob or was it just an expression of his youthful exuberance? The truth was most likely to include both factors.

Sir Arthur sat behind his reproduction Chippendale partner's desk and gazed rather mournfully at a faux copy of a Constable oil painting hanging on the opposite wall, and in so doing he pressed a button on his internal telephone.

'Edwina, I want you to bring me the petty cash book please; it seems we are spending far too much money on tea and biscuits and I have to write a report to the Foreign Office.'

1975 OXFORD

Having spent his youth with his nose firmly attached to an academic grindstone, university life for Arthur was like the sudden removal of the cork from a champagne bottle. His pimply world suddenly exploded into a fizzing bubbly party, where mutual admiration and academic achievement went hand in hand with his sudden self-awakening. From being a nerdy youth and a sluggish caterpillar, he now saw himself to be a beautifully enlightened young man; a butterfly with all the attendant mores and desires brought about by his recent morphosis. This of course meant girls. But the self-awakening process also introduced the young Arthur to politics, and so as most undergraduates he was inclined to review the political choices on offer.

Being a student his attention was first drawn to Marxism and the Labour Party, whereupon his often duffle coated fellow students would regale him with the fundamental achievements of current socialist realism. Hadn't the slums of Liverpool and Manchester been cleared of infested capitalist hovels from the Industrial Revolution by the building of good solid system-built thirty-story panel flats? Weren't these the brainchild of the Soviet Union, heroically bringing modern living standards to the masses and improving the workers' lot? Wasn't the present Labour party represented by a bunch of pipe smoking losers, peppered with blue rinse bluestockings with wobbly bottoms? What would put the Great back into Britain was a centralized government with five-year economic plans; surely he realized that?

Smoking roll-ups made Arthur cough, and as a matter of fact he was now actually beginning to doubt that a carping and shiny faced socialist hag could ever fulfil his domestic ambitions! Because Arthur—heavily revealing his practical lower middle class aspirations—was beginning to make plans for the future. He was not sure he could care less about the workers, let alone actually becoming one of them, and as to having a relationship with a card-carrying member of the Socialist Workers Party, that was never going to happen. So the sea of idealistic and evangelistic shiny faces and their attendant political doggerel fast became a matter of personal history and gradually faded away altogether.

Because history was what he seemed to be best at and to love the most, he wondered how the gesticulations of a rabid trade unionist could possibly compete with tales of the Peloponnesian War, how the idealistic witterings of Carl Marx could ever compare to the dreamy stories from the Iliad or the historical accounts by his favourite historian Herodotus. The stones of Drama beckoned, and the oracle of all knowledge now seemed destined to be a comfortable middle class one, with no cloth caps or ferrets, and no Jarrow marches either!

Arthur then turned to the more comforting views of the Conservative Party, which by any yardstick seemed far more palatable. No more shouting about and unnecessary threats, just the comfortable ease by which young people—used to enjoying authority—quietly discuss things, and take the reins of power with total confidence and occasional indifference.

This was more his style, and anyway, in the company of these often seemingly bored young people, he enjoyed their complacency and assumptive thinking. He also noticed that the women were much more confident and better presented. Far removed from the passion of the streets, these creatures exuded poise; not just self-assurance through their political views, but also in their view on life as well.

Arthur was still very naïve—despite being the veteran of the occasional hanky-panky in the back of a Morris Minor with a bit of the local Croydon totty—and he had never really met such sophistication in women who were quite unlike his mother Myrtle. She read novels by Neville Shute and watched Victor Sylvester on their monumental TV set, still with a giant magnifying glass attached.

And his father? Well, he was usually to be found in the garage making clay pots with wonky bits, which finally ended up in the garden shed.

Did he enjoy the Dadaist painters, what did he think of Lenny Bruce and what were his views on Nihilism, or was he a Humanist? What did he think about the Cold War? Questions and more questions followed until one day a Latin scholar casually spoke to him in the college bar about his views on Communism. Arthur was quite adamant, stating that if a load of horrible thirty-floor leaky flats in Liverpool had anything to do with it, the Soviet Union could sod off! He never spoke to him again.

After about a year, and during the annual Oxford summer ball, he found himself standing on the lawn next to a very tall and imposing woman, who introduced herself as Annabel. Undoing his white tie and collar stud, he offered her a cigarette from his rather pretentious orange box of DuMaurier, which she smilingly accepted.

The weather was very warm for an English summer and standing there gazing at the river Thames—with the sound of the Edmundo Ross orchestra playing in the background—he looked into her deep blue penetrating eyes with interest. What was she studying?

Although she was very secretive about her life, at the time Annabel Pergamon was deeply engulfed in the Humanities, and held many views about her studies, all of which she relished daily. Was Arthur a postmodernist in his views? What did he think of Wittgenstein's confusion theory, and did he understand Kierkegaard's views on ethics and logic.

All of this and another DuMaurier cigarette led Arthur to see that he was finally and firmly ensconced in academic society and at the centre of world learning. He reasoned that if he were able to bed this rather large but not unattractive female scholar, it would mean the end to all those banal discussions about football which he detested, and the other blokey subjects expected from him on his occasional Friday night visit to the Stoat and Radish public house in Croydon. Because, what has not been mentioned so far, is that Arthur Cumberpot was a total wimp!

At just over 5'2" tall, many people called him Ronnie behind his back because of his likeness to Ronny Corbet the comedian, and the similarities didn't stop there. With his national health horn-rimmed glasses, his grimy teeth, and a tendency to procrastinate, he seemed much older than his years and rather schoolmasterly in bearing.

He also had developed an effete slur in his speech, much against his voice tutor and speech therapists' instructions, because he wrongly believed that it added to his indolent middle class image, all of which was totally fictional.

'Mind your P's and Q's!' Miss. Prendergast would tell him, as she phonetically explored his nasal cavity, for any sign of the Home Counties.

Despite his social pretentions and his physically challenged appearance, once again he was approached in the college bar. This time it was by a tough looking red faced man with a hearty laugh.

'Collingwood's the name,' the man said, pumping Arthur's hand with unreasonable force and considerable strength. 'Have you ever thought about rowing?' To which the perplexed Arthur said, 'No, never,' and left it at that.

'Well we are looking for a cox for our second eight,

and you seem to be the right size and weight for it. Ever been on the river have you?'

Historically Beaumont College was the first college to take to the Thames in boats, although times had changed and sleek Polish manufactured plastic lightweights could be seen daily anywhere on the Thames from Letchlade to the Thames Barrier. And it was also the Beaumont crew who would normally challenge the Cambridge rowers at the annual Boat Race in London.

What Collingwood was offering Arthur was an opportunity to win a Rowing Blue by participating in this very English sport, something he would never have dreamt of achieving in the normal course of events.

At grammar school he was confined to acting as a long jump judge, and his only claim to fame was coming second in the throwing the cricket ball competition, for which there were only three contestants. Now the thought of adding sportsman to his rather thin CV was sufficient for him to agree to test for the position as cox for the second eight.

He was immediately accepted, much to the surprise and amusement of his fellow students, but it also became one more reason to distance himself from his parents and the ladish incumbents of the Stoat and Radish. He couldn't have them turning up on the river bank cheering him on.

In his weekly letter home he mentioned nothing of this event, preferring to moan about the treacle pudding or brussel sprouts served up at table in the historical dining room of Beaumont College. In common with many from similar humble beginnings, he was quick to complain of any minor infringement of culinary skills which did not comply with his mother's exacting standards and the stodgy overcooked food of his most recent past. For reasons which are clearly self-evident, Arthur was also rather inclined to expect perfection in others, despite his rapidly improving self-esteem.

What about Annabel, where did she fit in? Despite their difference in height disposition, and as it turned out her foggy background, they somehow become entwined as their studies progressed. By the end of the second year and out of college digs, they now shared a small but comfortable studio flat on the Headingly Road in Oxford.

Although she occasionally missed the friendly community of Lady Mary Hall and the pretty views over the river Cherwell, she was pleased to be able to have what she perceived to be a normal life. This was something which she had never really known in the past, and to be away from the constant activities and sounds that are the characteristic of college life, also seemed to be a great blessing.

And Arthur was also happy to be away from the cosseting and old ways associated with two years of Beaumont, the personal restrictions and the male-only free-for-all. With blissful weekends and constant companionship they soon became an unusual but devoted couple.

Annabel Pergamon had spent much of her young life away at school, far from her adopted parents' family home at Hambledon. Nevertheless she still had occasional glimpses into her past, a vague and almost legendary early childhood. It seemed her real father—working in either the Foreign Service or as a journalist abroad—had rarely been a proper father to her or any of her siblings. Nor in all likelihood, a proper husband to her strangely distant mother. On the rare occasions they were together he was impossible to talk to, and seemed to have great difficulty in answering even the simplest question; but still, he was her father.

She was barely three years old, and her father—always known to everyone as Jim—spent more and more time abroad, until one day he simply went away forever. She never saw him again. When her mother died and she was effectively made homeless, she was sent by relatives to live with a family friend in Hambledon. The Pergamons' told her that her father was also dead—which wasn't true—and that it would be wise for her to change her family name to theirs. And so the childless couple adopted her.

When she was a little older, Lionel Pergamon explained to her that there had been some talk of her natural father being a Soviet spy. He told her that because there were so many unkind reports of her father's activities, it would have affected her future had she not been given a new identity. From that moment onwards Annabel realized what it was like to be an orphan, with all the subterfuge it involved. When she was entered at 11 years of age into Roedean junior school, she was entered as Annabel Pergamon.

Arthur knew very little about this part of her story; after all, she too had become used to secrets and simply didn't tell him. She told him that her real mother was now living in Argentina, but she didn't know where, and had lost touch with her. This just left her brother John, who she described to Arthur as a carpenter and who now lived in London with his family.

Little more was said about it. When it was absolutely necessary she would tell people that she was the ward of a distant uncle who was a book publisher. Rather conveniently Arthur was also disinclined to discuss his family, but for quite a different reason.

Consequently the days passed, and life seemed very blissful for this strange couple. With particular pride and happiness it would also be the year which Arthur Cumberpot would describe as the best year of his life.

1996 SOFIA

The phone rang. 'Hello, British Ambassador speaking.'

In a split second the supercilious look of self-satisfaction disappeared from his face, to be replaced by one of grovelling supplication.

'Oh! It is you dear; I thought it was Dr Lind the Swedish Ambassador. We are having some important discussions at the moment concerning the Bulgarian import tariffs on cheese. I errrrrr!'

He abruptly stopped in mid-sentence, which was not unusual these days, while the receiver barked out some onerous instructions causing him to hold the receiver about half a metre from his right ear.

'Well, the diplomatic container has not arrived yet dear, but I will have a look in the stores to see if there is a spare jar of Marmite.' The barking continued.

'Yes, of course, and did you say Branston Pickle too? Of course, my dear, right away; I will organize a comprehensive search immediately.'

His unsteady hand quietly replaced the receiver and composing himself, the supercilious look gradually returned to his face and once more he pressed a button on his internal phone.

'Edwina, have you heard any more about our embassy container? Lady Cumberpot is expecting some parcels, and I am told that I also have a special delivery from my father. Oh yes! He is much better now he has retired to the country, it gives him so much more time for his pottery, and he tells me that he is also busy with his sculpture too.'

It was a great problem for him to discuss his family, and an even greater one to keep them away from the embassy. But this was not so when it came to friends in the diplomatic service and his many foreign office colleagues. Annabel very successfully managed to keep them all away, with her bullying personality, her barking voice and her appalling cooking.

'School food is the best food,' she would declare.

'Never did my family any harm. None of that foreign muck for us, thank you very much!'

1978 OXFORD

The Isis is a tributary of the Thames and is the name of the Oxford University boat club. Made up almost entirely by Beaumont rowers, membership was extremely agreeable to the now maturing Arthur and to Annabel on those occasions when ladies were also welcome at the rowing club soirees. These days Annabel and Arthur were becoming as synonymous as cheese and biscuits, although on some occasions it was noted that the couple were becoming more like Brahms and Liszt, as the evenings drinking progressed. Because Arthur could not hold his drink at all and Annabel—who was quite a Tomboy—never touched a drop.

Often during these seminal moments she would become over aggressive by joining in the more boisterous rough and tumble games which the young rowers enjoyed as the evening progressed. From a distance her booming voice was often heard above the rest, her raucous retorts easily identified by her cry: 'You rotter, I will get you for that!'

And so the year progressed, and all these occasions were fondly noted in their shared recollections. Henley and Shiplake, Wargrave, Reading and Putney Regattas, were duly attended with gallons of bubbly being guzzled on the footpath and elsewhere. Striped blazers, boaters and white trousers, were everywhere to be seen littering the beer tents and the champagne and oyster bars along the towpaths.

That year proved to be a very successful year for the rowing team, and Arthur was regarded as a considerable asset, and despite his size and disposition he managed to bark loudly enough at his crew to keep them on stroke and remarkably well motivated.

Annabel's tuition in the 'barking department' was invaluable, as was Miss Prendergast's diction and rounded vowels. In the end Arthur finally got his rowing blue and a medal for participating in the University Boat Race. And Annabel? Well, she became pregnant!

Academically, things were not so glittering for Arthur, due to the many domestic and rowing distractions. The rippling Thames and the rolling bed had to be reconciled somehow, and it was clear that their beautiful sunny view was destined to be distorted by a few dark clouds. Not so much a storm or a tempest but rather more, a damp summer's day!

The reality was rather a poor degree for Arthur, but a surprisingly good First for Annabel, due no doubt to the domestic downtime she experienced whilst Arthur took to the water. It was said that in the absence of his Rowing Blue, his degree might well have been absent altogether.

But none of this mattered if academia was to be bypassed by Arthur, and there were no internships or research opportunities for one with a lower second. There was however an outside chance for Annabel to go on to further her studies and to get an MLitt or even a DPhil. It rather depended on whether she could continue to prevail upon Lionel Pergamon, her somewhat obscure adopting father and silent benefactor.

In fact it was without doubt a very convenient solution for the up and coming Cumberpot family's continued existence. She could continue to pursue her studies at Oxford, whilst Arthur took the civil service examination, which was his only real remaining option.

The long summer rolled on, but by now the willows of the Thames represented a lonely picture for Arthur, with the pressing reality that he now had to make a living to support his newly acquired family. It was also becoming a great dilemma for him as to how he might explain matters to his doting family and their tribe of unfashionable and uncouth friends and relatives.

Arthur was not about to squander three years of social subterfuge any more than Annabel, but for two very different reasons. Although never a word was exchanged on the matter it was clear that both would opt for a quiet wedding without too many contemporaries swooning around them, and with just a few college friends and close family.

The result was a quiet and discrete service at St Giles church on the Woodstock Road. For the young Cumberpots the venue was a particularly cogent one, due in general to their respective interests in art and history, and so the small and select congregation met in

Lady's Chapel to celebrate the wedding of Arthur and Annabel and their yet unborn infant son; soon to be named James Norris Lionel Cumberpot. And so the first chapter of their young lives was concluded in a shower of confetti, but with considerable apprehension.

Myrtle and Norris Cumberpot stood largely ignored on the periphery of the wedding reception, as did the decrepit figure of Lionel Pergamon. He seemed to know Annabel far less well than had been presupposed, and appeared to be someone she treated more like a bank manager than her adopting father. But he was cordial towards the Cumberpot parents, and expressed his support and pleasure in their son's newly found union. He also said that he was in a position to help the young couple, being the trustee of a legacy bestowed on her some years before.

'Was it from her real father?' Norris Cumberpot inquired innocently.

'No no, nothing is from him! Nothing is ever from him, Mr Cumberpot, and we never ever mention him!' Lionel Pergamon was not going to be dragged into any further explanation.

The wedding reception was held at the miniscule White Hart pub in Broadstreet and the wedding party was mostly a student affair. The enigmatic Lionel Pergamon shuffled off towards the crowded bar, returning with two pints of draft St Austell Tribute beer and a Babycham for Myrtle.

'He was a bounder, I'm afraid, and I would rather not talk about him if you don't mind.'

And they didn't mind, because as the celebration pressed on it was time to squeeze around one of the tiny tables in the bar, and a very large plate of fish and chips. Next to them a red faced man called Collingwood seemed to be very friendly.

'Extraordinary chap that Arthur. Never seen a boat before in his life, or even been near the river,' he guffawed, 'Mind you, he kept throwing up a lot in the beginning I seem to remember! Anyway, we have no complaints at all because finally we won the race, and all was well. Jolly good chap that Arthur!'

The Cumberpots senior were increasingly baffled by the constant babbling, the talk of rowing, and the mystery woman who their son had married. After the lunch was over, they made their excuses and returned to their room at the Randolph Hotel. As they left the pub they could hear Annabel's voice booming out:

'They have proper English grub here, you see. None of that foreign muck! That's what we need; good traditional fare, just like we had at school!'

1996 SOFIA

When the diplomatic container finally arrived, there was quite a lot of excitement amongst the embassy staff and the Ambassador seemed greatly interested too. He knew that there were some important items for his wife; including articles of clothing from Harrods and Marks and Spencer, and some riding apparel destined for home from Barkers of Kensington.

The rest generally consisted of the sort of condiments one might associate with the average working man's café. But they were enough to temporarily satisfy Lady Annabel's culinary needs, and would also help to explain her undoubted siege mentality.

According to the Ambassador's wife, little seemed worth buying from the ever multiplying shops in Sofia which were generally described by her as being full of overpriced Turkish rubbish. To Lady Annabel, the British Embassy in Sofia was the bastion of all things western including culture, language and, of course, good plain food.

Sir Arthur wondered what had happened over the intervening years, during the long passage from Oxford to Sofia. What had changed the aspiring MA History of Arts student from those far off days? Where had this overbearing know all come from? When had things started to change?

Struggling through the door to his office his assistant Edwina arrived carrying a bulky parcel. Wrapped up in copious amounts of bubble pack and brown paper, it was firmly secured with duct tape, and attached to it was a sticker saying 'Extremely fragile, open with care.' The parcel was from his father who was now fondly referred to by the embassy staff as the sculptor!

'Phew, that is heavy,' she said, 'I think it is from your father Sir Arthur, he mentioned it to me on the phone the other day. It's very strange though because it comes with some secret instructions from MI6 marked Top Secret! This is most mysterious.'

It was quite a difficult matter to open this very well wrapped parcel and Sir Arthur had to clear his desk, and to find some scissors and a handy Stanley knife in order to do so. When he finally removed the last layers of bubble pack, what lay before him was a hideous garden gnome.

It had a red hat, a blue coat green trousers, and yellow shoes with orange pompoms. It also had an inane and absurd grin, and a very lengthy list of instructions concerning where to put it in the Embassy garden. The missive ended with 'Love from Daddy' and a PS saying: 'Please Follow the Instructions Carefully.'

'I know where I would like to put it,' mumbled Sir Arthur.

Sir Arthur Cumberpot was so appalled at this horrible shiny grinning symbol of suburban naffness, that he immediately called Dirty Macintosh to his office in order for him to explain the connection between his father's ghastly gnome, and Dirty Macintosh's beloved MI6.

'Well,' said Macintosh, 'it seems that this is the newest gadget from GCHQ. It's an advanced communicator and the first of its kind in the world!'

They all stood round the gnome and quietly stared at it in wonder! Why was it so special? This was something they were soon to find out.

CHAPTER TWO

1996 SOFIA

A VERY RED-FACED Sir Arthur presided over the security meeting which he chose to have in the secrets room. This was in the basement of the Embassy, next to the library and opposite the Embassy pub bar.

The bar was home to some of the expats on a Thursday night, and was where they purchased very expensive Newcastle Brown Ale, Smiths crisps, pork scratchings and pickled eggs. One wag who had recently thrown up in the street outside the Embassy remarked, 'Nostalgia is not what it's cracked up to be in Bulgaria, not at this price!'

It was however one of Sir Arthur's more welcoming gestures to the dull and dwindling British community, who often felt isolated and in need of the happy-go-lucky banter of their fellow countrymen and women. Many an affair blossomed between the lonely and often frightened people on assignment from British companies, their presence in Sofia also regarded as a punishment for some past misdeed or perhaps the consequence of a regrettable memory that they hoped to forget. This and the post-Cold War environment made many people develop a shocking siege mentality, especially the embassy staff themselves.

Thursday night was full of half-truths and inventions about success and triumph, or the pioneering trials and tribulations associated with the often baffling Bulgarian character. Fred the tailor from Pleven said, 'They are like a cracked mirror, all back to front and distorted!' Milena his wife seemed to agree with him although heaven knows why?

Meanwhile Sir Arthur was also baffled. How had his father's ghastly gnome suddenly become the object of MI6 scrutiny? Why should the embassy be plagued by this ugly contraption? Ned Macintosh was adamant:

'That's the whole point Sir. You see, it seems our Masters in London believe that it is so vulgar and ostentatious, that nobody in their right mind would consider it suspicious or unusual in any way, just funny!'

'Funny? Funny? I bloody well don't,' snorted the Ambassador. 'I will have to look at it every bloody day, I mean, what will people think?' He didn't mention his friends because the truth was he didn't have any worth mentioning.

When Norris Cumberpot sent his gnome to the Crown Agents to be inspected for inclusion in the diplomatic consignment, a very junior security operative—seeing what it was—phoned up his contact at the foreign office who in turn informed the duty officer. By the time the word had got out, the story had become so exaggerated that it bore no semblance to a garden gnome at all. One might have imagined that it was a creation by Barbara Hepworth or even the great Henry Moore. When finally inspected by a senior member of the security service, they all fell about laughing until one of their number remarked, 'Just imagine that pompous ass Cumberpot's face when he opens this parcel—he will have a fit!'

In the end it was agreed that MI6 should be officially informed, and they immediately took the offending article away for further inspection by their internationally famous Advanced Technical Department.

Back in the secrets room Ambassador Cumberpot's red face said everything as he pompously lifted his nose as if a bad smell had pervaded his cosy world of refinement.

'I'm not having it and that's that.' He banged the table with his fist. 'He is my father and it's my gnome, and I can do what I like with it. So they better watch out in Whitehall because it has got a very pointed hat on, which could do someone a lot of damage.'

Dirty Macintosh, Colin the first Secretary and the embassy security policeman Mick simultaneously coughed and spluttered, trying hard to cover up their sniggers as the details were unfurled.

'You see it now contains some very expensive and

sensitive equipment Ambassador, and some extremely advanced and secret technology. It must be worth thousands of pounds.' Dirty Macintosh waved his written instructions from MI6 in the air, and went on, 'It might have been originally made by your dear father Sir, but it is now the property of the Crown, and less I am mistaken as loyal servants we must do as we are officially directed.'

'Well, what does it do exactly?' Sir Arthur was not very technical and mobile phones had only recently appeared in Sofia. 'And why has it got a socket in its bottom like an electric kettle?'

Macintosh had been extensively trained at GCHQ and knew quite a lot about computers and telephones. He was aware that most people didn't know the half of it. They had no idea that they could be tracked by their phones, and pinpointed at any address in their area. Westinghouse had exploited this weakness and sold many tracking units to various government agencies and for considerable amounts of money too.

Information could also be transferred and received as well as phone calls. What made this colourful gnome unique was that these messages could now be encrypted if need be, for or by any clandestine operatives. It all seemed a bit of a doddle and terribly hush-hush. But, was it?

'You see Sir, if we put this gnome by the front gate of the embassy as they have suggested, our secret operatives can transfer their intelligence reports to us, without having to leave them at secret drops or dead letter boxes. It is a marvellous invention, and this garden gnome can do all this. Afterwards we can disseminate the incoming information and nobody will be any the wiser!'

At last Dirty had finally got a proper job of work to do other than to follow the ambassador around all day plugging up his gaffs.

'And we can also give these clandestine operators their instructions too, by using the same advanced technology, meaning no more direct contact with any of them.'

'What secrets?' The ambassador's red face now looked extremely perplexed.

'There aren't any, you said so yourself. All that bullshit you and your office staff read each morning in the newspapers—I mean, who believes any of it? It's all pure tosh, and probably left up to the reporters to invent each morning before they go down the pub!'

'Well ambassador, we British have got our information gathering down to a fine art unlike the Americans who haven't got a clue. Their entire spying network seems to be about spying on each other most of the time!'

In order to justify his salary Ned Macintosh had been warned by his masters in London, that it was important for him to look as though he was doing a specific project, due to certain forthcoming budget cuts in the security service.

'So how does it all work, Macintosh? Do we have to keep this monstrous garden ornament plugged in all the time? Surely people will notice that it has got something stuck up its bottom?'

Dirty was becoming exasperated with the ambassador and his boorish behaviour. As he stared at the vacuous face before him, he could now see the resemblance to the gnome in question. Perhaps his face was a little ruddier, but there was no doubt that his supercilious look had been accurately recorded by his father.

'Herodotus, as it is now known by MI6, has got a light cell in his head, so we only have to plug it in to charge it up in the beginning—for ten hours or so— rather like a mobile phone.'

The ambassador's eyes rolled in wonder as he tried to imbibe this highly technical information. Perhaps MI6 was right after all. Perhaps this could be the breakthrough they had all hoped for, now Bulgaria was on its way to join NATO and the EU, because it was imperative that Britain be kept up to date on all the possible threats to UK national security. Maybe things were looking up for him as well, and possibly his father's garden gnome could be the answer?

1979 LEWKNOR

His first days at the Foreign Office were to say the least hard work. Finding their first proper family home turned out to be a far more difficult proposition than he imagined, now that young James was a part of their daily routine. Children in rented property were not always welcome.

It was the weekday schedule that was the challenge. Not the weekend family routine which he rather enjoyed, especially on lazy Sundays by the river in Oxford, or more recently sitting in the garden of the Leathern Bottle. The little pub was just a few minutes away from the small but comfortable cottage where they presently lived in the nearby Oxfordshire hamlet of Lewknor.

Each weekday morning Arthur would diligently catch the bus to Oxford from the village and from there by train to London. Along with fellow commuters from the local area he was delighted to be a part of an army of sartorial lookalikes. Sporting the famous city of London uniform—a battered briefcase, the inevitable umbrella, and the ubiquitous bowler hat—he would stride off to the bus stop with a look of considerable pride. It was an image which told of his burgeoning status and the growing self-belief that he finally belonged in Middle England.

To Arthur it was also a highly visual announcement, especially to the workers he now so heartily despised, that he had finally attained his longed for middle class status in life. His father's baggy raincoat and floppy fedora hat had so often in the past made him look like a refugee from a Moscow Mayday parade, and time and again caused Arthur considerable embarrassment when they met.

Now dressed in his pencil thin pinstriped trousers, roomy jacket and waistcoat complete with grandfather Cumberpot's gold watch and chain, silk pocket handkerchief striped shirt and his adored university tie, Arthur believed that he at last looked the part!

He wore this never varying uniform each weekday morning with increased satisfaction as he progressed past his six month probationary period, finally becoming fully employed in his new permanent position as a clerk in the planning department of the Foreign and Commonwealth Office.

Annabel was a very strict mother whose only understanding of children was to closely subscribe to certain Victorian principals. This meant that a so-called nanny was employed to attend to the more gruesome daily aspects of child minding, while Annabel made the half hour journey to Oxford by car, to pursue her on-going studies.

Due to his very normal and loving childhood, Arthur found it hard to follow the somewhat stern views held by his wife on bringing up James. But he gamely followed the routine which his wife proclaimed a perfectly normal upbringing. This included children being seen but not heard, and to know their place within the somewhat pocket-sized Cumberpot hierarchy. But there were some obvious shortcomings to this rigidly domestic regime and the daily rules which she had imposed upon them all, because Arthur was only allowed to have a full English breakfast on Sunday!

Up at 6 o'clock on weekday mornings with a quick cup of tea, there was only time for Arthur to grab a slice of Marmite toast before he had to walk rapidly down to the bus stop, in time to hear the sound of the struggling Leyland diesel as it drove around the corner and into the village. Hot from the nearby little town of Watlington, timing was crucial in order for him to catch this bus which took him to Oxford train station, closely followed by the 7.20 morning train to Paddington.

His arrival at the station usually left him fifteen minutes or so to buy his daily copy of *The Times* from Smiths, the station newsagent, and a wrapped sandwich from the station buffet for his lunch. As he ran for the train he would stuff these items into his practically empty briefcase, containing a copy of the *London A to Z*, a Swiss army penknife, and the occasional apple which he brought from home. This was generally a matter of luck, because Annabel regarded food shopping to be a rather tedious if not insignificant task in her often self-indulgent daily itinerary.

James was now an innocent accomplice to the daily mincing of yesterday's leftover vegetables, care of a rather large Moleneaux food grinder. On her arrival at 9.30 sharp Doris from next door, who was now rather grandly referred to as the Nanny, would pulverize the glutinous ingredients and when James had been washed and bottle fed, she would spoon this oddly coloured concoction into his grinning face.

Up until then Annabel, who was reluctantly in charge of James' administration and unlikely to respond to his cries, would look sternly at the kitchen clock whilst she waited impatiently for the reassuring sound of Doris's knock on the kitchen door.

This would be followed by a series of barking orders, and although in return she would leave a remarkable and beautiful silence inside the cottage, Annabel would then leave in a flurry of unnecessary fuss, flounce out of the house and climb into the somewhat unreliable green Volkswagen beetle which was parked outside.

If it started at all, more often than not it would do so with an ominous puff of black exhaust smoke. With the engine screaming and the rear wheels spinning the postgraduate student would then drive like a bat out of hell to her continued studies in Oxford.

Much of these early days were partly subsidized by the genial and enigmatic figure of Lionel Pergamon. He had visited them only once before, which was just after the lease had been signed with the Hill Farm estate. Farmer Arbuthnot Grimmer had little further use for the flint stone cottage having replaced most of his workers with enormous tractors and combine harvesters.

At the time farmers believed that their future lay in heavy plant and machinery, and great glossy photos of big red and yellow leviathans filled the pages of the *Farmers Weekly*, virtually announcing the end to manual workers. It was the beginning of the gentrification of rural England, the death of traditional village culture;

all too soon to be replaced by commuters and invasion by rich Londoners.

The Rev Nicholson tried gamely to keep the dwindling church community together and despite the changes, St Margaret's remained a thriving church and was attended by the Cumberpots some Sundays. Although both Arthur and Annabel were by virtue of their Oxford studies self-declared agnostics, it did not mean that they had discarded their Christian values. Annabel's school imposed compulsory church services on its pupils, which were held twice a day and three times on Sunday.

Arthur, on the other hand, had only experienced the muddled multicultural Grammar School version of religion, and although obliged to attend a weekly religious instruction lesson, it was generally watered down and pitted with apologies to Massoud, and Shar, Ikbal, and Randhawa Sing. Croydon's virtue was that it did not exist in isolation from the realities of a cosmopolitan society.

But Lewknor did, and so did Watlington. The inhabitants of Watlington were up in arms one day when an Indian family took over the Coop supermarket and turned it into a seven-eleven. Although it raised considerable local resentment the shop prospered, selling vast amounts food and alcohol to the winging locals. Recently they had become very popular in the town due to their Super Saver and pensioners discount schemes, which were a great success.

During that summer, the Cumberpots having sunk into a cosy domestic routine, Annabel's brother John came to stay.

1996 SOFIA

'Well, if we put Herodotus by the Embassy gate, will there be any blinking lights which people can see? We don't want it to look like a bloody Christmas tree, do we? That would be a bit of a giveaway!' Sir Arthur was quietly mellowing to the thought of this electronic spymaster. 'I mean, how much maintenance would this creature need? What happens if he conks out?' In his own mind he continued to see the ghastly gnome as a sort of glorified electric kettle. 'You can't keep wheeling him in and out of the front door, it will look too suspicious!'

'I am sure that our Mr Beamish can more easily explain things to you Sir. As you know he joined us last week as a local employee, and because he is due to become the Embassy IT expert it will be his job to download all the crucial information we receive and to analyse the results.'

By now Dirty Macintosh was beginning to think of this new project with some comfort, in the knowledge that as the Embassy spook he would now take all the credit for any forthcoming success Herodotus might bring, but also that he now had someone else to blame if things went wrong.

'Beamish is a very skilled technician sir, but at the moment he is not cleared for this new intelligence project. You see Sir, the whole project is presently based on a need to know basis, and he doesn't need to know yet, does he? Do you see?'

He didn't see, but then he rarely did in such matters, because the intelligence jargon was all gobblegook to him and technically he was totally flawed. He had a drawer full of digital watches at home in England which he couldn't work, that's why he still used his Grandfather's Tissot pocket watch. Anyway, it fitted his personality more than a silly electronic wristwatch and gave him something to fiddle with when he was thinking. What was wrong with that?

He knew he might be a bit cack-handed when it came to technical matters and hadn't got a clue about electronic intelligence, but neither had a lot of people. In his opinion the expression 'intelligence officer' was generally misused and often appeared to be a contradiction in terms.

Herodotus was finally plugged in, and the following day Ambassador Cumberpot inspected his father's grinning gnome for any tell-tale giveaways. He seemed just a bit hot that was all, but with a rubber grummet inserted in his electronic bottom he looked to all intents and purposes like a standard garden gnome who aimlessly stared at people. The following day ten special Benefon telephones turned up in the Diplomatic Pouch all of which were destined for Dirty Macintosh's office.

They in turn were charged up, and so the trials began.

1980 LEWKNOR

John Kilbey was a hard drinking and a somewhat enigmatic man, given to grand statements, but showing little or no ambition. As a student at Hornsey Art School he had studied painting and sculpture, but without any great enthusiasm or success. In those days like most students he was very left-wing but he had absolutely no interest in Communism, which he saw as a socialist contortion. When he finally turned up on the doorstep of the little flint and wattle cottage in Lewknor, he was just an amiable jobbing builder and cabinetmaker.

'Anything you want fixing while I am here Annie, just ask! My tools are in the van.'

Annabel and Arthur where quite incapable of doing most practical things themselves, which included cooking and even mowing the lawn. And so they either put-up with it, ignored the problem, or got some alleged expert from the public bar of the Leathern Bottle pub to come round if anything important needed to be done. This normally resulted in an empty drinks cabinet whilst the heady matter of building maintenance was discussed at length. Sometimes claiming a hangover or even terminal amnesia, it was generally the case that the enlisted help failed to appear at the appointed time.

John's offer to help cheered up to the bumbling

Cumberpots, but also brought a sigh of relief from the hapless couple. John was keen to know more about their young son.

'What about young James? Are you going to Christen him? It might help you to get more involved in the local community if that's what you want to do.' John Kilbey was clearly fond of his small nephew.

Glancing through the window at the frosty garden he found it very reassuring to be seated next to the glowing embers of the kitchen stove. The door of the elderly Rayburn cooker was open exposing the red hot anthracite, recently supplemented by a small but spitting apple tree log. On the hob the kettle was spluttering and ready for tea.

'If you do, I would be very happy to be his Godfather, despite everything which has happened in the past. You could say that I was just a family friend!'

Once again Arthur was perplexed. What was the secret they shared? Was it Annabel's permanently demonized father, the eternal skeleton in the cupboard? Nothing had been mentioned since that unforgettable Summer Ball at Oxford.

'You will need some more bookshelves too. I notice your books are piled up on the staircase. I can do that for you tomorrow. There is a hardware store I know in Bourne End, and I can pick up the stuff we need tomorrow morning. You had better decide today where you actually want them, so I can measure up.'

The weekend passed, the cold dry snow filling the

country roads which by Monday had become impassable. John said, 'I suppose I will have to stay a little longer if you don't mind? Arthur will be all right because the trains and busses are still running, but the A40 motorway will be a nightmare!'

As if by a miracle during that weekend all the books and the unkempt bundles of notebooks and files were neatly stacked on bookshelves in the cottage entrance and along a part of the little hallway. Early on Tuesday morning the overnight thaw having cleared the A40 John took to the road in his builder's van and drove back to London and to his workshop in Kings Cross. That evening Annabel said to Arthur, 'I had to change my family name because otherwise it would have cast a very long shadow over all our lives. Why should I be blamed for my father's crimes? All his children were innocent!'

1997 SOFIA

It was some months on, and the Embassy trials had reached a point where the future arrangements needed to be discussed. Back in the secrets room the Ambassador and Macintosh were now joined by Beamish, the new IT expert who had been recruited locally and who was now cleared by security. He had a pixiesque face which beguiled his true demeanour, because as an ex-Royal Navy weapons expert he was well versed in the technology of telephones and communication equipment.

'Well Beamish, if you would kindly explain to us all how this system works, and without too much techno-babble please, so that at least the most basic information can get through to us. Keep it simple as possible, and we can then all go home for lunch early!' Sir Arthur instantly realized the folly of his last statement and the gruesome food awaiting him.

'Well Sir, what we must first realize is that your local mobile service in Sofia is an NMT system which means that radio communication presently travels great distances from a base station, depending on how strong the radio signal is and if there are any obstructions.' Ron Beamish had given this talk on numerous occasions.

He went on: 'It is actually quite a primitive system by today's standards where the most popular mobile system is in fact a cellular one. Cellular signals can only travel short distances, and are thus transported from cell to cell, if you are on the move, and as you travel through different base station areas. Most people either don't care or don't know how these two systems differ. This brings me onto the matter of radio frequencies, because each mobile telephone company operates on a specific radio frequency, which limits any intrusion by outsiders except if you are a genuine user.'

Beamish was proud of his immense knowledge on the subject, which caused him to look pleased with himself, although his captive audience did look a bit sleepy.

'Herodotus, as we now know him, operates on a wi-max system and functions like a mini-cellular base station complete with his own very high frequency waveband. He is the transmitter and a receiver of packets of information, as we call them, be they speech or data. Incidentally he does not care what it is because we still have to decode it in-house or send out coded messages through him.'

Beamish's eyes swivelled around the room, his pixy face full of expectation, whilst the Ambassador's eyes clouded over as he gamely tried to absorb the information while simultaneously thinking of the ghastly lunch awaiting him.

'I see, Beamish, that was very clearly put. I am sure we are most grateful to you for this detailed explanation.'

Sir Arthur realized he was now lying through his teeth by saying that, but he didn't want to appear to be a complete nincompoop. Grasping for his next question, his eyes oscillated across the ceiling, as though in deep thought whilst searching for the right words.

'And the rubber plug-thingy stays firmly stuck in Herodotus' bottom whilst all this is taking place, I presume?' The look of merriment clearly showed in Beamish's pink pixy face, or was it a look of total incomprehension? Beamish continued:

'The ten telephones we now have recently acquired have been cleverly adjusted in order to look exactly like the current Benefon model, and largely operate in the same way as normal telephones, but with these phones the text message section is transmitted on a different frequency than the mobile phone itself; can only be received by Herodotus by no other base station, and absolutely nowhere else.'

In common with the technically floored, most of the important questions remained unasked by Sir Arthur, and consequently remained unanswered. Dirty Macintosh and Ron Beamish would have to take responsibility for the details, a matter now very clear to them both.

The Embassy spook smiled at his boss rather condescendingly. 'Leave it to us Ambassador,' he said, 'that's what we are here for!'

The meeting finally came to a close and they all got up to leave. It was strange how the objectionable smell that had so recently lurked beneath the Ambassador's nose seemed somehow to have been replaced by that of summer roses. The supercilious look once more returned to his face, and he began to relax.

'Well, that's good, I am glad we cleared all that up,' he said as he reluctantly tottered off to his wife's school food and her usual barrage of probing questions.

After the three had left, Mick the Embassy policeman carefully inspected the room and then locked the entrance door. His next job was to inspect the stock in the little bar opposite to see if any Newcastle Brown Ale was missing, and to count the pickled eggs. At home in England, when questioned about what he did, he would proudly announce that he was a diplomat.

'Not exactly the Ambassador of course, but something very close!'

CHAPTER THREE

1998 LONDON

THE BULGARIAN AIRWAYS Tupolev 154 took off from Heathrow airport accompanied by the smell of kerosene. A few of the regular passengers on the flight understood that the No Smoking sign really meant business. The sign telling passengers to keep their seatbelts on added even further weight to the previous instruction. The suspicions surrounding this aging Russian airplane were legion, and the true statistics well hidden by the authorities. So although it was not considered the safest means of transport, it none the less was Bulgarian, free to most and represented a grim but thoroughly authentic homecoming.

In the first class area at the front of the plane and notable by the fact that it had more cigarette burns on the upholstery and matted carpets than the economy class, it was where returning diplomats and journalists sat imbibing their free half bottles of Stolichnaya vodka. Surrounded by clouds of acrid cigarette smoke from their Kent cigarettes if they were spies, and Victory cigarettes if they were not, their Balkan humour was pitted with black irony and a general disbelief in the prevailing political system they so cheerfully represented at their London embassy.

Most were wise enough to keep their mouths shut when there were strangers around, and to only ridicule the virtues of their ex-Communist paradise, when there were not. Between each other the truth was very clear. In Sofia they were regarded as class heroes whilst in London they were just poor East Europeans.

Philip Filipov was on his way home in disgrace. He had been the Charge de Affair of the Kensington embassy for only a short while. That is until the foolish Colonel Katrandjiev had stolen a military flying helmet from the Royal Air Force stand at Farnborough Air Show. Posing as a journalist, he was still being interrogated by the British police. The silly man didn't have a diplomatic passport and had therefore been branded a common thief, although the helmet had long since travelled to Sofia in the diplomatic pouch.

Filipov was forced to make a humiliating apology on the steps of the London embassy, and to inform the gathering reporters that Bulgaria was more than just a bandit nation in Eastern Europe, and that it had much more to offer the world than thieves and assassins.

The murder of Georgi Markov in 1978 on London Bridge had been exaggerated to the point where if you counted the number of people claiming to have been standing next to him when the lethal pellet had been shot into his leg by his killer's specially adapted umbrella, there would have had to be a hundred busses parked nearby to accommodate the hordes of willing witnesses. But there was only one bus and no real witnesses.

Sitting in a row of seats on his own, Filipov leaned back against the Topulevs window, and lifting the arm rests of the adjoining seats he managed to put his feet up and shut his eyes. 'Give a dog a bad name,' he thought!

As a staunch advocate of the old regime he had spent his life slowly and carefully climbing up the ladder of the communist party hierarchy finally achieving his position in London. What annoyed him intensely was how his unblemished record could be besmirched by a bandit like Katrandjiev, that it had all happened on one day, and turned his life upside-down!

Filipov's country was falling apart at the seams because there was no true leadership any more. And judging by his nearby loud-mouthed compatriots and their ceaseless bragging and drunkenness, it was probably time to abandon the scum which now inhabited the Sobranie Parliament and their various acolytes. But what was there left for him?

Little remained of the old order, and the structures had been broken down once more into Byzantine cronyism and nepotism. Why had all the good things been squandered, and where had all these gangsters appeared from, who now called themselves businessmen?

Michael Gorbachev had a lot to answer for, and Todor Zhivkov the old communist leader was right. Russia had let them down and opened the door to opportunists and criminals, so much so that it was difficult to see the difference between the present members of parliament and the gangsters who surrounded them!

In his way Filipov was an elitist from The Good Old Days, as it was fondly referred to by the old guard when they were enjoying a few Rakia's at the Podly Pitta restaurant by the forest in Borova Gora. There they drank in the Russian way, making toasts to their heroes and finally to The Russian Officers.

He was an old-fashioned conservative in the communist sense and brought up to believe in duty and service to the Party and his country. How similar he had felt to the British Foreign Office officials when he met them during his embassy tasks. Privately he believed that they had far more in common than his masters realized, despite the prevailing agenda and the political changes. The problem was Bulgaria! Even the current Prime Minister Kolev had laughed at his own country in the press.

'Bulgaria is the nearest thing I know to Alice in Wonderland,' he announced one day on TV, appearing to enjoy the confusion and the deceit that surrounded him!

But what did that make him, the Mad Hatter? Or was he the Jack of Hearts, siphoning off pre-accession money from the EU which he claimed Bulgaria needed in order to join? Now, what other choices were there? Nobody had any new ideas, even the White Rabbit, whoever he was!

At the airport in Sofia, Philip Filipov bypassed customs and immigration officials, and walked down through the special tunnel under the airport building and up the stairs to the entrance. Climbing into a Lada motorcar which had been sent by a friend from the Bulgarian National Television, he was driven home to his third-floor apartment in an area called Bekston. Just past the Russian Monument and along the Greek road three tall blocks had been especially constructed for reliable party members in the 1980's.

Nowadays the surroundings were unkempt and there was litter all about, thrown out of the windows by people who no longer cared. But the apartments were big and considered very exclusive at a time when you were rewarded for your loyalty and hard work for the Party, and often by the old dictator himself.

Zhivkov was now a footnote in history and had been thoroughly demonized, although living in comparative luxury in his daughter's house in Boyana and allegedly under house arrest. The old people liked Zhivkov, especially those who lived in the country districts to whom he felt close, and they to him. They liked his jokes and anecdotes, his bottle thick glasses and his diminutive stature. He often said that only short people ran the world, quoting Mitterrand and Brezhnev, Jimmy Carter and Yasser Arafat, and finally Margaret Thatcher.

The people said that when he smiled his face would open up like a beautiful flower. And his shrewd observations were still coveted, and many people visited him in secret or at night to ask him his advice. The government claimed that he was under house arrest but his jailers looked more like servants. Perhaps all that he wanted was to be left alone?

Filipov's homecoming was uneventful and silent. Kzenia his wife was still at work; she was a half professor at the Institute of Foreign Literature in Doctors Gardens. But the apartment was warm and very clean. In the old days the Gypsies had their place in Bulgarian society, and they still worked hard if you paid them properly. The water heating was centralized and was pumped to the block from a nearby power station. Philip Filipov decided to have a long restful soak in his commodious bathtub to cleanse himself of the grime of politics.

Home once more to a depleted but affordable socialist paradise, the best part for him was to return with plenty of cash in his pocket. This he inevitably did, but as a career spy he occasionally came home with some very valuable and interesting secrets.

1978 LEWKNOR

What Annabel had also neglected to tell Arthur was that before she met him at Oxford she'd had an affair with a fellow student who was studying Politics and Geography. Robin Caruthers was in his third year at Jesus College and seemed very glamorous to her in his hand stitched suits and tailored shirts. She also adored being seen with him speeding around the city in his bright red MG TC Midget.

With the soft top down and sporting a rather raffish white golfing cap, from the onset he seemed very masculine and confident. With a rakish bow tie and a Captain Peterson pipe, it made him seem even more attractive to this ex-Roedean and post-modernist scholar. Parking in unobtrusive places he knew by the Thames, the MG's bench seat proved to be very comfortable and ideally proportioned for Annabel to experience some early experiments with sex.

Fun was also called the Lansdowne Lounge Lizards Jazz Band in which Robin played the trumpet. It don't mean a thing if you ain't got that swing; Robin Caruthers sweating in his striped grandpa shirt, a suede brogue shoe perched resolutely on an empty beer crate, would blow great swathes of notes which the adoring Annabel could only regard as love letters from the angels.

Punting on the Thames at Letchlade, hidden from the sun by a weeping willow tree, they would lie in complete silence listening to the occasional screech of a Moorhen and the splash of a rising Pike or Perch. Two bottles of light Chardonnay cooling in a string bag dangling in the river; it was the taste of freedom which was the most delicious.

As dusk descended Robin would sit in the back of the punt sucking on his pipe, the burning Gold Block tobacco making a small red circular light in the darkness of the river. To Annabel this was the greatest moment of her young life. To be in love and to be loved, away from the stultifying dark and cold house of her fictitious father

Lionel Pergamon, the man who had created the enigma and the tissue of lies that protected her from her past.

Suddenly it seemed the right time to tell Robin about her family secret. One night parked outside Lady Mary College she blurted out the truth about her father only to be met with a stony silence. A minute later Robin Caruthers leaned across her and opened the passenger door.

'Get out please,' he said, and moments later as she stood shaking by the side of the car he shouted, 'I never want to set eyes on you ever again, you communist bitch! Go to hell and take your disgusting communist family with you.'

Then all that was left of their glorious three-month relationship was the revving of the engine, the grinding of gears and the disappearing red tail lights. Whatever happened to Robin Caruthers she would never know— or would she?

1980 LONDON

What impressed Arthur was how much he had in common with his fellow clerks, some of whom he had known at Oxford. The rest were Cambridge graduates, and somewhat superior at times when the matter of degrees and the level of passes were discussed. There was clearly an embryonic cult of intellectual snobbery manifesting itself amongst his fellow government scribes who were beginning to realize that hubris was part and parcel of their chosen career.

However, they still took it in turns to operate the aging photo-copying machine and to file important papers. At the cutting edge of government service Arthur occasionally made the tea, and diligently distributed the daily ration of McVities digestive or ginger-nut biscuits to his fellow empire builders.

Despite Miss Prendergast's nasal investigations, it was clear that Arthur also needed to further tidy up his diction. He was therefore immensely relieved when his Principal enrolled him at a training school near Victoria station where he was told he would learn to conduct interviews and make statements to the press. Public speaking was a very important attribute for the upwardly mobile Foreign Office official, who was politely encouraged to 'speak proper,' as his elderly principal cogently referred to it! And that was how Arthur developed his plummy accent.

'You must learn to speak through your nose, Arthur.' Miss. Dorithea Throdlington was adamant.

Tired of silly girls walking around with a book on their head, she no longer preened and prodded the ungainly daughters of successful entrepreneurs. Coming out was a thing of the past, the world had changed and she was now fully engaged in the gentrification of government employees and certain dim-witted politicians, all of whom generally had far too much to say for themselves.

At the Colebrook Studio where she worked, she was fondly known as *The Queen of all the Windbags*, although her official title was Chief Government PR Interlocutor, a title which served to underline the importance of her position. Generally seen wearing an alluring gold lame dress, her scent was a subtle combination of Chanel Number 5 and Booths London Dry Gin. Nevertheless she was regarded as one of the more attractive members of staff, although she did totter about on her high heels from time to time.

On the other hand Annabel's diction was perfect, having been honed on the verbal last of Roedean. However as she had aged, it wasn't so much her pronunciation which had changed as her method of delivery. Gone were the throaty purrs of early romantic girlhood, now replaced by a fair reproduction of Lady Bracknell, played by a slightly deaf Dame Edith Evans.

Would he now have to learn to tremble under her arrogant and noisy domination? Or had Arthur become impervious to her gradual change of character? Because there was no doubt that he seemed to enjoy it well enough, and being told what to do at home was perfectly acceptable as far as he was concerned.

What Lionel Pergamon thought was rather a different matter entirely. In the past he had known Annabel's father James, and could see many of his undesirable characteristics seeping into her inherited psyche. Was it the penetrating blue eyes, he wondered, the frightening self-assurance, or was she a woman of character settling into early middle age?

'*Well, for a start she hasn't got anything much to be*

devious about,' he thought, *'perhaps she is just a bit horsey, and that's all?'*

To the enigmatic but bookish Lionel Pergamon horses and sports were a total anathema. He hated to be asked about sport for which he had no interest. During all those years as Annabel's guardian, he had been oh so reluctantly introduced to Gymkhanas, Polo matches at the Hurlingham Club or Windsor Great Park, and the inevitable school hockey days. There was no one else to cheer her on now that her mother and father were officially declared dead, and he and his wife Susan would stand and shout approval along with the rest, not even knowing why half the time!

Pergamon now regarded himself as a kind of minder, sent to watch out for her and to wait for any signs of change or indeed any unwanted contact from abroad. He had been a part of that world himself for many years. But due to a bad car accident in East Germany in the 50's and many months spent in hospital, he was content to be regarded as an accommodating and patriotic retired publisher, looking after his adopted daughter. Now there were no more secrets, and the child of the traitor had finally come to know who she was and what her father had been.

John would later willingly attend his father's funeral in Moscow. He had been dubbed a Soviet Hero when he finally died in 1988 at the age of 78. But rather like his contemporaries, Lionel Pergamon could but reflect that, despite everything which had happened, he was still *'one of us.'*

James Kilbey used to say, 'To be a true patriot, first you have to belong!' Well he belonged to them and had paid the price, but so had his children.

1984 LEWKNOR

One morning Arthur was practicing his diphthongs in the bathroom. It was a place where he was able to carefully inspect his facial contortions as he mouthed his way through Miss Throdlington's phonetic exercises. He no longer lived in a house but a *'hice'* which was now situated in its own *'grinds'* and not in its grounds. He also tended to go *'rind'* the corner to the Leathern Bottle, from time to time for a beer and a chat. But not that often, since Annabel had started to perceive him as a kind of extracurricular skivvy, with or without any phonetically inspired alterations and amendments, because to her it was all irrelevant.

'When you were in Victoria Arthur, did you go to Gorringes to buy some of their marmalade?' Arthur's heart dropped as his omission was exposed.

'No dear,' he spluttered, 'I'm afraid it slipped my mind; you know, important Government work!'

'You mean sharpening the bloody pencils, don't you?' Annabel's contempt for his present employment was deepening.

'You have been there for five years now, and you are still buggering about! When are they going to promote you and send us off somewhere a little more interesting?

I'm sick of bloody Lewknor. There must be an embassy somewhere that needs a dogsbody or fourth Secretary, whatever they call it; somewhere with a bit of sunshine!'

'The review board meets next month, Annabel. They have to assess my work to date, and then make some recommendations to the Principal. There might be an opening in Helsinki; it all depends on who moves on or retires.' He did not sound over convincing or very sure of himself.

'Very often people are moved because they are getting a divorce, or if they have done something wrong. They call it a sin. Their idea of punishment is to send you somewhere horrible!'

'Well, Helsinki sounds pretty horrible to me, and bloody cold too. Aren't there any openings in Bermuda or the Seychelles?'

Annabel Cumberpot was becoming increasingly impatient with her husband who she believed to be indolent and complacent. He was always short of money, and trying to survive on his miserable civil service salary was becoming increasingly difficult. She did however receive a monthly payment from Lionel Pergamon which she regarded exclusively for her own use rather than for any household bills.

Arthur; who was ever courteous to his wife, omitted to remind her that since she had finally received her Master's Degree from Oxford, that she too was available for work as a teacher or even a research assistant. However the thought of work had never crossed her mind, believing strongly that as James' mother she could remain a lady of leisure for as long as she wanted.

Recently her main complaint stemmed from the fact that she needed a new challenge to occupy her mind, because after three weeks of being housebound with her son James and Doris from next door, she was slowly going round the twist. Increasingly bored and frustrated with the trivial observations and banal conversations to be had in the village, it seemed to be entirely populated by domestic harridans and halfwits. She had not spent six years of her life studying to waste it all on discussions about the price of fish fingers, or what happened in last night's edition of Coronation Street.

Although she found it hard to actually define her relationship with Arthur or her emotional connection with James, she claimed in her own thoughts to be loyal dutiful and completely devoted to her marriage. But it was the connection which bothered her, because no matter what, she found it very hard not to put her own interests first. This was why she was now prepared to consider anything to escape from the repetition and predictability which described the boredom of her recent three-week existence.

Consequently, after years of continued academic life her mind now turned back to her girlhood obsession with horse riding. With the help of the local Yellow Pages and farmer Grimmer's helpful wife, one day she found herself driving to the town of Wallingford and the Highclear Riding Stables.

1997 SOFIA

Lurking just behind the wrought iron gates of the British Embassy in Sofia, Herodotus the Garden Gnome greeted every passer-by with a supercilious grin. Peeking around one of the pillars he could well have been carrying out an undercover surveillance of the local area. It was not a casual observation however, because Herodotus was not only a highly technical state of the art electronic spymaster, but the most complex operative employed by the British secret service. From now on he would be considered the Jewel in the Crown of MI6.

CHAPTER FOUR

1998 SOFIA

DIRTY MACINTOSH sat in his little office staring at a recently acquired bronze sculpture by Stavri Kalinov. It comprised a figure not dissimilar to a Henry Moore knob head, which appeared to be gazing into a number of staggered fanned coffin lids, which bing-bonged together when someone went past in a hurry, although he strongly suspected that they were not supposed to. If you really got them wobbling they sounded like clanging church bells. But for the princely sum of $3,000, it had recently occupied a lot of his attention.

The Bulgarian Orthodox Church was also of interest to him, if only because of the tragic neglect of some of the older churches, many of which could be found hidden on hilltops or in a derelict village. One spectacular example could be seen on a steep road leading to the Vitosha Mountain, which he would visit with his wife Janice.

His favourite place, however, was a little monastery

dedicated to an obscure woman's order. It was perched deep in the forest on the mountain of Little Lozen. Almost derelict, the monastery itself seemed close to collapse, and was only preserved through the kind support of the local village builder and a considerable amount of scaffolding. Eight very decrepit nuns lived there led by a charming but practically blind Abbess. Ned Macintosh found it a very spiritual place, and often went there with food and provisions for the neglected nuns.

Rather like Thrace in northern Greece, many present-day Bulgarian churches were newly built by businessmen or politicians, most probably as a penance for certain perceived misdeeds or crimes of which Dirty Macintosh was only partially aware.

Although he was reasonably proficient in the Bulgarian language—having spent three months living with a local family in Plovdiv—his relationship with almost anybody outside the Embassy was marred by suspicion and innuendo.

His wife Janis was the Embassy doctor, and as such was pleased to see any British subject who needed immediate treatment at $100 US per visit. She also found it hard to have any meaningful association with local families with or without children, and only seemed to connect with anyone at all when attending the local branch of the International Women's Association. This was where she would meet other wives from the foreign community to discuss the trials and tribulations of living in a so-called hostile environment.

Nothing seemed good enough for most, and although it was clear that they were living in considerably better conditions than they were used to in their home country, they complained bitterly about everything. Together with cars, drivers and servants, their luxury homes tended to be situated on the periphery of Sofia in spacious villas still owned by the ex-leaders of the old regime. They in turn occupied their city apartments in Doctors Gardens and comfortably lived off the villa rents they received.

What a lot of rot these wives talked. Both Dirty and Janis were all too aware of the paucity of good local information or anything that might be of interest to the British Government, but instead it was all mindless gossip and scandal.

'Perhaps they should change the name from MI6 to MG6,' Janis remarked one day whilst enjoying one of the many well-earned rest days from her Embassy duties, 'Gossip is about all you hear from these silly cows. Don't you ever get any real secrets?'

'You ought to listen to some of the nonsense I have to!' Dirty was getting sick of drinking cheap wine and guzzling egg mayonnaise sandwiches at various embassy receptions. 'All these silly Ambassadors talk about is regurgitated cold war propaganda, bits of James Bond and Graham Greene, peppered with stuff from Smiley's People.'

Dirty continued, 'I thought about writing myself once Jan; just imagine the title—*The Case of The Half-witted Ambassador by Ned Macintosh*—I am sure it would sell thousands of copies.'

Despite their misgivings, embassy life was very comfortable due to the English bank holidays and the many Bulgarian holidays which they were obliged to recognize. Because of that and with early half-day closing on Friday, it left long weekends each week so there was a lot of leisure time to occupy. And it was during this down time over one long weekend that Ned Macintosh puzzled over the question of what to do with Herodotus the gnome.

But what he didn't expect was how popular and well known Herodotus would become as a consequence of unimaginable telling circumstances—because, it wasn't long before his presence had been officially noticed by the President of the Sofia Garden Gnome Society.

Mr Andrey Antov had spotted the grinning plaster midget one day whilst passing by the embassy on his way to a nearby cake shop. Impressed and totally overjoyed at the international re-emergence of the once popular post-war Bulgarian tradition of Gnomiclature, he recognized that it could well be a matter of great political and cultural significance for those with a keen eye on history.

Due to the contempt that Ambassador Cumberpot had for this grinning creature, for a time it might have looked like curtains for the spymaster gnome; but now, and for some quite unexpected reasons, it was to be the beginning of a long and successful career for Herodotus the Gnome of Sofia.

1985 London

Although Arthur had been well educated in the classics, rather like some Americans he had met, his knowledge of geography was practically non-existent. He knew where he lived, where he came from, and that the UK was north of France. He also knew a lot about the classical world, the Ancient Greeks, Romans and the Persians. So he was spot on with most things which happened before the death of Herodotus in 440BCE, and that of Plini the Younger in 112 AD.

He also knew and understood the Classical Mediterranean like the back of his hand, not only due to his Oxford studies, but also from school trips to France, Italy and Spain with Croydon Grammar rambling club. The rest was a bit of a blur, and was further reason why he had ended up with a lower second, a bowler hat, and a daily trip on the 7.20 a.m. train to Paddington.

'It seems that you have attended to your work quite well,' Arthur's somewhat Pooterish principal observed, laying his transparent liver spotted hand on a dusty file full of carbon copies. Casually lifting the buff coloured cover, he stared at it for a moment and then observed, 'And your time keeping also appears to be excellent too!'

Removing a Fox's Glassier mint from his waistcoat pocket, he swiftly unwrapped it, and popped it into his mouth.

'Furthermore Cumberpot, it seems that you have also made very few gaffs; a guiding principal at the

Foreign Office.' The peppermint made a number of circuits around his mouth. 'As you know the FO can't abide gaffs, nor do they reward or even acknowledge initiative either. In fact they expect you to remain practically inert.'

The transparent peppermint oscillated around his ill-fitting dentures once more as he stared somewhat indifferently at his expectant clerk. Arthur's heart was jumping with eager anticipation.

'So Cumberpot, I am recommending you for a small promotion.' His grey eyes looked tiredly at Arthur's eager face, knowing that he himself had lost the race, and only had his Civil Service pension to look forward to. 'Perhaps we could find you a position in Africa; many of our young men like the adventure, and of course the challenge.'

Clasping an old battered copy of Wisden, the Principal cast his eyes over the Times cricket scores, running his finger down the batting order of the day.

'That will be all Cumberpot. I'm afraid you will just have to wait your turn.'

Annabel was not at home when he returned early evening, and he was greeted by Doris in the kitchen.

'Mrs Cumberpot has prepared you some potato soup, Mr Arthur,' she said, glancing under the saucepan lid. 'Or is it just potatoes? It's hard to tell. I expect there is some sliced gammon left in the fridge if you are lucky.' James was playing with his dinky toys on the floor by the Rayburn.

'Well, I will be going now sir,' continued Doris, 'I

expect she will be home soon; she only went to Wallingford. Will you be alright on your own?'

Arthur assured her that he could manage to feed his son and himself at a push, and she quietly closed the kitchen door behind her. On the table Annabel had left a note:

'*I have gone to see a Mr Caruthers at the Highclear riding stables in Wallingford. I thought I would talk to him about taking some riding lessons. Mrs Grimmer the farmer's wife said they are quite a professional bunch there and I used to be a good horsewoman once. So I will be back home about eight o'clock and then I can tell you what has happened.*'

1998 SOFIA

At the Ministry of the Interior in General Gurko Street the second floor room was full of cigarette smoke as usual. Philip Filipov sat with his newly acquired briefcase which contained his written report and the many other sensitive documents and photographs that he had acquired during his final stay in London. He was furious. Looking at Colonel Sabev, it was easy to see how his term as Minister in Charge at the embassy in London had been cut short.

From the outset it was evident that he was talking to a fool who saw his country's reality through the comic strips of the Dnevnik newspaper. The over-simplification, an inability to perceive any change in the world order, and the absurd escapades of Colonel

Katrandjiev had brought any serious diplomatic discussion between Britain and Bulgaria to a grinding halt. It was also clear from Sabev's attitude that the Balkan mentality was alive and well, and living in Sofia.

Sabev was a peasant from the Vidin region, who regarded people from the rest of Europe as the *Infidel*. They were there to be used and lied to. How a clown like him managed to circumnavigate both the Foreign Minister, the President and himself could only be explained by the intervention of the wily General Kovotchev. He ran the Ministry of the Interior like a private security service, but nevertheless Filipov remained unimpressed.

The answer was to be found in two simple words: *political chaos*. It was a prevailing situation where he saw little hope for himself, realizing that he now lived in a country bereft of any firm policy, where the political antics were often described in the press as democracy in action, when it was clearly the Theatre of the Absurd!

However this farce was not being performed in the theatres of Rakovski Street, but in the Parliament where the weasels and crooks were babbling their demagogic nonsense, and plying their political tricks. There were of course a small number of well-intentioned but impotent honest brokers around, but most were just gasbags who tried to monopolize the television debates on the government channel which broadcast their mindless rhetoric each day. The parliament had become a Circus and was treated as a huge joke by even the gypsy street sweepers, who laughed at the clowns and performing acrobats.

Colonel Sabev thought he was cleverer when in fact he was just a fool and a bully. Like most bullies he knew three things: how to intimidate, humiliate and finally to threaten people. When that didn't work he gave up!

'You do realize of course that I could have you arrested?' Sabev hated Filipov because he was from the old school.

'Oh really,' he replied, 'And what would that be for?'

Philip Filipov remembered this twerp as an Embassy guard in Sweden, or was he one of the drivers? These basic Bulgarian characters all had the same look about them. He was a thick headed peasant straight from the pages of Bay Ganyo by Aleko Konstantinov, and extremely proud of it.

Colonel Sabev's whole objective was to somehow humiliate Filipov. The Balkan inferiority complex generally found its way into most things, with the desperate need to push down someone's head. Sadly it was supposed to make Sabev feel good about himself, but it never lasted for long.

'You have brought your country into disrepute.'

The Colonel leaned back in his chair and passed his hands over his shiny shaven head. He was going to enjoy this interview; or so he thought, and had been looking forward to it for days. Filipov stared at him for a moment.

'And how did you come to that conclusion Colonel, I would be very interested to know?'

A smirk found its way onto the policeman's face. 'Because, forgive me if I am wrong, Gospodin Sabev, but aren't you supposed to be responsible for everything that happens at an embassy if you are the ambassador?'

His absurd attitude and hubris was very irritating, and Filipov desperately looked forward to wiping the superior look off Sabev's silly face. Since the so-called changes, it was clear that these basic characters had taken over the police force in most of the regions, and were also inside the Ministry of the Interior too. Philip Filipov went on to the attack.

Laughing at this muscle-bound policeman, Filipov asked him, 'Excuse me for asking Colonel, but aren't you the officer who ordered that raid on the British mobile phone company in Mladost last month? What was it? Oh! Yes, I remember now, it was because you found a mobile device at the scene of a crime somewhere. That was you, was it not Colonel Sabev?'

Sabev looked a little shocked, the smug look gradually disappearing from his face. 'We are not here to discuss other matters, but to address your incompetence and negligence.'

Sabev tried to regain his position of authority. 'So what is your answer, Gospodin Filipov? Are you or are you not responsible for these actions? Answer my question please?'

Filipov studied the expectant face before him. 'Firstly, your operative was acting outside any diplomatic protection, which you know as well as I do.

Secondly, the Ministry of the Interior gave him the order to steal this item. And thirdly, and unfortunately for you, I can also prove it!'

The look of restrained hate was plain to see on this puffed-up thug, who then said with a look of exaggerated innocence, 'What do you mean proof—what proof?'

'Unlike you Colonel Sabev, the Metropolitan police in London respect all the usual diplomatic rules, and they kindly gave me an official copy of his confession which I intend to give to the President today; that is of course if you don't arrest me and lock me up. Unfortunately this confession names you, Colonel Sabev, as one of the instigators!'

'Can I see this alleged confession?' asked the Colonel somewhat more timidly. Filipov smiled in a dignified way knowing that the Colonel only understood Russian as a foreign language and not English.

'By all means, I have a copy here for you to read at your leisure. Why else would I be here, Colonel Sabev, please tell me?' He handed over the Photostat copy, marked with the logo of New Scotland Yard, which even the oafish Sabev could read and understand.

Philip Filipov continued: 'And then what happened? Oh! Yes, I remember now! You raided the office of the British telephone company, handcuffed the entire staff, and locked the company chairman Lord Coleman in a broom cupboard? Is my information correct so far Colonel? Your country must be very proud of you, I am sure!'

Rising with dignity from his chair, he wished the

blustering policeman a courteous Good Morning, and then walked out of the building. At the rear of the Ministry he found himself in the gardens situated next to the old church in Graf Ignatiev Street, and wondered just how much longer he would be able to operate inside the present maverick political system.

He bought a coffee from a little stall in the garden, and sat for a moment on one of the dilapidated park benches, and watched the people going in and out of the church. Getting up, he stopped for a moment to buy some fruit from the street market, and clutching his new pigskin briefcase close to his chest, he finally jumped onto a rickety yellow tram which took him all the way to Bekston and back once more to the tranquillity of his home.

1997 SOFIA

Sir Arthur sat back and looked at the ghastly Constable painting before him. Whilst it reminded him of the country which he dearly loved, he didn't love the same corny view day in and day out.

'Can't you find something more colourful?' he once remarked to Edwina his assistant. Next day she produced a Pirelli calendar, and hung it on his wall instead. 'Very funny Edwina, I think I will have the other one back if you don't mind? What will people think?' Edwina believed that people might think him to be quite normal for a change.

On his desk was an unopened envelope—embossed with a grinning garden gnome not dissimilar to Herodotus—and bearing the acronym SGGS. It was addressed to Her Britannic Majesty's Ambassador to The Republic of Bulgaria, and marked Delivered by Hand.

It was from a certain Mr Andrey Antov who claimed to be the President of the Sofia Garden Gnome Society. He offered his fraternal greetings to a fellow enthusiast of Gnomenclature, and requested a meeting in order to discuss the possibility of starting a bi-lateral association for the appreciation of Gnomes. He had read that they were very popular in the UK, especially in Swindon and Slough, and that as a post-Cold War gesture of peace, friendship and reconciliation, it could help to foster mutual bi-lateral respect and understanding between the two nations.

Sir Arthur regarded any intrusion from the outside world to be an infringement of his undeniable right to diplomatic privacy, and so—since the subject concerned Herodotus the Gnome—the whole matter should obviously be handed over to the proper authority and to Dirty Macintosh in particular.

It was suggested that Dirty and Beamish might take Mr Antov out for a quiet lunch somewhere and to discuss the finer details. It was also conceded that some kind of frequent event might be invented as a possible cover for their star spymaster, who was currently undergoing performance evaluation and operational tests. This could be the breakthrough they were all hoping for, and one which the gallant Sir Arthur could now step aside from altogether.

'It's all yours now Macintosh,' he said with glee.

1985 LEWKNOR

When Annabel finally returned from the riding stables, she was ecstatic. She said that she had found a kindred spirit in Mr Caruthers—the man who owned the superb Wallingford stables. She told Arthur that he had excellent horses and tack, that he was a very interesting person, and was dying to meet him. It turned out that they had briefly met in the past, and that they shared some mutual friends from Oxford. She seemed very pleased with herself, and was for a change quite girlish.

Whilst she consumed some of the glutinous potatoes, complete with a sausage which somehow Arthur had missed in the fridge, he in turn described his meeting with his aging Principal at the FO. Looking as though he had personally discovered the meaning of life, his face was full of the passion of success.

'Annabel, you won't believe it, but I have been offered a promotion today. My Principal summoned me to his office, and told me that because I have recently had some good results, he was going to recommend sending us abroad! Isn't that wonderful?'

'It rather depends where it is, doesn't it? It has to be somewhere civilized surely?'

Arthur hadn't thought it though very carefully, and

amazed by his good fortune and the fact that he had been noticed at all after five years of drudgery, the subsequent implications of his promotion had eluded him.

'He said that there might be a post in Africa somewhere. He said that it would be quite a challenge and an adventure for us.'

Arthur pictured himself wearing a sweaty shirt, khaki shorts and a bush hat, and squinting down the twin barrels of an ominous looking box rifle at a charging elephant.

'It might be an adventure for you, but what about me and James? What about tsetse flies, malaria, and Ebola? Have you thought about that? Then there is dysentery, cholera, and rampant tuberculosis. That is not to mention food poisoning, riots, revolutions and invasion. That wouldn't be so good, would it?'

Arthur now pictured himself driving a beaten up Land Rover through the jungle, past screaming natives carrying spears, and on his way to some seedy port. Then carrying the two unconscious bodies of James and Annabel on-board a grotty tramp steamer, and begging the drunken captain for a passage to safety. But his heroism didn't last long.

Annabel wiped the last bit of tomato sauce off her plate with the remainder of the sausage, and looked up at him with pity. 'Couldn't you get a nice easy job in London, you know, as a desk officer or something?'

In Annabel's mind, she was cantering around the heated indoor paddock of the Highclear riding centre with the handsome Robin Caruthers as the ringmaster. He hadn't changed a great deal after ten years absence, and in fact seemed to her to be more handsome than ever, despite his thinning hair.

Arthur went on, 'Well, he said I still have to wait my turn, so whatever is offered to me is still up in the air! But I will get a better salary which happens anyway if you go up a grade, so that at least is good.' Annabel lifted her eyebrows in thought.

Certainly this would help the family finances, and might even pay for a few additional riding lessons. The problem now was how she was going to manage an affair with Robin Caruthers, should the old lusts from the past somehow resurface.

Meeting after all this time she told Robin about her life, Arthur and James, and how she was married to a rising diplomat. From his remarks it was obvious to her that the memory of that night outside St Mary's College in Oxford had paled considerably with the years. He told her that his wife had been ill for some time and was being treated in a clinic, and that since then he had been living alone.

Annabel saw this as an opportunity. She calculated that if in time a romance could be conveniently rekindled—and if she played her cards right—at some point she would have a good chance to continue the affair where they had left off all that time ago.

Surely the significance of her father's treachery would now act in Robin's favour—since it would lay her open to all sorts of moral and domestic blackmail? And if an affair were to flourish, the dark world of secrets would keep things under wraps—of that she was absolutely certain.

1998 SOFIA

The rotund figure of Andrey Antov stood outside the Party Restaurant in Patriarch Evtimi Boulevard. It had taken him more than an hour to reach his destinations despite its closeness to the City centre. This was mainly due to a compulsive disorder he was afflicted with. Seldom admitted to strangers, he was pathologically addicted to cakes and pastries.

In the normal course of events he found it difficult to bypass a single patisserie, which he entered with uncontrolled abandonment. He knew exactly what was good and bad in each shop or café, and always ordered the specialty of the house. Due to his obvious dedication to these sweet tasty cakes and pastries, he was popular and always warmly welcomed by the owners.

On this particular occasion, Andrey Antov had navigated his way towards his ultimate destination by a very circuitous route; in fact one might almost suggest that he had little or no sense of direction at all. But there was a method in his madness, because by taking that morning's course, he had managed to visit four sources of his favourite confectionary before arriving at the Party Club Restaurant.

Although the strong espresso coffee he had incidentally consumed—by which he washed down his numerous sweet and flaky pastries—had left his head buzzing a bit, he nevertheless found himself looking forward to a good lunch, paid for he sincerely hoped by the British Embassy.

As his tummy emitted a long and satisfied rumble, he casually turned to see two smartly dressed young men arrive at the entrance of the restaurant. Introducing themselves as Macintosh and Beamish, First and Last Secretary to the British Embassy, and official representatives of Her Majesty the Queen, it was to be the beginning of a very fruitful—unusual and largely unknown—association between the President of the SGGS and the British security services.

Mr Antov as it happened also suffered from an advance case of selective amnesia. In his halting English he explained that due to his on-going diet he could only eat wholesome food with very few calories, and so it took him at least half an hour to inspect the vast choice on offer from the restaurant menu. After a long discussion with the waiter, it was soon discovered that very few items were actually available in the first place, and when the food finally arrived it was further discovered that it was not for them, but for three people sitting at another table in the restaurant who had inadvertently already eaten their order, and were getting up to go. Therefore, since the choice was to take it or leave it, it was decided the simple expedient was to take it, whatever it was!

'I was in what you English call the funeral business. I ran a state funeral service before the changes, but now I am just an ordinary businessman, and what you might call a tax consultant.'

In the end the dreadful restaurant service didn't seem so important, and the choice of food was more or less forgotten. What seemed important to him was that everything had to be chewed thirty times, something which he had read was good for the digestion, and which also gave him plenty of time to think. The magazine in question had also extolled the virtues of exercise, at which point his eyes had glazed over, and the magazine contemptuously dumped into a convenient dustbin.

'I was also a Bulgarian chess master,' he opened his man's-bag and removed three identical telephones, one of which he answered, and then switched off. 'I don't think we need any interruptions,' he said, inserting a forkful of Dirty Macintosh's aubergine salad into his face.

'I once played against Boris Spasski, although that was some years ago, and I was one of many at the time. There were about twenty of us I seem to remember. It was at NDK; you know, the People's Palace, and everyone in the audience watched it on a big screen. That day I think he beat... well, everybody!'

This time a piece of rather bony fish was chewed up, as his thoughts went back to his glory days. 'I only play chess on my computer these days, and never with actual people,' he said by way of an epitaph whilst removing an annoying bone from his mouth.

'What made you take an interest in gnomes than?'
The bright eyed pixy-faced Beamish was back on track,
wondering what this roly-poly creature's reminiscence
had to do with him. Antov's fat fingers curled around a
fork, which was then thrust like a rapier into the only
remaining black olive.

'Well, it was the gravestones. They are so sombre and
sad, with those sepia photographs of people attached to
the headstone, and all those improbable youthful faces
smiling at you from the grave. I just thought that the
sight of a few garden gnomes might cheer everyone up.
So I put twenty of them around the graveyard. They are
such cheery fellows!' He took a swig from his wineglass,
his little finger poised in the air.

'What happened then?' By his concern it seemed that
even Dirty had been lulled into an unusual suspension
of his disbelief.

'What? Oh, they sacked me; after twenty-five years
of service, they just kicked me out!' At which point the
potato chip which Ron Beamish had been chewing
propelled itself across the room, attaching itself to a
somewhat ostentatious screen depicting a Spanish
bullfight.

With his eyes watering but without the slightest
external sign of amusement—due to a course in
emotion management at GCHQ—Dirty managed to
blurt out, 'What happened then, Mr Antov?'

'Well, I took all the gnomes home with me and put
them in my spare bedroom.' He smiled at the black

irony and the cogent memory of the misfortune that fate had dealt him. 'And that's how my collection was started; it was the only good thing that came out of the whole debacle! I now have over 500 gnomes at home,' he said as an epilogue to the sad story.

At this point Beamish was rolling and coughing on the floor, and gasping for air. But straight-faced like a dyspeptic County Court Judge, and only heaving with merriment internally, Dirty Macintosh finally managed to say, 'And how do you think our two countries can co-operate, Mr Angelov? I would be most interested to know how?'

Being a chess master, Andrey Antov was used to thinking a number of moves in advance, and his answers and general responses were well rehearsed in his head.

'Well, I thought that we could have an occasional meeting in the front garden of the embassy, so the members of the SGGS and their English colleagues could bring their favourite gnomes to meet one another.'

'You mean the garden gnomes meeting, or their proud owners meeting each other with their gnomes? I don't quite understand.'

'Well, both actually,' he smiled at the obvious misunderstanding. 'You see, and you will have to forgive us, but we gnome owners believe that our gnomes are real and we give them names and bring them into the house when it is cold and wet. They mean a lot to us, Mr MacDonald.'

'The name is Macintosh actually! So, let me just

précis this down a bit. We all meet in the Embassy garden, about—well, what can I say—once a month or a week, eat a few egg mayonnaise sandwiches with the odd glass of white wine, and discuss... well, errrrrr, garden gnomes, and introduce these various gnomes to each other. Is that about right?'

The look of total happiness on the fat man's face told them everything they needed to know, and it now seemed to be the perfect time to pay the bill, and to discuss the final details with the Ambassador himself.

Dirty, took his wad of cash out and left the approximate amount on the table plus an extra 10%. The British Embassy was not a parsimonious institution when it came to matters of national security.

CHAPTER FIVE

1985 WALLINGFORD

THERE WERE THREE practice arenas at the Highclere Riding Stables—one an open paddock which is perfect for pupils to ride around during the summer months, another old barn which was originally the main building for the stables, and thirdly there was a newly built aluminium clad structure. This had staggered plastic seating on three sides around the arena, a single story office to the right of the entrance, and a fully equipped kitchen with two WC's to the left of the entrance door. It was the main building in the complex and the venue for all the wintertime training sessions, for show jumping and the general running of the stables.

Robin Caruthers employed two grooms—both young enthusiastic girls from Wallingford—and a groundsman who also looked after the tack. The whole environment was tailor made, and the surrounding trees, grass and bushes were planted with a good eye for layout and design. This was not an average riding school, and seemed well run and properly organized.

There were ten horses that occupied an old block adjoining the original arena, with cobbled brick floors, wide channels and deep drains. This part had obviously been a stable for many years and although newly painted, the chew marks on the door frames indicated much use in the past. The previous owner specialized in retraining three year old steeplechase horses, which had not quite made the grade on the turf, and which he then turned into show jumpers.

Next to the stables was a small farmhouse with pretty Georgian sliding sash windows. It had a large porch with two benches either side of a white painted and panelled front door with a horseshoe brass knocker. The house stood next to the open paddock. Being summer, there were various small jumps laid out, low and wide apart, and suitable for a novice jumper or for the local gymkhana. The tack-storehouse was next to the office and attached to the main building. It was where the visiting farrier shoed the horses and where there was a small electric furnace.

The tack was not new, and so it was comfortable and sturdy. All the saddles were English, and were dubbined and well cared for. A large tin shelter nearby contained bales of hay and straw that was stacked up to the roof, an old Zetor tractor parked alongside with a loading bucket attached to the front fork. The feed was kept in a big steel silo that stood next to another small covered area where there was a big pile of sharp sand and many bags of wood chippings.

At various points around the grounds there were farm implements and carts and an antique farm wagon stacked with potted plants and flowers. The track leading to the complex was gravelled, and at the entrance there was a newly made hatch gate. By the gate was a sign with the times of business, the telephone number, and the proprietor's name.

Robin Caruthers sat in his office juggling phone calls on his only telephone line. His business and private life were interlinked so that the inconvenience was unnoticed most of the time. Whilst not exactly single, the only obvious difference from the past as far as Annabel could see, was that he no longer drove a MGTC Midget but a rather battered Series I Land Rover pickup. To all intents and purposes, since Oxford he had become a peaceful hard working landowner with a thriving horse stable business. Dressed in roll neck sweater jeans and Jodhpur boots, with a hefty pair of green Wellington boots waiting for bad weather in the corner of the office, he seemed to have changed little in appearance. Maybe his cavorting womanizing and hard drinking days at Oxford were now a thing of the past, or perhaps there had been some event in his life which had changed him into this more docile state.

Unlatching the hatched gate, Annabel entered the smallholding and shutting the heavy gate behind her she walked down into the stable area, leaving the battered

VW outside on the nearby grass verge. She smiled as she entered the office.

'I will need to buy a few extra things Robin, and I wondered if you might have a spare hardhat that I can use for the time being and a small whip. Hard hats are a bit tricky and I need to try it on before I buy one. Arthur said he would go to Barkers today and get a few things for me which I need. He has my waist and inside leg measurement for some Jodhpurs, and I thought a nice Harris Tweed hacking jacket, some good waterproof riding boots and maybe a Barbour jacket as well?'

She was pleased to be doing something which was not academic for a change. Strange as it may seem, her classical education was beginning to quickly fade away, as was her interest in her most recent Master's degree. At best she felt that it was a measure of her intellect, but at worst it held the prospect of some puny teaching job at a minor girls' private school which was something that appalled her.

Annabel was a social snob as well as an intellectual one, which meant that she would never consider the prospect of teaching at a state school any more than becoming a vegetarian! In truth, the idea of working at all was also becoming a pretty unpalatable one!

'We have got a big selection of hard hats here Annabel, including plastic jockey hats, which most people prefer because they stay on and are not too heavy.'

The banal details of everyday life at a riding-school were far outweighed by Robin's love of horses. It was the animals themselves which made it all worthwhile. They managed to fill up the gaps left by his tragic marriage to Sarah, and gave him the will to go on and to do something positive with his life. As to his friends; they had gradually disappeared over time, and few had managed to survive his wife's mental illness and the problems which she caused.

Now his trumpet playing was reserved for the odd gig at a Wallingford pub, or playing along to his Ruby Braff recordings when alone in the evening. He could not remember the last time he had spoken to his fellow musicians from the Lansdowne Lounge Lizards Jazz Band, although two had moved away from the area that he knew of.

'I haven't been on a horse for years,' she said. 'Do you think I will be OK?' For some reason, being in the company of Robin made her more compliant and away from Arthur, far less dogmatic. 'I really need to be told what to do,' she said for the first time in years.

'You'll be OK Annabel, but let's get you up on a horse first so I can see what you can still remember, and how you sit.'

Walking out to the horse stables she could see one of the stable girls leading a docile piebald into the centre of the ring. It was snorting and steaming a bit from being exercised earlier.

'Let's me get an idea of your competence and riding standard, because my experience of school-girl riding lessons at places like Roedean, is that you all go round in circles and the horse does what the trainer tells it, and not you!'

Annabel's jeans and Romanian cowboy boots looked the part but were very uncomfortable to ride in, the seam of the jeans catching her on the inside leg when she squeezed the horse to stop it from moving.

'It will be better when I have got the right gear, Robin; it doesn't feel right in jeans somehow.' He got the horse up to a canter and she held onto the mane for dear life as she tried to stand in the saddle. When she dismounted he smiled at her.

'Try and come back tomorrow if you can because we are not busy at the moment; that is if hubby has bought your stuff from Barkers. Give me a call in the morning and let me know if you can come, and at what time.' Walking was a little uncomfortable after her first ride in years.

Driving back in the VW she remembered the heady three months she'd spent with Robin, and the reason why he had dumped her. Although nothing had been mentioned by either of them about this episode, she nevertheless believed that with the passing of the years he had matured and had generally become less brittle.

1987 LEWKNOR

When they at last bought the cottage in Lewknor from farmer Grimmer, they proceeded to enlarge it by building an extension at the rear. The cottage now possessed a third bedroom and a new bathroom on the first floor, thus replacing the old ground floor bathroom with a nice big airy kitchen area with windows on three sides. The old kitchen was now the dining room, and the lounge area stretched from the front to the back of the property.

There were some pretty French windows at the rear, which led directly into the garden via a veranda which was paved with sandstone slabs, and the building work was easy to achieve in the Cumberpots' absence because whilst both she and Arthur were officially residing in The Bahamas, her brother John was keeping an eye on the construction in Lewknor.

They were now billeted at the old Government House in Nassau, Arthur as the third Consul and she as a part-time public relations officer and full-time party giver. Not exactly a time-consuming occupation, but it filled up the days when they weren't socializing with decrepit fat Americans, or the few remaining and spoilt aristo's who had first arrived on the island pre-war on a Sunderland flying boat.

The Bahamas was partially independent from the UK by then, and in 1973 Prince Charles on behalf of the Queen officially handed it over to the existing government of the islands as a British Dominion. This meant that the islands still owed certain allegiances to the Crown, but retained the Queen as the notional head of state.

At the time it was still a relatively poor country, and although popular with American tourists, it continued to have a colonial flavour and strong memories of the

Duke of Windsor who was the Governor General during World War II. He and Mrs Simpson reigned—through a plethora of parties and a sea of Gin and Tonic—over the dwindling British community.

Americans could now be seen roaming the streets, busily cursing Fidel Castro whilst smoking very large Cohiba cigars. Their frequent threats of nuking Cuba, a country only half an hour away from the island by plane was a familiar one, but one that did not demonstrate much local knowledge, nor would the sudden absence of Cuban cigars have pleased them if they managed to achieve their mindless goal. It was clear to the Cumberpots that some American thought levels were quite restricted, and that their general perception of geographical awareness was paralyzed by considerable ignorance.

Despite the beautiful weather and the sandy beaches, these were very boring times for them both. By now their son James was boarding at a prep school in Oxford, which allowed greater freedom for them to do as they pleased. While Arthur inspected passports and interviewed travellers destined for the UK, Annabel took to the American Club and the trivia of post-colonial chatter, whilst bravely ignoring the continuing clichés concerning Cuba.

Back in Lewknor for a regular free home visit, Annabel was entertaining her brother John. Now that the paint had dried and the furniture was uncovered, a lot of her time was spent rediscovering lost trinkets and personal belongings. It was also a good time for her brother and her to rekindle some of the fading memories of the past.

'I was studying at Art College at the time when I heard about his defection—I wasn't surprised. It was bound to happen. He was a complicated man with a very complicated mind which had somehow to be used. Once he was convinced by the Soviets his life suddenly had new meaning. He was comfortably off, very middle class and inquisitive. He might have been a traitor in our eyes but through his eyes he was on an ideological quest.' John lit his seventh cigarette and sipped his breakfast tea.

'Imagine what he would have been like if he had admired the Nazi's instead,' he laughed. 'He probably would have become a close friend of a certain previous Governor General of the Bahamas had that been the case. One has to remember that he was also very English with unquestioning loyalty towards his regiment. The problem was that his regiment was called the KGB!'

'You get on with him John, because you are both very similar characters. I know that you have visited him in Moscow on a few occasions; and we all know you both like a drink and a gossip.' Annabel cleared away the detritus of an English breakfast and piled the plates in the new steel sink.

For once there was enough hot water and the house was warm from the oil-fired Aga cooker and the new central heating. But more importantly she could now speak her mind, something it was impossible to do with anyone else except her brother, and very occasionally Lionel Pergamon.

'Well, I like him,' John said. 'A lot of people do, because he is funny, clever and very entertaining. If you can forget the circumstances of his exodus, he is the sort of father any man would wish for. And he is a gentleman, very English in his tastes and attitudes, and he could be sitting here with us right now and not seem the least out of place!' John had no qualms about his visits to see his father and couldn't care less about the politics or the alleged shame. John was a carpenter, not a bloody diplomat.

'I still can't talk about it to Arthur, although I suspect his bosses know everything. So we go on pretending that it never happened and try to be a normal family. Anyway, why shouldn't we?'

Looking at the kitchen clock she suddenly went into another gear, 'Where's that bloody woman?' Annabel's relationship with Doris, her ex-nanny who was now called the daily help was very pre-war, with quite a lot to do with the class war as well.

Annabel never really got over her stint at Roedean, the memories of a very short family existence in East Sussex, nor her mother's premature death aged 47. It was said that she actually died of shame, not alcoholism; not that Annabel could remember anything about it because she was still a very small child; but that too had become a huge family secret. To this day none of the children had the slightest idea of where their mother's grave was situated, and they were forbidden to attend her funeral and nobody would tell them. She just seemed to fall off the map. It was as though she had never existed at all, which to her errant husband Jim Kilbey was probably only too true!

'Papa Lionel was good to me, but he was very distant and rarely said much about our father.' She stopped speaking, when Doris walked through the door with a cheery good morning ready to attack the endless mess which seemed to permanently accumulate around them.

'*God knows what they would do without servants,*' Doris thought, as she remembered the fuss and the accusations she put up with concerning little James. Mrs Cumberpot could be very rude and arrogant, and if she hadn't needed the money Doris would have left them to their own devices.

'I'll start with the washing up if you and your brother care to go into the sitting room.' Doris liked them both to be out of the way; in any case, he flicked cigarette ash everywhere!

Having settled up with her brother by paying the last tranche for the building work, Annabel waved goodbye to him and watched his white Ford Transit as it made its way towards the main road past the Leathern Bottle and on to the A40 London road. How strange it was that he was so practical and dexterous with his hands and able to accomplish all that building work. Neither she nor Arthur could do many household chores, let alone wield a hammer.

'Father always admired me because he was totally impractical, and had never put up a bookshelf in his life!' In his father's eyes John Kilbey was one of the workers, although Annabel and Arthur were by their own volition, decidedly not.

The VW beetle was now replaced by a red VW Golf GTI, and a considerably faster and far more useful car. It was kept under the covered parking area which was attached to the house, a tarpaulin covering the car when not in use, with the battery disconnected. These were the firm instructions from Mr Noakes at Albion Motors where she had purchased her newish second-hand car after the VW Beetle had finally conked out. He had generously part-exchanged the Golf by offering her 50 Pounds for their old wreck.

When she arrived at the riding stables, Annabel parked her shiny new car by the tack store. 'It's so fast,' she said to Robin by way of a greeting. Smiling at her he held her in his strong arms.

'Good, you're back then! It's seems such a long time!'

1998 SOFIA

It was time to visit the secrets room again to recount their conversation with the very eccentric President of the Sofia Garden Gnomes Society (SGGS), Andrey Antov. The red-faced ambassador was extremely annoyed.

'He sounds a bit of loony to me,' was Sir Arthur's only understandable comment after copious streams of expletives had been exhausted. 'Believe me, I'm not going to hang around the Embassy garden talking to a load of bloody gnomes or their owners for that matter.' A little bit of froth had formed itself in one corner of his mouth. 'You can sod that for a game of soldiers, straight away!'

'Let's be reasonable, Ambassador.' Dirty Macintosh was more concerned with the practical issues than Sir Arthur's feelings. 'You have to admit it would be an excellent cover for our informers, and would allow them to download their secrets to Herodotus without any suspicion.'

He was trying to keep their meeting on track. 'You see, hidden amongst a load of weirdo's and gnome fanciers, our informers won't stand out one little bit Sir. It is the perfect solution when you think about it.'

Sir Arthur did not want to think about it. 'What about the costs? I mean, not just the sandwiches, but if I follow your logic, we would also have to buy our spies a gnome each, wouldn't we? I mean, I assume that they are not cheap, and I am not getting my father involved in espionage; he is 83 years old for God's sake!'

Dirty had the answer at his fingertips. 'Surely the big question is how do we distribute these gnomes to our operatives without attracting any suspicion? And Beamish has come up with the perfect solution. He believes that the simple answer would be to have a raffle at the forthcoming Queen's Official Birthday party, and to fix it somehow so that our informers win a gnome each. Nobody would smell a rat and even the gnomes will be happy!' His eyes twinkled mischievously at his last remark.

An annual event and much regarded by the British ex-pat community, it is considered a great privilege to attend. On behalf of Her Majesty the Queen the Ambassador invites a large number of eminent Bulgarian leaders, many of whom have distinguished themselves in various ways, and a considerable number who have not. Apart from them, there are the also ran's who somehow manage to get themselves onto the approved guest list for no particular reason other than to consume the food on offer, which invariably means fish and chips. This latter category usually doesn't say much, and they vacate the premises early on when they are full up.

For some unholy reason fish and chips are regarded by most incumbent British Ambassadors as being a particularly national dish, whilst it is regarded by most discerning Bulgarians as being a particularly disgusting one. That, and gallons of cheap white wine, has a singular effect because as soon as the boring speeches have been completed, the great majority of guests make a beeline for the exit.

'Where do you buy gnomes anyway?' Sir Arthur was becoming bored with the whole subject.

'I believe Germany has the most prolific number of gnome owners in Europe.'

Dirty's wife had surprised him one day by putting one on the balcony of their flat in Pimlico, much to his horror and disgust. Theirs was not the sort of neighbourhood one might expect to see a gnome, but even he had to admit the world was changing fast.

'There is a factory in Dresden that makes them, I believe, Sir; my wife has a catalogue somewhere which we can have a look at.'

Macintosh was not going to admit to such an item being on the manifest of his London home, nor was he going to be accused of being common.

'I daresay we could get a special price on say twenty units or so, with various demeanours. They don't all stand around grinning at you; in fact I am told that some of them even like fishing!'

'Well, all right, you can go ahead with it but leave me out of it.' Sir Arthur had bigger issues to attend to in his diplomatic duties. 'You two deal with it; and Macintosh,' he glared at the embassy spook. 'I mean it; leave me out of it, I have got a reputation to maintain.'

Dirty Macintosh and Beamish looked at one another knowingly, realizing that the great gnome conspiracy had finally begun and it was down to them to make it work.

1999 SOBRANIE SOFIA

The king looked up to the heavens, and smiled. He was a man who seemed to have a private dialog with God. Listening to the overtures of the new Parliament, the protocols and the noisy speeches, he smiled at the sight of so many hardened communists and gangsters, turning to symbolism and pageant in order to establish themselves as the true leaders of the people.

Three months before, there had only been lies, pointless promises and galloping corruption. Now, with his magic wand, Gregory III had created an enigma which these *other people* could not cope with. Looking carefully at the sea of faces below, all he could perceive was wonder and confusion. How had it all come about?

Everyone was sick of the Balkans and generally sick of war. Years of turmoil, the unending TV reports on Bosnia Croatia and finally Kosovo, had finally put paid to a sympathetic idea of war as a media event. Granite faced generals were economic if not parsimonious with the truth, and grass root politicians with their new media opportunities burbled on about human rights. Always in terms which they themselves didn't really understand, and often to a bewildered western viewing public who prior to the event, probably didn't even know where the Balkans were. The history of a Greater Europe was a blank sheet to most people.

Few young people had ever heard of the Archduke Ferdinand, or the existence of the Austo-Hungarian Empire. History in all the schools of Europe and America concentrated on current history and the concept of a fairer post-modernist existence. But then, what on earth could be more important than the interest paid for a bank overdraft, the buying power of one's credit cards, and the cost of an apartment in Kensington, Manhattan or even Swindon? They had no notion of the Balkans being the historical powder keg of Europe, and the place where so many damaging wars had started.

But violent events were still happening on the doorstep of new cushy Europe, and recently rather too close to some well-established holiday destinations.

But the vast majority didn't have a clue, nor did they care less, unless of course they were investment bankers. These vultures had a different perspective, because with war comes change, and change brings investment opportunities. Their fundamental belief within their lopsided concept of a modern political democratization is that money is the most important ingredient. Characteristically, they called it the emerging market syndrome.

As the newly elected speaker stumbled over his form of words, some of the red bourgeoisie tried to heckle him like uncouth football supporters from the terraces of some forlorn and dilapidated East European football pitch. But today they were shouted down by the more moderate amongst them, and those who could see quite clearly that their fifty-year term of office had just expired.

It had been a long journey for many. Fighting their way to the top of the greasy pole of socialism had been very difficult to achieve, despite the nepotism that existed within the post-war communist parties. Now they were older and perhaps a little wiser.

Their children were at American French or British universities, and studying the very subjects that would put paid to their corrupt pursuit of personal fortune, one which the last so-called government had so effortlessly managed to achieve. Now the theatre in which they acted would have to reflect the inconsistencies of their performing art, and in the future the hero they might choose to play would not only have to speak for them, but for some of their voters as well.

The King sat next to the aging ex-President, and together they carefully observed the current title-holder who seemed isolated and alone. They noticed how he gamely tried to maintain his composure and to add poise to an occasion that presently occupied the hearts and souls of the Bulgarian TV viewing public. The people were sick of the old ways and the deceit. Ten years into an alleged democracy, all they had to live on was a diet of innuendo and rising prices. The food which they consumed was mostly imported from Greece. Zendov, the previous president, turned to the king.

'Do you think they know what will happen?' The king looked at the ceiling of the parliament building as if looking for some divine inspiration and then turned to the older man.

'No, do you? You found it almost impossible to deal with these bastards when you were President. But now, thanks to you and as the new Prime Minister in waiting, at least I now know who to trust and who to get rid of; and that is an important start!'

Looking over the balcony at the assembled members of parliament, he saw the thin and stooping figure of Kolev, the outgoing Prime Minister, noticing how grey and mawkish he had become since his party had lost the elections. His sly face had a look of disbelief, and the black bags under his eyes were evidence of many sleepless nights. He sat and glared maliciously up at the King.

'*Bloody foreigners,*' Kolev thought, '*coming back here and winning an election. How did he manage to win the election and a bloody king too?*'

Kolev's mind twirled with theories of conspiracy and revenge. His foxy eyes darted from one person to another, from one familiar face and then to some total stranger.

'*Who the hell are you?*' His thoughts raced. '*You were just a clerk three months ago asking me for favours, being made to wait for hours in my outer office. You were nothing, just some toady knocking on some westerner's door and hanging around business receptions looking for a bloody job.*'

He hated these creeps. They were the maggots that lived off his flesh, the ones who now told the hated foreigners a new version of the truth. All of a sudden they had become terribly brave, but only because he was leaving office. Yesterday they wouldn't have even dared to talk on the phone in case someone was listening to them.

But as the outgoing Prime Minister there remained one small conciliation. Until the new government took power in six weeks, he would still retain control of the country and be able to complete his final business deals before stepping aside. It would take a very long time to break down his network of informers, and all the old intelligence structures that remained in place from communist times. It made him feel safe.

'I cannot understand why these people still think

they are in control!' The King knew that Zendov the intellectual had been kicked out of his job as a lecturer at the Sofia University in the early 1970's because of something he had written. Perhaps his punishment was to have become the first elected democratic President. The king continued, 'But old habits die hard here in Bulgaria Professor Zendov, now we will have to see.'

King Gregory III had always known about these people. They used to visit him in France, where his family had chosen to live after the communists had taken power in 1948. Maybe it was truer to say that the communists had thrown his family out.

From early on he was always open to meeting Bulgarians of any persuasion. Hard-nosed communists, woolly minded intellectuals, and young people trying to escape to another country. They were all made welcome by him no matter the true reason for their visit. They kept him in touch with Bulgaria, and so he began to understand the psychology of a people who he hadn't lived amongst since a child.

Zendov lifted his hands, and turned down the corners of his mouth with a look of benign acceptance. 'They think they do because in the past we let them. After the fall of communism as President I had no power to speak of, I was like a puppet. All I could do was to give the people hope that there would be changes, but these changes never came. The people learnt not to trust in politics, although they never spoke of anything else. It was absurd. Now all they understand is that there are red and blue communists!'

Gregory looked at his companion, and touching his arm gently he said, 'Yes my friend, but you personally never lost hope and now you can see fear in someone else's eyes for a change. They won't get away with it for much longer, and in the end they will end up in jail. Most of them are greedy fools and greedy people make stupid mistakes. It is easy to prove that they are crooks if you totally control the banking system, and I will!'

Sitting apart, the current President Chavda Stanchev rose from his ornate throne of office, and summoning as much dignity as possible he made his way slowly down to the floor of the parliament building and took his place on the rostrum. Four years as president had made him confident, and many visits to the west had improved his wardrobe. The immaculate white smile was also very good advertising for the newly acquired skills of Bulgarian dentists, many of whom had imported good second-hand equipment from Germany together with shiny Mercedes motor cars. As he looked at the many different faces before him—Bulgarians, Turks, Jews, and even one Gypsy—he carefully adjusted yet another pair of trendy spectacles which he then perched on his long aquiline Armenian nose.

The perspiration of a warm summer's day blurred his vision, and mixed with his tears of defiance, he knew that his own future position was very much in doubt. It was accepted that he would not refer to the King as such, but by his family name of Gregory von Augsburg. He was not about to fool himself into believing that the King wouldn't one day want his country back.

'Mr Speaker, members of parliament, ladies and gentlemen. I would like to start my speech by welcoming you all to this the forth parliament of the New Democratic Republic of Bulgaria and to the first sitting of our democratically elected membership. I would also like to compliment the National Party of Gregory von Augsburg, on their remarkable victory in the recent election in which they won more than fifty per cent of the seats. Although this will mean that a coalition has to be formed in due course, as the largest party in this Parliament, as president I now call upon The King's Party to form a new Government—according to the laws of the Fourth Republic—and to officially nominate a new Prime Minister and Cabinet.'

Stanchev's words seemed so trite, because he knew that he didn't deserve all the crap left by Kolev and his cronies. The stolen accession money, the mansions, the corruption, the kickbacks and the cash in foreign banks; it all had to be accounted for. It was the total loss of any credibility at home and abroad, that made him feel sad about his term in office.

The people thought that he was a part of it, but it was not true. In reality he had less today than when he started his presidency in 1996. The new millennium would put paid to all his chances, his career as a lawyer and who knows, to his marriage as well. He hated corruption but he had also become a part of it despite his endeavours.

'You don't want to judge him too badly,' the King

said. 'In a way he is exactly like you Zendov, because all he can really do now is to make patriotic and dignified speeches. All he has now are his principals and ideals, a bit like a dog with no teeth!'

Gregory buttoned up his twenty-year-old Seville Row suit, stretched his legs, and lay prone on his chair gazing once more at the ceiling. 'Sometimes my friends say that it is better not to take prisoners. But maybe he could serve another term, as long as he plays ball with us. It is his choice.'

Gregory recalled the childlike pureness of Stanchev's self-discovery and how it all seemed so very profound to him. He was attending a discussion in Paris about Human Rights and they had met on the side-lines. It was a refreshing change from the mindless religion of communism which rotted the very being of ordinary people in his beloved Bulgaria.

The first lieutenants of communism often came to see him too in various guises, and sometimes just to practice their lying. He knew they were trying to deceive him, to discover some kind of weakness in his character and to understand who and what he knew. But he said nothing. He was polite, he was calm and sometimes generous, but he always studied them very closely. When they laughed at life's great ironies, he had held out his hand in friendship, whoever they were and whatever their motives. But Stanchev was different, because he was actually a good man.

Outside the heavens opened up, and a great sheet of rain almost drowned the citizens of the capital. Those brave or determined enough to stand outside the Sobranie that morning, simultaneously ran for cover into the cafés and the shops in or around the Narodnie Square. The taxi drivers, who had been waving posters of Gregory, jumped into their cabs and started to sound their car horns. The Hussars in their white plumed uniforms stood patiently in the rain. The police disappeared under the nearest tree, smoked their strong Balkan cigarettes, told each other that nothing would change, and laughed at their misfortune to have been born in such a hopeless place.

'When will you tell us who will be the Prime Minister? Who will be in the cabinet?'

It wasn't just the local media who were interested, but it seemed the whole world had its attention on Bulgaria, and for the first time ever. Gregory simply said, 'When the time is right, I will tell you.' He was not a man to be rushed.

1988 WALLINGFORD

Annabel urged the bay mare into a canter, and then proceeded to circle the arena for twenty minutes or more. She then did three figure of eight manoeuvres bringing the horse round and then started cantering in the opposite direction. She had to maintain this course before returning back to the trot, which Robin insisted should be held in a sitting position.

Back to a walk, it was his intention to get her to make the transition smoothly from walk to trot, and from trot to canter. This way she would have full control of the horse at all times, without any clumsy shifting in her riding position. It is important that at the very least, a horse knows who the boss is, because an experienced horse can always spot a novice rider in the saddle.

After half an hour she dismounted and proceeded to walk the mare around the ring to cool it down, finally leading it to the stable where it started munching bran and foraging in the hay. One of the girls was brushing another horse in the yard.

'Sharon, will you take off the saddle, do what you have to do and put everything away? I've got something important to discuss with Mr Caruthers.'

The red-haired girl immediately took the bridle, led the mare round and then tied the reins to a metal hoop in the stall. '*I bet you have, you old bag*,' she thought to herself.

Taking the saddle off, Sharon placed it on a nearby trestle and, removing the blanket, she proceeded to rub down the horse with an old towel. 'She's had a lot of exercise today, I expect the poor thing is tired,' said Sharon who was mainly on the side of the horses. Annabel picked up her kit and, impervious to the girl's last remark, strode off to the new building where Robin was sitting as usual in his office.

'You can't begin to imagine just how boring it is in these diplomatic postings. It was much better when Arthur was buggering around at the Foreign Office. The good bit is that he is there and I am not!' Annabel looked at Robin and waited for a sign of sympathy to appear, which of course didn't happen.

'You won't believe all the tripe and the meaningless small talk,' she continued. 'I simply do not know what gets into these diplomats and what's more, they all appear to enjoy it.'

Robin stretched his tired body. Exercising four horses a day had its downside as well as its delights. 'Well, they don't have much of a choice really. As you say, they are there and you are not!' He closed his eyes, and ran his fingers through his thinning hair.

'I would leave him if you wanted me to, Robin.' Annabel stared purposefully at Robin and then crossed her arms as though a cold chill had suddenly blown through the office even though it was high summer. 'All you have to do is ask, Robin, you know that.'

'We have had this conversation before Annabel. I can't leave Sarah—she needs me and I am all she has.'

His regular visits to Fair Mile Hospital in Wallingford were a weekly chore for him. It was not easy for him to sit and listen to her often incoherent ramblings, although recently she seemed perfectly sound in mind, easy to talk to and perfectly normal.

But it had been a very long time since he had experienced a welcome home, a waiting meal, or to any kind of human warmth at all. Annabel gave him sex and companionship when she was in England, but definitely not consolation.

'What would she do if you divorced her?' Annabel was not the most diplomatic diplomat's wife. 'Surely she wouldn't care too much after all these years?' Robin looked deep into the past. He was from an old-fashioned school which believed in duty and loyalty. 'I mean, you don't have any children, do you?'

Robin turned to her with angry eyes. 'Annabel, don't come here and lecture me on what I should and shouldn't do, please. Don't you think I've been through this time and time again?'

He got up from his desk and looked through the window at the handyman as he drove around the grass paddock on the motorized mowing machine. Dusk was fast approaching and the working day was drawing to a close.

'Annabel, you have a son and your silly husband has a job.' The simple logic defeated him sometimes. 'If you left him he would never become an Ambassador or anything worthwhile, and you would always be chasing him for money. Don't you think the best solution is to leave things as they are? You don't want to destroy him, and there's always the possibility of your father's past misdeeds to be reintroduced into the equation by some vindictive shit! You'll never know when, or why!'

Robin was sure that his wife Sarah would eventually find a way of killing herself if she understood that he was even considering a divorce. It would be something for which he could never forgive himself if it ever happened. She had tried to harm herself before. Before, that is, she had been diagnosed Schizophrenic.

How she managed to disguise her developing disability was hard to imagine, and the extent to which

Robin's patience was tried and tested was also a truly remarkable feat. The survival of their short relationship was quite an achievement in itself, but in the end the solution was down to the local doctor who reluctantly sent Sarah to the local Psychiatric Clinic for evaluation.

During her evaluation as a voluntary patient she ran away on three separate occasions, so in the end it was agreed that she should be sectioned under the 1983 Mental Health Act. Since then she had been detained in hospital on a long term basis. It was as simple as that.

'But, what about us?' Annabel had never really got past her own interests. 'Don't I bloody matter then?'

CHAPTER SIX

1998 SOFIA

DIRTY MACINTOSH held the view that the British security service was the best in the world. If the information received from various clandestine sources was a load of rubbish, it was because there was no genuine intelligence available in the first place, and as his wife Janis had so accurately pointed out, the rest was just about scandal and gossip.

In order to convince his masters in London that he was doing anything at all, he had perfected a system of reporting which couldn't be scrutinized or verified by anyone. Frequent visits to the bars, restaurants and clubs inhabited by the foreign community bore little fruit, other than the usual speculation and occasional attempts at revenge. It was his position at the Embassy which restricted his activities, and why he reluctantly came to rely on the various foreigners and expats for information.

These expats happily attended any event requiring

the prodigious intake of alcohol, especially if it was free. His reason for relying on these proxies was that he had only been given one liver, and that he would like to keep it intact if at all possible. Consequently various full-time imbibers were enlisted as informers, who then attempted to recount the confused but occasionally revealing comments made by fellow imbibers or imbibees, and their Bulgarian counterparts.

Subsequent accounts were often a minefield of inaccuracies, with date, place and name errors, but as the hangovers subsided and the memory function returned for just a brief moment in time, it was up to Dirty to unravel these events and to report back to head office in London.

This generally unreliable information could occasionally have some passing interest, but only if it was subsequently verified by an indigenous source or someone close to the Bulgarian Government. Suspicion and speculation was the enemy, and if taken too seriously would only lead to a work of fiction. And fiction would perfectly describe Dirty's work to date. Every morning both he and his staff would read the local papers to see what revealing information could be dredged out of the rambling local rhetoric, which he would then report as fact.

The most valuable information sources were local people who worked purely for money or favours. The problem was how to manage these valiant spies, and what's more, how to be sure they were working exclusively for Dirty and not the local internal security services. So the choices were limited and he invariably had to rely on drunks, fools and double agents, with the occasional honest man or woman thrown in for good measure.

All very confusing you might think, but to a mind like Dirty Macintosh's the truth was often to be found at the bottom of a wastepaper basket, or to be retrieved from the domestic detritus of an aspiring politician. He also possessed a well-developed lateral thought process, rather in the mould of Prof Edward de Bono. Often a lie was better than the truth to Dirty, who was able to dissect the information received with some clarity of thought, as he had been trained to do by GCHQ in Cheltenham.

It was less important what the military were doing, because the actual truth was nothing. If he wanted details on what resources they had, he simply looked it up in *Jane's Fighting Vehicles*, which told him everything he needed to know. So it was the businessmen and the politicians who were the greatest threat to the world order; as he would like it to be known, and were the people he concentrated on mostly in his perennial quest for secrets. Then of course there was the illicit arms trade to consider. Now the country was in chaos. Because of the historical ties to the likes of Saddam Hussein and Colonel Gaddafi, there were those who still pursued this unwholesome trade.

Dirty knew his was a deadbeat job in a famously lousy posting, and all because of a sin from the past. Not unlike Ambassador Cumberpot, he realized that if he was held responsible for one more balls up, he would be driving a desk next to a blank wall in South London for the rest of his career. This was not an option to be lightly considered, and why he was clasping at his final straw—Herodotus the Gnome of Sofia.

'Ron, have you got Herodotus working yet? I finally got those mobiles out this week, and they all have one now.'

This had also been a problem, but the Mobilnet Company was very helpful, and they set up a provisional office at a central Sofia hotel exclusively manned by a trusted English manager. The whole program was presented in the press as a market research project, prior to the opening of a branch office for their expanding retail network. It was a very good cover.

'We have already got my first message Dirty. It says, '*Hello, I am Boris and I am very preeminent.*' Do you have any idea what that means?'

Ron Beamish was privately a little sceptical about the Herodotus project, because to him it could only be as good as the operatives involved. What if they were all idiots? This presented a danger to him personally, because the FCO would blame the IT staff for any mistakes made which was only him at the moment!

'Oh! Yes, it's that writer bloke; you know, the one who wants to live with his sister in Barnsley; the one who told me he's a big fan of Allen Bennet. He says that he has read *Single Spies* and *An Englishman Abroad* twice, and that he has compiled a dictionary for idiots.' Dirty sat and thought for a moment, and then he went on by way of an explanation.

'He showed it to me once. It's difficult to describe really, but if you can imagine—you know—where any old dictionary describes a bicycle for example. This guy has gone a stage further. First he has the word in English with a description of what a bicycle is; then the same description in Bulgarian or Russian, and finally all this stuff is followed by a drawing of a bicycle. He says he can sell it in Africa! But frankly, I think he would be better off trying to sell it here; I think the people in Africa are far too intelligent!'

'What about the word *testical*, what does that drawing look like?'

Ron Beamish was experiencing the expected shortcomings of his new computer program. 'Why do they make these things so complicated?' He rattled out his instructions to the computer on his keyboard. 'Where did you meet this twit anyway?'

'I met him at the book fair in Plovdiv. He told me that he was a writer, and that he was very clever. Can you believe it? He told me he was very clever!'

Ron Beamish rattled away on his keyboard once again, and then sat back to admire his work. 'I have never heard anyone say that before! What is he, a fruitcake, or some kind of galloping narcissist?' He sat back and puffed at his cigarette. 'Or is it the famous Slavic inferiority complex kicking in? Some of these people are so—pathetic!'

'I don't really care much either way, Ron.' Dirty slurped some Tetley's tea from a cup advertising Bovril on the side. 'He says he needs a work visa and a one-way ticket to Heathrow.' He casually turned the page of a glossy catalogue full of German gnomes. 'However, the important person is his father. That's who I am trying to get to; he was the old communist president's lawyer!'

'So his son Boris can be as "*preeminent*" as he bloody well likes, as long as he buggers off to Barnsley!' Beamish stubbed out his third cigarette of the morning. 'I wouldn't want to do your job, Dirty! Where do you find them, or do they find you?'

Dirty scratched his head for a moment. 'What I have to do now is organize the bloody raffle during the official Queen's Birthday bash at his nibs' residence in June. I also have to track down some gnomes—with various character dispositions—ready for presentation to the nominated winners.'

This was not a matter to be considered lightly and was a crucial part of this very secret mission. Things relating to the size, cost, demeanour and colour, were all of great importance. These details were due to be discussed with Ambassador Cumberpot within the week, by which time it was important to finalize the intrinsic costs and details in the forthcoming presentation.

Sir Arthur recently claimed that there were only limited funds available in the embassy bank accounts, which were mostly needed to purchase large amounts of fish and chips for the official Queen's Birthday celebration.

'How can we be sure that the right people will win the raffle?' Beamish's pixy face was full of mischief. 'We don't want some old hag taking a gnome home by mistake and sticking it on her front doorstep. Perhaps we ought to buy twenty gnomes in order to hide the ten who are spooking for us, and to keep a few spares for the future? You never know, you might get a huge diplomatic discount!'

'What, you mean so we can have another ten or more loonies attending the monthly Sofia Garden Gnome Society garden party, as a subtle cover for our legitimate operatives, not forgetting Mr Antov's own bunch of nutters? The Ambassador's answer I know will be no, Ron, but I agree it's a very good idea.'

Ron the IT specialist stubbed another duty-free cigarette out. 'The ambassador will throw a giant wobbly when he knows how much it will all cost!' And a few days later, the Ambassador did throw a giant wobbly.

Sir Arthur's face closely resembled a spluttering red traffic light, and his spittle practically blinded his co-conspirators as he repeated his full and practiced list of expletives, which was quite a feat in itself, as well as a comprehensive and detailed inventory of English slang.

'Twenty grand!' He banged the table. 'You expect me to agree to spend all that money on some bloody gnomes, and those demented halfwits from the Sofia Garden Gnome Society? You must be bloody mad!'

He wiped the dribble off his humourless face with the back of his hand. 'I'll become the laughing stock of the service if I let that happen.' His morose face gazed deeply into the future whilst his alter-ego considered if he even had a future.

Dirty was of the opinion that the ambassador's behaviour had been considered rather hilarious for a number of years, and that this new operation would make little or no difference to his Foreign Office CV, which he knew to be full of derisive comments and satirical remarks.

'Well Ambassador, our masters in London are quite adamant and—subject to the final figures being produced by us—they have already given us the green light. It is now on the books as an on-going operation. I'm afraid it's too late to stop it now!'

1992 ISTANBUL

Arthur Cumberpot controlled the activities of The British Consulate in Istanbul with dexterous and skilled clerkmanship. He was wise to the continual stamping process which so redolently reflected the often mindless bureaucracy that had always existed in European Turkey since the beginning of the Ottoman Empire. Passports, visas and documents—commercial and personal, importers and exporters of all sorts and hues—filled his days, but with the ever-present suspicion of deception.

With the Iraqi wars just a matter of a few years away,

Turkey was—as it had always been—an easy point of entry for terrorists and blackguards of various descriptions and nationalities. Sandwiched between Iran, Iraq, Syria and the Orthodox Christian state of Greece, Turkish Trace was a very busy entrance and exit route for all kinds of traffic, both legal and not so legal. Its entrance point into Ex-Communist Bulgaria was not so well documented however, and there remained rather a blank sheet regarding these activities, especially from the British government point of view.

Trucks and cars drove through Central Europe via Bulgaria, Romania and Hungary, on their way through to the sophisticated markets of northern Europe and the UK. Turkish people were employed in large numbers in Germany and elsewhere in the car factories, and were also considered an integral part of the retail shopping and catering industry almost everywhere. Turkish was spoken in the street markets of Brussels and Hamburg, London and Zurich; and anywhere where hard working people could make good.

But, Turkey was also a strong barrier between Saddam Hussein and the rest of Europe. Saddam would have become the next door neighbour of the European Union, if Turkey was allowed to join. Considering the character of Bulgaria's leadership, it seemed strange that they could ever be considered for accession into the EU, and not their hard working neighbour Turkey.

Arthur was generally committed to the political realism of the day, but also concerned with placating his wife's continuous criticism of all things foreign and the so-called unbearable inconveniences of her everyday life in Istanbul. Occupied with window shopping in the Kasbah and the many little shops close to the Consular Office and the Government Residence, it was she who was agitating for a change of address in England. Annabel claimed that the house in Lewknor was far too small, and no longer big enough for the tree of them to live in or to house the many antiques she'd accumulated over the years.

These days she was inspecting Damascus silk fabrics which she imagined might adorn the regency casement windows of a rather rambling house which now had her attention. Griffith and Partners, the estate agents, were adamant that it would suit the Cumberpots, and she read out the estate agent's details with considerable emotion to Arthur.

'This beautiful five-bedroom Regency house stands next to the tennis courts in Watlington—known as the smallest town in England—and will make an ideal home for a diplomat or businessman and their family. In need of some light renovation and decoration, this unique building—which is surrounded by the beauty of little England and the spectacular Oxfordshire countryside—was built in 1820. The house, which stands out against the adjoining properties in Watlington, is a Grade II listed building, and as a probate sale it is offered with full vacant possession on completion.'

Annabel looked at Arthur with the dewy eyed expression of the soon to be, landed gentry. 'Watlington has got all the shops we need,' she said, 'and a very good butcher which I have used for years. The Chequers seems an excellent pub too; not full of those Neanderthals who almost live in the Leathern Bottle, but people like us!' She had passed the house on her way to see Robin Caruthers during her last visit home and looked over the wall.

Unfortunately, her visit had been somewhat marred by a pointless argument, because Annabel was becoming increasingly more aggressive and demanding of Robin Caruthers. Of course Arthur knew absolutely nothing of this, but being of the same mind—in an upwardly mobile diplomatic way—he too relished the idea of becoming the pre-eminent family of Watlington.

'Oh! That's nice dear,' Arthur replied, 'but what about our house in Lewknor?' It seemed the matter was out of his hands. 'What does James think, or don't we have a say in the matter?'

This little bit of provocation was ignored, because she was well aware of the duplicitous nature of her quest. She was convinced that Robin would be far more enthralled with the prospect of a permanent relationship if she had somewhere special to live. The thought was always there, that once ensconced she could keep the property for herself and James, without the inconvenience of having Arthur around. She had only recently returned from the UK and was feeling a little bitter. It was on this occasion that Robin Caruthers dropped the bombshell that Annabel had been most dreading for many years.

'Sarah seems to be much better these days, and Dr Coates has said that she can leave the hospital soon, as long as she lives in what they call a half-way house somewhere in Reading. That's like a guest house with permanent medical staff; but it means that she can come here during the day if she wants. Dr Coates said that horses are very cathartic for mental patients because it helps them to relate to something other than themselves. It seems that Sarah can control her condition with a drug called Prozac, now she is a bit older, and of course with regular therapy and counselling.'

'When did all this start, Robin? I thought we were going to be what they call these days, an item? I can't believe that you still have feelings for Sarah; after—what is it—over ten years now?'

Robin fixed her with an all too familiar look. 'The trouble with you Annabel is that you have a very selective memory, and you always have done. I made it quite clear to you from the very start that I have no intention of dumping Sarah, because unlike you, she really needs me; you see, I am all that she's got. And, I also made it abundantly clear that all you and I have is a comfortable arrangement, and no more. You are married with a son for Christ's sake, so what do you expect? Don't be such a selfish cow!'

As Robin shouted at Annabel for the second time, it all became painfully clear to her. Robin went on, 'But you are not having it, are you? What the hell do you think, Annabel—that the world is only about you? Well, it may come as a big surprise for you to know that it bloody well is not! Other people live in it and some of them need help, and that means dear Sarah!'

On the flight back to Istanbul, Annabel thought long and hard. She hadn't truthfully looked in the mirror for years. Perhaps it was time she did and to reassess her life now middle age was well in the assent and possible defeat on the horizon. Maybe Robin was right when he said that she was a selfish cow, but she already knew that perfectly well, and fast becoming just like her father James.

Something ominous was stirring inside her. Was it the beginnings of hate, a need for vindication, or the horrifying portent of loss? It was hard for her to explain to herself, but she perfectly understood the anger and resentment towards Sarah, someone of whom she had very little knowledge or any real concern. She could see that any attempt at manipulation was presently very dangerous, because, on the one hand there was Arthur's career to consider, and on the other there was also the strong possibility of Sarah harming herself.

It was clear that right now, nothing was to her advantage. Despite her well-developed sense of self, she was not inclined to become *the other woman*, nor was she about to sabotage the fanciful acquisition of her newly discovered Watlington manor house. If the worst came to the worst, she would now be forced to concentrate on more worldly matters and less on the affairs of the heart. She sent a fax to Griffith and Partners:

'As you know my husband is Head of the British

Consulate in Istanbul, and only able to make a short visit over one weekend in order to view Orchard Manor in Watlington. Meanwhile, I think it only wise that you inspect our present house in the village of Lewknor to assess its market value and sales potential, whatever you people call it. Our next door neighbour Doris has the house keys, and you will find her telephone number below.

Obviously we would need our current house to be at least under offer before we exchange contracts on a new purchase, should we agree terms. However, because we are in the diplomatic service, we have easy access to bank finance and I have already spoken to our bank in Oxford and they have agreed in principle to offer a bridging loan, in order not to lose Orchard Manor to another purchaser. On which account we must surely be considered as a good prospective purchaser. Perhaps I might telephone you in the next few days, to make a weekend appointment to look around the house?'

How strange it was that she could be so down to earth, when her emotions were so up in the air? But the program was very simple. Firstly Arthur had a very secure job in the Foreign Service which would encourage a good sized mortgage to be agreed by a bank or a building society. This was because they knew that overseas government employees exclusively lived on their expenses, and pocketed their salaries—minus UK tax of course—almost intact, so from a banker's perspective they were a very sound risk.

Secondly, since she was the only family member who was free to organize the move, it would be a very convenient opportunity for her to remain in England. She would of course report back to Arthur about the costs and the progress, but she would simultaneously be able to pursue Robin without the fear of exposure.

Thirdly and lastly, she would use James as a further excuse for spending even more time away from Istanbul, which she hated for the same reasons she disliked Nassau. It was full of boring self-important wittering twerps whose conversation was bordering on the infantile! They called it small talk, but how small could it get?

Was the diplomatic world exclusively populated by provincial oafs in suits? Were all the so-called British businessmen working for Price Waterhouse or KPMG? Surely there must be other entrepreneurs and empire builders who didn't want to fawn around her husband; but where were they?

It was as though he was actually a member of the very royal family he claimed to represent. When would they see diplomats for what they really were—a gaggle of public servants hopelessly scheming for a knighthood?

1999 SOFIA

Philip Filipov felt very comfortable sitting in the president's office. It was a much safer place than the Sobranie, and a sanctuary where he could minutely reflect on his country's home security without intrusion. He was not there because of his politics, but because he was respected and knew the rules. Despite the debacle of the flying helmet, now largely forgotten, he was generally regarded as a solid and reliable assistant to the beleaguered President Chavda Stanchev, and therefore a worthy member of the Presidential cabinet.

President Stanchev was a man who was far better suited to appear in court as an advocate, than to carouse with the butterflies of politics. By now he had become totally distracted from his true vocation within the world of human rights. Forced to shake hands with and make futile speeches to an assortment of international politicians, in actual fact he was more of a professional dinner guest than a president. Most of the visiting acolytes would be forgotten men and women in the very near future, generally to be seen rehearsing their demise on the TV screens of the capitalist west. As Harold Wilson, a past British Prime Minister, had famously remarked, '*A week is a long time in politics*'—and this was mainly true of the fading stars of diplomacy which he had to put up with.

At first, Stanchev had thought it a great honour to be President, until he realized that he now rarely met anyone of any substance, except when he was invited to attend EU meetings in Brussels, or as a guest at the many American jamborees. Nevertheless, he dearly needed to know the realities of life inside Bulgaria— quite independently from the parliament—and outside the clutches of his own political party which was now in power. Kolev, the Prime Minister, treated him with contempt and regarded him as a very small part of the Bulgarian circus of which he himself was the real ringmaster. That is why Stanchev chose Filipov in preference to any of the clowns who performed daily in Parliament—or whenever they could in order to get in front of a gullible TV audience—because he obviously was an outsider.

Philip Filipov was proud of this, as was his wife Ksenia. It was she who had convinced him that the past was practically over and that it was time to put away the old prejudices and to look forward to Bulgaria's inevitable move into the EU.

'Don't look back Phil; it never happened, and it doesn't help! I have got the same problems at the Institute. I don't know how long it will be before the witch hunt starts, and if I am to be unceremoniously turfed out for a more politically acceptable and probably younger lecturer, or whatever those uncouth morons regard as an improvement. We need to keep one salary in the family at least, and to try hard to and steer clear of these so-called home grown democrats.'

She was right, because once more it was a return to the now familiar Byzantine story, where politics seemed to creep into every available nook or cranny. Even the newspaper shop where one bought a daily copy of *Dnevnik* or *Trud* marked you as supporting a particular political party. And the newspaper itself also gave prying eyes further clues as to your political affiliations, especially if you bought a copy of *Pravda*.

But with politics came abandonment, as individual MP's pursued their own interests and tried to make some money. The people in the provinces—well, who cared about them? As one Businessman's Block MP arrogantly remarked, '*They have all got a TV, they can watch me on that. I'm not interested in them!*'

'The old attitudes are still there Phil, nothing has changed with the ordinary people; it is just that the propaganda and the media are now controlled by these wicked demagogues, and the people don't know what is happening.'

Ksenia was not just being conciliatory to Philip, because she too realized that—whereas it might seem to be a nominally functioning society to a casual foreign observer—it now seemed to be a zoo to Philip and to her.

'We shall see Zenny, because I now have certain subtle powers, and I can do something about it for a change.' But was it a forlorn hope, or a chance to even the odds?

To say that Philip Filipov was a disappointed man was for him to admit failure. As someone who'd spent the better part of his life somewhere in the middle of the political spectrum, he was by his own account a very successful survivor. What the new political arrivals could never totally understand was the concept of political longevity. His was a career spanning some thirty years; they were like insects which might live another day, to fly away into oblivion, or get squashed.

That was today, but yesterday was very different. In the back of his mind were the revealing facts of his past. Yes, he had been recruited from the first English language school in Sofia; yes, he had studied at the Institute of International Relations in Moscow, together with all the Cold War ramifications that these facts very simply implied. And he was not innocent, but he did not have blood on his hands and he did not hate anyone.

In the past he had met James Kilbey, both in Moscow and once on holiday in Varna when he was with his English son John. On Sunny Beach they had drunk together, and laughed at the crumbling Bulgarian infrastructure and the terrible hotel and restaurant service. But he was quite different from the famous English spy, because he did not rely on the Soviets for anything nor was he in love with the ideals of communism. To him it was all a means to an end, and the end stopped firmly with his family, because he was not for sale.

As they drank they talked about England and his defection, but what Philip couldn't understand was why this rather pompous Englishman had sacrificed his family and a comfortable job working for the British government, all for a two-bedroomed apartment in a Moscow panel block and a lifetime—or what remained of it—of contempt and suspicion? Apart from the deaths of various faceless and nameless British and American trained operatives—none of which seemed to bother him much—it was hard to understand why he was so pleased with himself. Was he simply an amusing buffoon?

Quoting all the corny remarks made by the *Passed over Majors* of Communism, he seemed more a parody of a Soviet spy than a first line thinker. But that was how he maintained his position, and frequently remarked that to be a true patriot, you first had to belong. He simply declared that he was an idealist, who now happily lived in the bosom of his chosen family in Moscow.

The question had always remained the same with Philip. Would Kilbey have done it all, had he known what to expect? Communism was not about ideals, it was about power, money and control. Now it appeared that his obnoxious younger daughter Annabel was in Sofia, blithely dominating her husband—the weak-chinned British ambassador Sir Arthur Cumberpot—and looking remarkably as though butter would not melt in her mouth. Perhaps it was time to speak to her about her father and to see how far the art of betrayal had affected her, and to see if she was in any way vulnerable to some well thought out coercion.

Annabel Cumberpot had not attended General Kilbey's funeral in Moscow on his death in May 1988, although her brother John has been present with an older sister. Was she even aware of his death at the time? Going back to the meeting in Varna, it seemed to Filipov that his son John Kilbey had remained on good terms with his family, and acted as a kind of filter through which his father's continued existence and his booze-sodden life in Moscow was occasionally recounted. The remaining twenty-five years of this so-called master spy's life was well documented in his autobiography, a period full of self-indulgent and pointless philandering.

These days, a plethora of western business consultants now littered the foreign bars and joints in Sofia. Whilst claiming to be able to help Bulgaria back onto its feet, there was very little proof of genuine activity to back up their claims. Nowadays it was not in the company boardrooms where they marketed their feasibility studies and business plans, but in the bedrooms of Sofia—the famous City of Sin—where they spent most of their hedonistic time!

Sofia had become a place which was often referred to in the western press, as the *Knocking Shop of Europe*. How sad it was for Philip and Ksenia to realize that the daughters of socialism were willingly selling themselves to the foreign scum who had invaded their country after 1990, now euphemistically described in the tabloids as bankers and businessmen.

To defame Sofia as "a *male menopausal destination for aging roués*" was to simply scratch the surface, and to expose little of the true moral decline of a once proud nation. These days it had become a place where young girls openly prostituted themselves in order to get through their university studies. To most of these foreign inhabitants of Sofia, Gordon Brown's famous *Moral Compass* must have sounded like a horse running in the 4.30 at Kempton Park!

With his new-found status as a Presidential advisor, Philip and Ksenia Filipov were cordially invited to attend the Official Birthday Celebration of Her Majesty the Queen Elizabeth II, to be held in the gardens of the ambassador's official residence in Sofia, and they naturally accepted. In his absence in America, they would be personally representing the Bulgarian President Chavda Stanchev.

CHAPTER SEVEN

1993 HELSINKI

ALTHOUGH James Cumberpot had studied hard at St. Toogood's prep school, and was by all accounts a bright boy, he was also given to melancholy. Unlike most of his peers he was a loner who rarely talked about his family, but when he did, they were presented as being rather distant and two dimensional; rather like characters from a dull and disappointing book full of social stereotypes.

Most of his contemporaries seemed to be from similar social backgrounds. Some fathers were in the army as officers serving abroad, some were diplomats like his parents, but many had been shipped off to school because they got in the way of their warring families, or occasionally a prosperous family business. James sometimes wondered why he was put into the world at all, and had very ambivalent views about his parents who these days generally treated him like a distant relative.

There were also a few dullard farmers' sons who needed poshing up, prior to going to some obscure boarding school, followed by a life spent down on the farm. But amongst the pupils there were some foreign children from the now independent ex-colonies. They were soon to be sent to Eaton or Harrow, and then on to become playboys or public relations spokesmen in their respective countries. Some simply disappeared off the radar, or returned to the coconut republics and dysfunctional regimes they originated from.

It was amongst these outsiders that James found his friends. In an odd sort of way, in so doing he was spiritually returning to his father's humble but more cosmopolitan pre-existence in the leafy suburbs of Croydon. This was where he spent most of his half terms and school holidays. Consequently, it was Norris and Myrtle Cumberpot who now represented the only close family he really had, the doting couple with whom he'd spent much of his early life. His parents were virtual strangers to him, and by this time were becoming the hardly known recipients of the once weekly letter he was obliged to send home about cats, dogs and various sporting activities.

It was now time for him to move on to his public school, which he had been *put down for*, many years before. Paid by the government it was of little importance to the state where he finally ended up, but his mother Annabel chose to send him—quite wisely as it turned out—to Summerlake College near Henley on

Thames. It was said that it was to be near to him for occasional school visits, but also because it had a very good academic record, and was also a perfect solution to James' obvious problems with dyslexia which he had been afflicted with since birth.

For Arthur's sake, the school was also known for its rowing. The school was situated on the Thames and had a very liberal teaching policy. James, at the age of 13 years, was looking forward to going to his new school now that he had passed his common entrance examination.

Grandpa Norris Cumberpot had been retired for some years, and relished the days he spent with young James. And it was he who took James to Barkers in Kensington High Street after his final term at St Toogood's, in order to be fitted for his new school uniform. A special day for most public schoolboys, it marked the passing of childhood and the final arrival of the teenage years. Together with ever-increasing and perceived independence, it was the time when a young boy started to become a young man.

The Summerlake dress code was simple because their schoolboys were allowed to wear an informal sports jacket, white shirt and school tie, grey full-length trousers and black Church's or Loak's shoes. In fact, although it was meant to distinguish them from other schools, on days out in Henley they could easily pass for quite regular young adults, once they had removed their school tie! James also liked his grown up dark blue school blazer, and was greatly pleased to see the back of the ghastly striped blazer and the school cap of St Toogood's.

Looking forward to the long summer holiday, he had at last received the British Airways plane ticket to Helsinki. Sent to him via the Foreign Office, it was accompanied by a consent form for him to fly as an unaccompanied minor, which both his parents had signed. Dressed in jeans, with a silk screened picture of '*Taz the Tasmanian Devil*' on the front of his printed tee-shirt, James was ferried by Grandpa Cumberpot to Heathrow airport in his dark red Morris Minor Traveller.

'Goodbye old chap,' Grandpa Cumberpot had said through tearful eyes, 'I hope that things go all right for you; if not, you know where to find me.'

James had never been to Helsinki, and was only aware of it as an obscure place marked in a school atlas. With this and some fairly meagre information gleaned from the local reference library, he had no real idea of what to expect, but what he did expect was to get to know his father a little better.

Flight BA 6079 was largely uneventful, but being an early morning flight British Airways offered a good English breakfast to their passengers. That and the friendly cabin staff made the journey a very pleasurable one for the 13-year-old James. What was a surprise, however, was an impromptu visit to the flight deck and a chat with the two airline pilots.

Arriving at Helsinki Vantaa airport at midday, he was met off the plane by a young woman from the airport staff, who navigated their way through passport control and customs. Arthur Cumberpot was wreathed in smiles as his young son emerged into the reception area, and after he signed a receipt for James' safe delivery, the girl promptly disappeared into the crowd.

'Hello old boy,' beamed the diminutive red faced diplomat, noting that his young son had grown and was now the same height as himself. 'What was the flight like?'

'It was splendid father, they let me into the cockpit and I sat next to the pilot.' As they walked to the waiting embassy car, which was parked at the airport entrance, James rambled on. 'He told me that he also taught flying at High Wycombe airfield, that's when he isn't flying commercially. Apparently there are two single wing Condor trainers there at the flying school which I can learn to fly in someday.'

The boy was full of enthusiasm and pleased to see his father. His father was determined to start a rather delayed bonding process, and was brimming with goodwill.

'When you go to Summerlake, I expect they will ask you to join the army cadet force at some point, but you can always ask to join the air force cadets instead. And if you do that—a friend once told me—as a cadet you are allowed to train officially with the RAF on motorized gliders from fifteen years of age onwards. This could be a very exciting time for you, James, if you wanted to learn how to fly; and free of charge too!'

Arthur was pleased that he and his son had something new to think about. It seemed now that Arthur might finally have a say in his young son's life; it made him feel useful again, and led him to suspect that it was time for him to exert more influence over the boy, and to do something other than agree with the tyrannical Annabel all the time. This was something which he had spent his entire married life doing.

Encouraging James to be independent was the way to do it, and with an absorbing interest like gliding—when he became a little older—he might spend his weekends somewhere like Lasham airfield, helping out at the gliding club which his friend Karl ran. According to him they could always do with an extra pair of hands during the weekends. That might also get his young son away from Annabel's clutches, and stop him from becoming too much of a mummy's boy.

'You didn't realize that I knew a bit about flying, did you? Well, Grandpa Cumberpot was in the air force during the war. He was a sergeant pilot and flew Mosquitoes for a pathfinder squadron. Didn't he tell you about his war?'

Arthur was looking forward to being able to talk to his son without all the usual bullying interruptions. Annabel was in Watlington organizing the garden and the final touches to the house decorations, which gave father and son Cumberpot a chance to explore the Finnish countryside.

As a schoolboy in Croydon, Arthur and his father used to look at old black and white photographs which he'd taken whilst flying over the Mona dam or elsewhere in Germany. In wartime, it was part of his air reconnaissance duties and carried out days before the dam became the target for a bouncing bomb.

'He was a very brave pilot James, and was mentioned in dispatches twice. He also received the *Distinguished Flying Cross* from King George. I don't suppose you knew that, did you?'

'Why didn't he become an officer, Father? I never could understand the difference between a pilot officer and a sergeant pilot. What was wrong with Grandpa?'

Suddenly Arthur found himself on the defensive. What could he tell the boy? That his Grandfather was lower middle class? This would confuse the artifice which Annabel had created around their respective backgrounds, and become an insurmountable problem for him due to the contrast between his own humble beginnings, and his outward appearance.

'Things were like that in those days James, and it was just a matter of chance!'

He purposely left the subject in a vague and uncommitted way. James was far too young to be bothered with his family's social aspirations, or by the somewhat pretentious nature of their current existence.

1993 WATLINGTON

Mr Griffith was a good, capable and professional estate agent, who held no truck with the uncouth youths in city suites and BMW's, who inhabited the flashy offices of the big national estate agents. He had nothing to prove to anybody, and regarded his purchasers as acquaintances rather than clients. Consequently Annabel found it very easy to purchase the Grade II listed building, given the complexities of the survey and valuation, and despite the mind-numbing procrastination of her sleepy Oxford lawyer.

It was clear that Mr Thwaits, of Jones, Jones and Thwaits Solicitors, was a man who stared at the mound of buff files before him each morning with hugely negative thoughts; and so he liked to take his time. The method he used each day in dealing with the somewhat repetitive task of Property Conveyancing was to start at the top and to work his way down. This meant that—on balance and as the day progressed—his most recent conveyances were dealt with first. If however he received a caustic phone call from a belligerent or neglected client, the buff file in question would suddenly be placed once more on the top of the morning pile. Thwaits regarded this as the perfect solution to his on-going dilemma, and had followed this principal throughout his entire working life.

Annabel however had an unexpected motivating effect on Mr Thwaits. Recently he had been spotted—by Phyllis his ever-vigilant secretary—holding the telephone receiver some three or so feet from his right ear, whilst he spluttered and prevaricated in a grossly humiliating way. She could not actually hear what was being said on these occasions, but she could see that it was quite serious. After a number of such incidents, she noticed that Mrs Cumberpots file became a permanent feature on the top of the morning pile, and that the purchase of Orchard Manor was completed—by Jones, Jones and Thwaits Solicitors' standards—in record time.

'Old Thwaits is due for retirement shortly,' Mr Griffith remarked. 'Most lawyers are a bit relaxed in this part of the world; we always have to bully them. They have rather too many clients and are a little bit spoilt I fear.' On completion Annabel gave Mr Griffith a bottle of Champagne for his troubles, his due diligence and negotiating skills, and of course he also received a good commission from the vendor.

John Kilbey was immediately summoned from London, this time to view Orchard Manor, the new Cumberpot residence in Watlington.

'Wow! You two are going up in the world! This is a big bugger Annie.' John Kilbey liked big rambling houses, and also lived in one himself in Kilburn.

Once more his trip from London gave them a further opportunity to mull over the past. It was the question she had always wanted to ask.

'Did daddy actually love us, John? Did we mean anything to him?'

John generally managed to keep his feelings to himself. Too much damage had already been done. 'Of course he did,' he said as convincingly as possible. It was what he didn't say to his sister that mattered.

'*Like a dog loves his dinner*,' he thought, but he kept quiet on that account.

'I don't know how I am going to do this John, or even if you want to help me out as before.' This time Annabel might have bitten off more than she could chew, and she knew it.

'There is a good local builder which Mr Griffith has recommended,' she continued, 'but I really need your sound advice on the whole matter, as somewhat of an expert.'

John was a practical man. 'What about Lewknor, have you sold that yet? You don't want to have that hanging round your neck for too long surely?'

As a matter of fact, that was a part of her plan. Whilst she did up Orchard Manor and pursued Robin Caruthers, Lewknor seemed a very comfortable place for her to stay for the duration, or at least for the next few months.

'Oh well! There is a lot to do here,' she said, 'and can you imagine the mess that will be made? One couldn't possibly live amongst all that debris and stay sane. Anyway, Mr Griffith is already showing people around Lewknor, and if it comes under offer sooner than later, we will just have to mess the purchaser around a bit; which they are probably used to anyway these days! They might also have something to sell too, who knows?'

Annabel's thinking, although on the ball commercially, was in truth merely prompted by her romantic ambitions towards Robin Caruthers, and was in fact, very personal indeed.

'I think you will need an architect for many of the little changes you propose, because the house is Grade II listed. That is always the downside of these lovely old houses, and not only that but any alteration to a listed house has to be reviewed by a committee, and you can imagine how they can be; long winded and bloody minded!'

He remembered in the past a similar building in London, and the problems he had over a particular sliding casement window. It wasn't exactly like the architect's drawing but very close, and he was made to remove it because of a nosy and vindictive neighbour who complained bitterly to the planning committee. That had cost real money.

'And, if you don't build it exactly as the drawings show, they will dog every move you make from then on. They can be a bit like private detectives; you mark my words.'

He was right of course, but he also knew Annabel's character, and how she was prone to try to bully her way through official red tape. But this was little England and quite different, so she had to get the message very quickly.

Having settled the purchase of Orchard Manor, in her mind Annabel had somehow transferred all her affections to Robin; despite his stern warning to her. The diminutive figure of Arthur and his bumbling inadequacies and his burgeoning self-importance, was quietly being replaced in her affections, and very secretly usurped by the man she really loved.

She knew that her hopes could be flawed in the long run, but in the foreseeable future; surely she should be allowed to pin her hopes on the attractive and sinewy presence of Robin Caruthers in her life, and not the shorter and more challenged figure of her husband Arthur.

After all, it had been many years since she had experienced any meaningful relationship with Arthur, their marriage having become more of an arrangement. She perceived their continuing marriage to be mutually companionable, but only in terms of those few social occasions when her husband needed publically to confirm a strong and reliable marriage and to maintain his credibility as a diplomat. The rest was about her.

Other than that, she held no qualms about her infidelity, and absolutely none about any property acquisition. It would seem that she was emotionally well equipped to feather her own nest, and also that of her poor neglected son James. In whichever way things panned out, she believed that Watlington was the perfect solution for everyone concerned.

How she pursued and attained her impossible dream relied on her duplicity and negotiating skills. Was that something she had unknowingly inherited from her father? As he had so successfully demonstrated in the past, she too found it hard to distinguish between being clever and being treacherous; which is the DNA of a successful spy.

1995 READING

Robin Caruthers was busy making last minute arrangements to collect his wife Sarah from the hospital, and to deliver her to the half-way house in Reading.

The building in Argyle Road was a transformed guest house. It had twelve rooms which were occupied by patients and where they continued their therapy and counselling during moments when they needed help. Dan the resident psychologist was an easy-going West Indian who had worked in the mental health community for many years and was considered locally to be one of the best.

He occupied what was the lower ground floor apartment, together with his wife Isobel who was also a professional nurse. Robin had visited him on two previous occasions, and they'd agreed that Sarah could occupy a large ground floor room at the rear of the property.

In the previous century the house had been the Reading School of Music and this room had a wide conical timber addition attached to the rear part, where the school grand piano had once stood for acoustic reasons. Now this part was occupied by a sofa, a coffee table and two comfortable chairs. The rest of the room was occupied by a large double French bed, a Victorian wardrobe and a broad chest of drawers with drop handles. There was a small adjoining bathroom, with a door leading onto the garden and car park, via some stone steps.

Dan explained: 'On a sunny day she can sit outside on the steps and read on her own.' Then as an afterthought: 'And it is very quiet around here, so there will be no interruptions.' He looked at the cars in the parking area, and lit a cigarette. 'Two of our patients have a car, and that is good in my mind, because it helps them to get out and to be a part of life again.'

Climbing the steps and back into the old music room, Dan smiled at Robin. 'We have very few long termers here like Sarah, but there is no reason why she can't adapt, and maybe get a little job somewhere locally. My task is to keep an eye on her, talk to her about her problems as she wants, and to make sure she takes her medication! The rest is up to Sarah and to you of course!'

It was agreed that Robin should only visit with her twice a week at first, but particularly on Sunday, because that was the day that all the staff were away.

'The patients like to make their own breakfast on a Sunday morning, which is a chance for them to get together and to help each other, but the rest of the day is free.' Dan was very simple in his approach to his charges' welfare. 'During the week we have staff in, and so our patients get three meals a day; unless of course they have a job.' He smiled, 'I know it is called a half-way house, but really it is a home from home!'

The medical report from the hospital was straightforward enough, and Dan was pleased because he did not want any uncalled for problems from his patients; after all, he also had a life of his own to live. Dr Coates' report read encouragingly:

"*With Sarah Caruthers we have achieved some remarkable changes through her treatment and her most recent medication, all of which has proved a great success particularly during the last six months. Over time her schizoid tendencies have become well controlled, and she is no longer prone to articulate incessantly, and seems able to concentrate on specific matters at hand. The usual tendency to flit from one subject to another has stopped, as has her occasional hysterical behaviour and uncontrolled anger.*

Her mood changes are less obvious now, and her anxiety and paranoia are less noticeable too. How she adapts to living in a community again—or indeed sharing a future relationship—is no longer a matter of concern. She can be a rather cold patient at times, and in the past has spoken about suicide. However, we believe that unless badly provoked most of her symptoms can be controlled and in time might disappear altogether, especially if the patient lives in a quiet and stable environment."

Long term patients were not Dan's most favourite guests, but Dr Coates had been quite clear in his report, so the rest was up to him. What surprised him was Sarah herself when Robin Caruthers brought her to Reading to look at her new accommodation. It was the day before she moved in.

Many patients, who received long term treatment were often drab and unkempt, something he was expecting having read the report from Dr Coates. What was astonishing was the arrival of this slender and beautiful woman with long auburn hair. Dressed in jeans with a Mary Quant top; although somewhat dated by the day's standards, she presented quite a stunning sight.

Walking up the steps to the raised ground floor entrance she seemed a little shy but quite self-possessed, as she hung onto Robin's arm for support. The cleaning staff stopped work and greeted her, and the patients, who were still in their rooms, came out to see this unusual creature who would be their companion for the next few months.

Dan went around showing off some of the features of the building; the ground floor TV room, the basement dining and sitting room, and finally her proposed private room at the rear of the ground floor.

As she walked around she inspected the bathroom, the curtains, felt the mattress on the French bed, and smiled. It was as though she was staying at a recently discovered hotel that came up to scratch. She also smiled at Dan, who could see her pleasure at being there; noticing the brown almond eyes and the curious warmth they seemed to generate, quite independently from any of her other features. Turning to her husband, she said, 'It is very nice here Robin and I can't wait to move in.'

To Dan she appeared more practical. 'I expect you will need to see my records and prescriptions before I move in tomorrow.'

She removed a fat buff envelope from her shoulder bag and handed it to the West Indian doctor, who took her aside and sat her down by the reception desk in the entrance hall.

'If you would be so good as to fill out this registration card, Mrs Caruthers, I will need to check out a few personal details with Dr Coates before tomorrow; if that's OK with you?'

On the way back to the clinic in Wallingford she spoke of the trauma of the last few years, and the fear and anger—at having sacrificed what had started out as a beautiful marriage—of a life that had turned into darkness and despondency, apparently for no real reason at all.

'Thanks for standing by me, Robin. I don't know what I would have done if I hadn't known that you were still there. But I was deeply troubled, and very confused and angry, because I didn't know why these things were happening to me. They were very frightening times for me, but thanks a lot—I will never forget it.'

She smiled as she watched the scenery pass by the side screen of the old Land Rover as it rattled its way to Wallingford and back to the nursing home. Robin looked at her with a wry smile.

'As the Americans say, let's hope that tomorrow is the first day of the rest of your life, shall we? Maybe we can see things more clearly soon. So let's keep our fingers crossed!' He did not want to give her too much hope.

1993 HELSINKI

The dark green Jaguar came to a halt in the forecourt of the British Embassy in Itainen Puistotie Street, and father and son clambered out, the driver carrying what little luggage James possessed through the security barrier and into the main reception area. A smiling girl passed by holding a pile of correspondence, which she promptly handed to Chief Consul Cumberpot, and then introduced herself to James.

'Hello, I'm Edwina; I am your father's PA here at the Embassy.'

Arthur grinned broadly at this pretty girl and, placing his hand on James' shoulder, said, 'Yes, this is my son and heir James, who will be staying with me for the summer. I expect you will both be seeing a lot more of one another!' Then the happy girl disappeared bouncing down the nearby corridor to her cramped office.

'She is very nice, isn't she James? And, when I am busy—which won't be too often now it is summertime—she has agreed to show you around the museums and art galleries. She knows a quite a bit about Finland. Did you know for example that Finland once used to be a part of Russia?'

1999 SOFIA

It was the beginning of June and the stage was set for the celebration of the Queen's official birthday at the

British Embassy in Sofia. It was a warm and balmy summer evening, and the official invitations, which had been carefully delivered by courier the week before, had been officially accepted in most cases. The whole matter had been left to Edwina by the British Ambassador, who relied on her good judgment and common sense. Over the years they had developed a comfortable working relationship, their shared confidence proving to be warm and friendly.

In terms of the diplomatic pecking order, Britain ranks itself second in importance to the Americans, a matter hotly disputed by the French who not unnaturally consider themselves to be the torch bearer for modern civilization. The Germans, on the other hand, know that they are unquestionably the financial engine of Europe and so don't care a damn what their two European contemporaries think anyway!

In general there is an unhealthy competition between the leading European countries, which—mainly based on the size of their Ambassadors' official residence—gives very little importance to any significant contribution to world order, peace or any human rights issues. It is where the invitees come from which is the guiding imperative. They absolutely do not invite representatives of coconut republics, nor dodgy conflict nations, or certain corrupt ex-communist regimes. This is because diplomacy is, as usual, the last thing on their mind. There are however, certain priorities in their choice of invitees and those they most want to cuddle up to.

Firstly, they invite their most important diplomatic opposite numbers. Secondly, they invite themselves; the entire Embassy staff, husbands, wives and associates. Thirdly, they invite the most prominent local politicians and certain respectable indigenous businessmen. And finally, they invite selected members of their expat community who may have contributed in some small way to the maintenance of any perceived national interests.

That evening, Sir Arthur managed to squeeze himself into one of his so-called tailor-made suits, which in actual fact was measured up by an Indian from Moscow, made up in a small sweatshop in Kowloon, and paid for in cash during the tailor's following visit to Sofia.

Recently, Sir Arthur had been overstuffed by Annabel's revolting school food, which by any definition was fattening. However, due to certain domestic disagreements resulting from her most recent visit to Watlington, his diet had lately been augmented by a considerable number of very necessary mind-numbing whiskies. The bottles, which were carefully hidden in the diplomatic consignment that arrived each month from England, now became an essential part of his evening ritual. He found that by gulping down this most precious of liquids, it was an easy—however temporary—escape from his wife's nagging, and continuously unreasonable demands.

It was easy for Sir Arthur to disguise the number of empty bottles his heightened consumption entailed, by secreting their contents into a plethora of crystal decanters marked *whisky, gin, sweet sherry, dry sherry, and port,* which sat on a mahogany butlers tray—together with some Waterford cut-glass tumblers—which stood next to the commodious sofa in his ample drawing room. By regular increments to the whisky and sweet sherry decanter, his recent consumption was very difficult to monitor by the prying eyes of his despotic spouse.

The butler's tray and turned mahogany stand was part of a considerable schedule of furnishings provided by the Foreign Office from their extensive resources. Furnishings in all foreign embassies are regarded as a necessary boost to the image of Britain, although the provenance was often in doubt. Over the years competent reproduction items had become distressed by their temporary users and subject to the ravages of time diplomats' families and their guests, these items of furniture had assumed the telling qualities of authenticity, as indeed had Sir Arthur himself!

The embassy garden was in perfect condition. The flowerbeds were brimming with freshly planted flowers and shrubs, the hedges trimmed and shaped, the lawns mown with the tell-tale signs of an aging Quelcast motor mower, and reminiscent of a well-loved English village cricket pitch.

Laid out in the garden were trestle tables which were festooned with the finest linen tablecloths, a great silver Bain Marie and bowls of assorted bits and pieces, much beloved by guests at the never-ending round of cocktail parties and receptions. The heated closed silver entree dishes were ready to receive angels on horseback and mini-Cumberland sausages, all of which were being prepared in the embassy kitchen, alongside the traditional English fish and chips which had become so much a feature of this annual event.

'Try not to get drunk too early, Arthur.' The rasping remarks fell so easily from the lips of Annabel as she draped her increasing girth with fashions recently gleaned from an expensive foray into a dog-eared copy of a *Freeman's Catalogue*.

'And, don't spend too much time with the American Ambassador; he already thinks you are becoming a bit of a toady! Try and maintain your aplomb for once!'

Wherever these words came from, they were most definitely not from the self-conscious and adoring woman he had first met by the banks of the Thames in Oxford, but more likely from the depths of some malevolent troll which had invaded her body.

The thought of trolls inevitably brought him back to the subject of gnomes, causing him to pause for a while to consider the well-rehearsed antics which Dirty Macintosh had devised for the distribution of these silly grinning garden ornaments which the Bulgarian spies were destined to win. The raffle would have to be well monitored by Dirty Macintosh for it to succeed, and would have to run like clockwork and involve more than a little sleight of hand by Ron Beamish.

Thankfully, Annabel was unaware of the plans for

that evening. Showing only a passing interest in the arrival of twenty cardboard boxes from Germany marked *Fragile, Handle with Care*, she had simply remarked: 'I hope those bloody things are not going to end up in the embassy garden Arthur, because, believe me, one is quite enough!'

As it was, that evening's events went quite smoothly. Annabel and Arthur received their guests in the embassy reception area, together with Dirty Macintosh, Colin the First Secretary, Andy Warren the Commercial Attaché, Ron Beamish, and finally Mick the embassy policeman who lurked in the shadows in case any uninvited guests needed ejecting.

Most of the important arrivals were timed at five minute intervals, because it was incumbent upon all important guests to arrive within the embassy portals in a large black limousine with some sort of flag attached, together with a flashing blue light. Very important people like the President and Prime Minister also had a police escort, whilst lesser Bulgarian politicians only had the flashing blue light, which was usually attached to an old banger.

The ambassador's staff was on best behaviour, and looked confident in the familiar surroundings of the embassy. They gladly shook almost anyone's hand including the waiters. All this bonhomie was delivered with a beaming smile on their faces, which was transfixed, but due to their temporary fame and fortune, it was one which they knew only too well, would disappear when they returned to grim diplomatic normality in the morning.

Traditionally conversation lacked any noticeable lustre—small talk is very small at such events—but no matter, it was a place to be seen and not heard. That was unless one was scheduled to make a grovelling speech, generally including such phrases as fraternal greetings and other simmering leftovers from the cold war.

Non-English speakers would enlist the translation services of the embassy translator, who was primed to leave out any controversial remarks and to add flattering embellishments of their own instead.

On this particularly agreeable summer's evening, the simultaneous translation was as usual rather confusing for everyone. That is, except for Sir Arthur, who couldn't have cared less, because the only thing on his mind was to get the successful distribution of gnomes over and done with.

Finally, the local expats would arrive; some from an afternoon drinking session at the Irish pub, but many came directly from their desks at KPMG or Price Waterhouse. Drinkers or workers, they all had one thing in common—they all looked extremely rumpled and worse for wear!

But it was during the formal mixing of these and other Sofia luminaries, that the raffle began and the problems started. It was mainly a problem of identification, and although it was easy to distinguish the diplomats from embassy staff and most expats, the Bulgarians themselves provided quite a challenge.

Due to somewhat unnerving recent fashion trends, the great majority of the men looked like gangsters, whilst many of the women would not have looked out of place at midnight on London's Charring Cross Bridge.

It was the fault of the Americans of course. With Hollywood's unending production of violent movies and other easily explained cultural influences, how else would emerging Eastern European society dress other than to look like one of their famous American screen heroes?

So, the distribution of garden gnomes seemed problematical almost from the very beginning. In their black suits, shaven heads and sunglasses, the De Nero or Al Pachino lookalikes were hard to distinguish from one another. They all looked so similar that it took a good eye and a memory for names to keep things under control, and was where Dirty Macintosh and Ron Beamish were supposed to earn their salary, although mistakes do happen!

The charity which the raffle supported was a very British one. It was for the protection and neutering of the many street dogs in Sofia. A popular cause for the dog-loving expat wives and girlfriends, they often become dewy eyed at the thought of all the beleaguered and itchy animals that roamed the streets of Sofia at night in packs, attacking the many vagrants that had begun to inhabit the streets in this newly found capitalist country. With little else to do with their unending leisure time, it became a hot topic of conversation at the International Woman's Club, whilst they sipped their G&T's and puffed on their duty-free cigarettes.

At the time they were not too sure what to call this new charity, and during their often thirsty afternoons under the umbrellas of the so-called Diplomatic Club in Boyana, many names were proposed. These included *Woofers, Paws for Thought,* and finally *Barking Mad!'*

The final suggestion was easily discounted due to its wide-ranging implications, and its immediate reflection on some of those present. The former was similarly rejected due to the inability of many of the ladies to actually say it so late in the afternoon, and so they all finally settled on title *Paws for Thought.*

This charity was dually registered as an NGO and publicized in the pages of the local expat English language newspaper, including heroic photographs of the organizing committee and various flea-bitten and snarling dogs. Thereby it was taken to heart by all the lost or ignored expat wives, and presented to the grinning Mayor of Sofia, Emil Sandanski.

Cowering in his office and surrounded by a large number of effusive and demanding foreign women was not his idea of fun. But it was his undying support which was required, in order to underline their noble cause, and not his approval!

'A neutered animal will not have any puppies and snarl at people,' Winona McTavish firmly stated with the verve and zeal of a canine Joan of Arc, 'and of course we will find them all good homes once the operation has been completed.'

The sight of all these hopeless women only served to provoke in Sandanski the thought that what these women really needed was a strong and healthy Bulgarian boyfriend, not a pathetic and hopeless cause. But he smiled and promised to support them whenever he could.

That evening he told the local police to keep shooting the animals at night using a suppressor on their rifles, but to make sure to move all the bodies and shell cases by morning. He did not want to upset the British Embassy or their canine crusaders.

CHAPTER EIGHT

1995 WATLINGTON

WHILST ROBIN was trying to deal with the very personal issue of Sarah, and adjusting to the possibility of a new beginning, Annabel was busy bossing the local builders around as usual, and being obnoxious.

Ambrose Dent, a local architect of some repute, was employed to design the alterations required at Orchard Manor. These were mainly cosmetic and concerned new replacement windows and frames for the main building, together with two sets of French windows and a new terrace at the rear of the property.

Internally there would be various changes required too, especially the creation of a new bathroom and dressing room for Annabel, and the opening up of the two smaller rear kitchen and scullery rooms into one rather large kitchen. This involved the demolition of a wall, the building of two brick pillars, the insertion of two rolled steel joists; many new electrical installations, and considerable amounts of re-plumbing.

The kitchen, which was also to be a major feature of the house and the consequent layout, was cause for many a harsh word from Annabel who knew little or nothing about cooking. Ambrose Dent on the other hand, knew quite a lot about the subject.

As well as being an architect, he was also a part-owner of the La Collonette Restaurant in nearby Caversham, and as such rightly claimed that he knew a bit about catering, and was said to be no mean cook himself.

'Mrs Cumberpot, just imagine for one moment, arriving from the supermarket carrying lots of shopping bags. The first thing you do is to put things down and then put them away. You then consider the menu which determines the order in which you carry out your cooking procedures. That means food preparation first, followed by cooking, and then serving up your meal.'

He continued, 'Finally, it is about bringing dirty dishes back into the kitchen, washing them up, and then ultimately putting things away once more. Now, if you get all these things in the right order, and the respective parts of your kitchen in the right place, it makes your kitchen much easier to operate.'

To Annabel, the salient facts were just a boring detail, and as far a she was concerned he could have been speaking Farsi; because, it had absolutely nothing to do with her already pre-conceived and somewhat conceited pronouncements on kitchen design. Whereupon it was abundantly clear that she believed in design over practicality, and her undoubted view that a kitchen was meant to impress one's friends, rather than to produce good food.

After all, she could use a tin opener perfectly well, and knew how to fry sausages and fish fingers in a professional and adroit manner. You only had to ask her bloated husband about her cooking skills for him to confirm them.

'I think you are talking a lot of tosh, Mr Dent,' she said with withering contempt. 'The Cumberpots do not eat any of that foreign muck you have just referred to, just good English cooking. Proper food! So, I will thank you to do what I ask if you don't mind?'

Ambrose Dent did not mind, but in his head he quite simply doubled his fee, and then smiled at his new client in an understanding and condescending manner.

'Of course Madam, I shall do whatever you please. There may be some practical issues concerning drainage and water services to consider, but no doubt I can find a solution in due course. Where there's a will there's a way!' he smilingly announced.

Consequently utter exasperation could wait—to be handsomely rewarded later—and so it was finally left to his experienced hand on the drawing board, and his well-practiced mincing of words to solve these tricky design problems.

He found it much easier when dealing with her brother John on the few occasions he came to visit Watlington from London. This was partly because he could use him as a conduit to express some of his misgivings about many of Annabel Cumberpot's absurd instructions, but also because her brother was an experienced builder and could understand many of the local building regulations and their obvious restrictions.

'Rightly or wrongly she is too used to getting own her way, Mr Dent, because in the Foreign Service one is permanently surrounded by sycophantic yes men and women. It has a slightly corrupting influence on one's perception of reality, but I am sure you realize that.'

Ambrose Dent was rather used to his own set of admirers, as it happened, in his capacity as Chairman of the Watlington Historical Buildings Association. Indeed, as far as he knew, that was the main reason he had been employed in the first place.

He was often retained as a consultant by many of the grand historic houses like Mapledurham House or Stonor Park, and could also be found on market days rambling on about the architectural features of Watlington Town Hall. Built in the 17th century, it was where the weekly food market was held, under the eaves of the raised municipal offices.

But all this was of little interest to Annabel who was mainly concerned with getting things done her way. There was however no argument over the external parts of the Manor nor the terrace, where Dent's word was final and flint stone walling his personal area of expertise.

It was also suggested that a pond with a small fountain might finish off the proposed external alterations, which could then be filled with ornamental carp, and perhaps a small fishing gnome. Annabel's gimlet eyes stared at him in disbelief at the last remark, which he then promptly retracted.

'Well, it was just a suggestion,' he said modestly.

Meanwhile, when she was able, Annabel still continued to visit the Wallingford riding stables, both for relaxation and in pursuit of Robin Caruthers. He was often not there, and on those days he was, he seemed very distant.

'What is the problem Robin?' she asked in a hushed and soothing way, maybe expecting the worst, but realizing she had to be subtle and conciliatory.

'Oh, nothing,' he would reply, 'nothing that should concern you, Annabel.'

As her regular visits to the riding centre made her more accomplished, she could now find her own way around the stables, and was generally content to catch her horse if it was loose in the paddock, or if not, to bring it from the stable block. She knew how to muzzle it and to put on the martingale, which stopped the horses head from bobbing.

The blanket and saddle now seemed less heavy than at first, because she had learnt the knack of swinging it onto the horse's back, and then firmly tightening up the saddle straps. With a familiar old saddle, she could shorten the stirrups herself and knew how many notches were needed to adjust the straps. It was only when she finished her two-hour ride and feeling tired, she would ask one of the grooms to put the horse away.

'Do you know where Mr Caruthers is this morning?' She was unsure of how much information she could extract from the girl. 'Is he coming back soon, and shall I wait?'

Sharon had no reason to be over helpful, and remained politely casual. 'I have no idea, Mrs Cumberpot; he just gave me my jobs to do, and said that he would see me later. You know how he can be sometimes—head in the clouds!' Sharon looked at Annabel, smiled and shrugged.

'Did he say where he had gone?' Annabel demanded.

Annabel felt the girl was becoming exasperating and stubbornly unhelpful, which was the exact moment when she rather stupidly blurted out, 'Well what do you know, Sharon? You must know something!' Annabel walked out of the stable block fuming. Kicking a passing marmalade cat, she heard Sharon's distant trailing voice.

'Now I remember Mrs Cumberpot, I think he said he was going to Reading.'

Silently laughing she thought to herself, *'What a nasty bitch she is! I really don't know what he sees in her! He is such a nice man. What a horrid cow she is!'*

Annabel sat at Robin's desk in the arena office, and wrote a note on the back of an official looking letter he had only recently received. In it she tried to be chatty and nonchalant but unconcerned.

"Dear Robin,

I have been spending a lot at time in Watlington recently dealing with the builders, but there are still masses of things to do before I can move in, so I am still in Lewknor most evenings. Your Mr Dent is a very good architect, although a little slow at times, and prone to procrastinate over small issue, involving plumbing and suchlike; but generally I am pleased with the way things are going.

I haven't seen you for a little while, and I hope that everything is all right with you and yours. Perhaps we could meet up for a drink later this week? However, I am planning to come to the stables for a ride on Sunday; if that is OK with you, and then we can have a good chat.

Yours, AC."

When he returned from Reading he found the note on his desk, scribbled on the back of an important letter he had received that morning.

After all the recent events concerning Sarah, the thought of facing Annabel and her incessant questions, was becoming somewhat daunting. Sunday would most certainly be off the cards, because it was the day he was due to take Sarah out for the afternoon.

A buffet lunch at The Bull in Sonning seemed rather a good idea, mainly because it would not be too busy at lunchtime, and afterwards they could go for a quiet walk by the Thames, and to sit by the water's edge and relax. It was clear from Dan's most recent remarks that there was still a long way to go with Sarah's rehabilitation.

'Just keep her quiet and try not to intimidate her in any way. She is very sensitive, and reacts to any perceived slight or criticism. Keep off any humiliating subjects concerning the past, because she is not ready for that yet. Imagine her as a teenager, who is full of all sorts of insecurities, and subtly build up her trust. It takes time Mr Caruthers, you must realize that?'

'Can't make Sunday I am afraid Annabel, I have got one of those family things to attend to, so it will have to be some other time. Saturday, perhaps?' The telephone answering machine in Lewknor had a strange and crackly message on it with a young boy's voice.

Robin was pleased that he could enjoy the anonymity of a recorded message, one which Annabel would receive that evening when she returned from bullying the builders. He went on. 'Give me a call at the office tomorrow early, and we can arrange another time,' he said rather unconvincingly.

Robin Caruthers had his mind on other things, and none of them were likely to involve Annabel for the time being.

1993 HELSINKI

'*Where had all the time gone?*' Arthur Cumberpot asked himself as he proudly visited the sights and sounds of the Finnish capital with his young son James. It seemed that he had missed out on much of his formative years, and that he had become a little bit of a stranger. With his steady progress up the diplomatic ladder through the various levels of Foreign Service hierarchy, although he had been diligent and hard working as a man, he may have seemed to be rather neglectful and lax as a father. But it was now a golden opportunity to put these matters right.

Finland in the summer was an unending choice of pleasures for young boys like James. Up until then he had lived mainly on a diet of boarding school, Croydon at half term and most holidays, a few weeks here and there in Lewknor, and the occasional summer break with his parents when in easy reach of Heathrow. His bossy mother was never really interested in him, and by her behaviour at least she saw him more as a distraction if not a nuisance when her own interests were at stake. His father seemed similarly preoccupied, but was he?

Now both of them were away from Annabel's clutches, it was to be one of few occasions they would spend together for some while. Arthur also felt that the occasion deserved some serious time spent in exploring the country in which, as First Consul, he was now a senior official UK representative. Surely, it was high time for him to get away from the Embassy, to use his credit card and the Embassy Jaguar, to get better acquainted with Finland, and to enjoy some of his Foreign Office perks?

'We have got quite a choice of things to see and do, James.'

Arthur had done his homework. 'It's summer festival time, so you can take your pick. There is opera in Savonlinna, folk music in Kaustinen, chamber music in Kuhmo, Naantali and Mustataari, organ music in Lahti and finally some rock and jazz in Pori.'

To James, his father had never really come over as a music buff, but that may well have been due to his mother being practically tone deaf. *Home and Gardens* or *Horse and Hounds* magazine rarely had any views on music, or the arts in general. It was all about middle-class style, and any music appreciation, if it had ever existed, had rather fallen by the wayside in recent times.

'What is your favourite pop group?' Arthur asked rather rhetorically, 'The Boom Town Rats?'

James looked at his father in disbelief. 'No dad, that was years ago; it's all changed now. I like Madness, Kate Bush, and Ian Dury because I'm into new wave funk. They are my favourites at the moment. What about you?'

Arthur had to think very hard, by delving into the mists of time and a miasma of music he had sought to ignore. He would not score too many points if he said Gilbert and Sullivan, so in his mind he continued to struggle for a popular music artist, finally coming up with the name Frank Ifield.

'Is he a punk singer?' James was getting into the bonding process.

'Well that sort of thing,' replied his somewhat flushed

father as he gamely tried to change the subject onto more familiar topics.

'Anyway, not to worry, let's make for the lakes James, because they are so beautiful at this time of the year and there is plenty to see.'

There are over 80,000 islands off the coast of Finland. There are also 180,000 lakes which exist across the country, which also incorporate a further 100,000 islands all teeming with wildlife, flora and fauna. During the summer months the sun can be seen from Helsinki for 19 hours a day, and in the very north the sun does not set for 67 days. Rather like Canada, it is a place for people who in summer like nature and the outdoors, especially in the Oulankajoki National Park, which is a paradise for hikers and fishermen.

Covered in natural woodlands and small rivers, the countryside is sparsely populated. It is said that the harsh winter conditions probably formed the character of the people who live there. In winter the sun never shines in the north for a period of 52 days, perhaps accounting for the Finnish character which is perceived as being stubborn, imperturbable and taciturn.

James' father was a careful driver, not given to high speed, and relaxing to be with, the trip was uneventful. From Helsinki they took the coast road to Kotka, then followed along the Russian border to Imatra and then inland to the lakes and the town of Savolinna. It was here where the opera festival was in full swing, and for which Arthur Cumberpot had recently received four complementary tickets from the Finnish Ministry of Culture.

They both agreed to stay in Savolinna for just three days, and so his father decided to push the boat out and to book in at the four stars Tott Hotel. It was close to the town centre and within easy reach of Olavinlinna Castle, the venue for the opera.

The opera which was being performed that night was The Knife by Paavo Heininen, and was announced as being a World Premier. Although the hotel was rather full due to the festival, they managed to gets a twin bedroom overlooking the town and the waterways. Once they had settled in they took the bus from the hotel on the regular local opera service.

Winding through the town, the bus took them over the long bridge which crossed the lake to the 15th century castle. Built on a rock, the huge medieval fortress was lit up and festooned with bunting, offering a portent of good things to come and hopefully a wonderful musical evening.

The result was rather disappointing however, as the truth about the composer and his deconstructive style left both father and son baffled from the very beginning. There was not an ounce of recognizable melody, just a cacophony of unrelated sounds, squeaks, tapping noises and occasional screeches. This caused the pair to stay away after the interval and to go back to their hotel. Before they did however, they looked at some of the exhibits in the museum, which was an opportunity to absorb some Finnish history painlessly without a dreadful musical accompaniment.

Arthur wondered how it was that the composer, who had allegedly studied at the famous Julliard Music School in New York, was only capable of such appalling sounds. So many other Julliard students like Aaron Copeland, Bud Powel and even Bobby Timmons, who were all contemporaries of this seemingly floored Finnish composer, had filled the world with such beautiful sounds!

Back once more at the hotel, they decided to eat at the café next door, mainly because they were exhausted from the journey but also the trauma of the opera. In an odd sort of way, the whole occasion had brought them closer together, and they laughed at their shared experience. The Magic Flute by Mozart was due to be performed the following night by a traveling Latvian Opera Company and this at least would be familiar to both father and son, and a lot less painful.

The next morning there was a knock at the door, and the hotel manager came into the room accompanying a vast breakfast trolley. Holding an enormous basket of fruit, he seemed very formal.

'We would like to extend a warm welcome to the British First Consul and his son James, and we hope that you enjoy your stay here at the Tott Hotel. Please, if there is anything we can do to help you, you only have to ask. We are always at your disposal. It is a great pleasure to have you to stay at the Tott Hotel.'

This was the first time James had seen at first hand the obvious respect his father received as a British diplomat when not under the shadow of his manipulative mother. Although by now he had become used to the way she tried to dominate both him and his father, ordering them about like servants, and telling them what to do all the time. With his mother away in Watlington, it occurred to James how easy and amenable his father seemed, now that they were left to their own devices.

'What would you like to do today, James?' His father was standing on the balcony, breathing in the fresh air of the lakes, and stretching his arms above his head. 'It is so relaxing here, I had no idea!'

'We could take the ferry and look at some of the other islands; it is a beautiful day for a long walk.' He had brought the boots he wore at school for cross country rambling. 'I think we could both do with some fresh air after last night's racket,' he said, laughing mischievously. Smiling, his father agreed.

Putting on a rather battered pair of walking shoes, his father proceeded to lace them up over a pair of thick socks that he'd packed in his traveling case. 'I brought my old rucksack too,' he said, 'so we can take some sandwiches and tea for the day.' He smiled once more at his son.

'I used to go rambling all over the place with the school when I was a boy. I have almost forgotten how much I enjoyed it. It is funny how one forgets!' He turned to one side, lifted his eyebrows and appeared to stare mournfully into the past. Was it with regret, or was it something else?

'That's why I have always wanted a dog, so I could take it for walks in the countryside when I am in England. Would you like a dog James?' Arthur Cumberpot had started to ask questions of his son, but how strange that this had happened so rarely before.

'We will need a guard dog in Watlington daddy, especially if mummy stays there on her own.'

The thought of a large black retriever appeared in his mind's eye, an apparition that pleased him greatly.

1999 THE QUEEN'S OFFICIAL BIRTHDAY IN SOFIA

Philip Filipov and his wife Ksenia networked their way around the British Embassy garden, shaking hands with many different people in his capacity as the official representative of the Bulgarian President. He and his wife were away visiting the US as private guests of President Clinton. Well clear of the yellow press and the Bulgarian publicity machine, it was now left to Philip Filipov and his diplomatic skills to reassure any interested British guests of the Bulgarian President's good intentions.

Greater detail about his country's good intentions would come from the incumbent Prime Minister, the erstwhile King Gregory III of Bulgaria, but that was his affair. He was networking in a different part of the garden, stuttering out his support for the on-going EU accession talks, and his continued commitment to the now famous 800 days; during which time he had promised the political and social transformation of the country.

In common with most Balkan Republics, the opposition—which Filipov by definition supported—was gleefully awaiting Gregory's dismal failure, his ultimate humiliation, and a prompt return to obscurity. However, Filipov did hold certain reservations on that account.

This was because the King had somehow managed to capture the attention of the world, as well as unearthing some previously hidden nationalists and royalists who had hitherto remained unrepresented within the political spectrum. This meant that Bulgaria no longer seemed beleaguered and set aside from the world by other leaders, politicians' newspapers, and western TV channels. Royal weddings or funerals and their attendant coverage continued to confirm his front page status as a prominent leader, despite his diminishing image within Bulgaria itself.

As he considered these on-going themes, the rather flamboyant and ample figure of Annabel was nonchalantly oscillating though the embassy garden towards him in the opposite direction. With the practiced glad handing of a diplomat's wife, she came upon the Filipovs with little genuine interest. Shaking his hand with a somewhat disdainful look upon her face, she enquired, 'And, what do you do then?'

'Good evening, Lady Cumberpot; my name is Philip Filipov and I am representing our President at your wonderful garden party this evening; and this is my wife Ksenia Filipova.' He handed a newly minted card bearing the address of the President's private office and waited for a response.

'Oh! So err, what exactly does that mean?' Annabel handed back the card as though it might have been his driving license. It seemed to Filipov that perhaps details might not be her strongest point.

'I am representing the President this evening due to his absence in the US, although generally I am an advisor within the President's Cabinet on matters of diplomacy and security.' He waited for a moment whilst he looked into her staring eyes.

He continued: 'Some years ago I was ambassador in London, so I know England quite well. It was because of this that he thought we might become better acquainted.' Annabel's penetrating eyes then turned to Ksenia Filipova who was smiling beside him.

'And what do you do Mrs Filipot?'

Annabel Cumberpot, attempting to look as though she was vaguely interested in this polite couple, gave a plastic smile, or was it a slight look of incomprehension?

'I'm a half Professor at a literary college in Doctors gardens. I understand that you are a Master of Arts yourself, Lady Cumberpot, and I hear you studied at Oxford. So you never know, we might find something in common to talk about!'

'Oh! That was many years ago. I'm just a wife and mother these days. Being a diplomat's wife is quite time-consuming. I expect that you too had masses of things to do when you were in London, Mrs Filipot. Where is your embassy now? Let me think, oh yes, Kensington. Close to the park I understand? How very nice!"

These and many other rhetorical questions glibly rolled of her tongue, which was her characteristic attempt to belittle almost anyone she came into contact with. Most would normally have tried to escape from her patronizing gaze and to disappear into the crowd, but Filipov was made of sterner stuff.

'Actually, we have been posted all over Europe in the past thirty years, and of course Russia. I met your father there once, Lady Cumberpot, together with your brother John.'

'You met Mr Pergamon in Russia? No, that's not possible, he rarely leaves England if he can help it; doesn't like to travel much these days—you must be mistaken, Mr Filipot!" She glared at him in a somewhat antagonistic way.

Fifteen years had passed quite quickly, but he remembered faces and places perfectly well; perhaps it was his punishment for being intelligent.

'No, Lady Cumberpot, your real father, General Kilbey. I met him on a number of occasions both in Moscow and on the Black Sea, together with his

Russian wife Rufa, and of course your brother John. Didn't you know about this?'

If ever a statement was successfully contrived to wipe the look of messianic self-importance off Annabel's face, Philip Filipov had succeeded brilliantly.

'This will of course remain a secret between the three of us, Lady Cumberpot,' he went on. 'I have no wish to embarrass you. It is not my intention to reveal your secret to anyone; I just thought you might like to know a little more about your father, that's all!'

'No, I don't, Mr Filipot. It is a matter that rests in the past. I am the innocent result of a loveless marriage for which I have been punished all my life. I am sure that even you can understand that.'

Her natural contempt returned once more, and without another word she turned and flounced away and stood next to the reassuring but diminutive figure of her prematurely puffed-up husband. Sir Arthur Cumberpot had a large glass of whisky in his hand and was standing on his own by the bar with his back to his many distinguished guests.

There was a faraway and somewhat benign look upon his face, one which vanished with the arrival of his flustered wife. He had never seen her look so frightened before which was an extremely ominous sign. It was also cause for him not to deliver his most recent revelations to his rather condescending and insufferable wife.

Ksenia Filipova finally said to her husband, 'I don't know who I feel sorrier for; him or her. They both seem quite horrible!"

He smiled ruefully at his wife of many years and said, 'Perhaps they deserve one another Zenny! Perhaps there is a God after all.'

PART TWO

THE END 1999–2000

CHAPTER NINE

THE RAFFLE IN SOFIA

DIRTY MACINTOSH was responsible for running the raffle together with Ron Beamish. Between them they had concocted a ruse which they believed would accurately distribute the assorted gnomes to their official spy network. It was very simple.

There were twenty gnomes available, and therefore twenty winners. There were 200 raffle tickets for sale for five Leva each making a total value of 1,000 Leva. Of the twenty winners, ten gnomes would be for the spies and a further ten could be for anyone else. The resultant dosh would be for the doggy ladies and "Paws for Thought."

What they devised was a system whereby only the prearranged winning tickets would be put into the hat when the draw took place plus ten others. This way the ten spies would automatically get their garden gnomes, and that no one cared 'two monkeys' about the remaining ten.

Pretty fool-proof one might think, because all they had to deal with in reality was to manage the transfer to the ten official raffle winners and to make sure that the rest of the draw looked genuine.

'It's a no brainer.' Dirty Macintosh the Embassy spook seemed extremely confident of the outcome, despite his reservations about the project as a whole. 'It won't take long; one of the "Paws For Thought" ladies can make the draw, the Ambassador's wife can distribute the gnomes to the winners, Sir Arthur can make a short speech, and then we can all bugger off home. No problem!'

The doggy ladies mingled amongst the assembled guests handing out some rather poorly printed leaflets. On the front was a photo of a moth-eaten looking dog, wearing a silk sash on which the motto "Barking for Joy" was emblazoned.

'Please give generously to help us in our cause to save these noble Bulgarian creatures,' one of the ladies was tearfully heard to say to the amazement of the indigenous guests. Waving his raffle ticket in the air, the smiling Mayor of Sofia put his arm around her and waited patiently for the photographer to finish clicking, 'You see, I always keep my promises,' he said through his shiny white teeth.

Ron Beamish carefully kept account of the receipts, whilst Dirty Macintosh stood by with his prearranged nudge that would denote an authentic spy whose ticket was to be kept separately for the draw. It was agreed that the ten random units were to be allocated at Ron's discretion.

'To whomsoever is in the right place at the right time and deemed appropriate,' was Foreign Office speak for anyone at all really!

And so the sale of raffle tickets began, and a process which took much longer than anyone expected, due to the large number of guests who were totally skint! But in the end the raffle tickets were all sold, and the plan put into operation. Now the rest was up to the doggy ladies to draw the winners, and to Lady Cumberpot to hand out the prizes.

Most of the winners were nondescript baldies wearing a black suit, a Hong Kong Rolex, and Rayban sunglasses. This was Dirty's most difficult section, due to problems with identification, but the older men and women were easier to recognize, because they did not look like gangsters or prostitutes. There were a few people who held their raffle tickets upside down like 16, 91, 18 or 81; but this was fast resolved by Ambassador Cumberpot's wife, who acted as the de-facto referee.

Any little problems or misunderstandings were easily resolved by her mild rebuke, 'Hard luck, it isn't you, and you haven't won,' which seemed to do the trick.

The only time she was nervous and reserved was when handing over a grinning gnome to Philip Filipov and his wife Kzenia. Thanking her profusely for his prize, she simply stared at him and said nothing.

Sir Arthur thanked everyone for attending, and

wished the fortunate winners of the raffle many happy hours in the company of their assorted gnomes.

'It is a great tribute to the new tide of democracy that is sweeping through Bulgaria, that we, soon to be brothers in the family of the European Community, can enjoy an evening together in fraternity and with such hope for the future. It is especially important that we bind this future together with the ties of social equality; one that is ever present, and bodes well for all Bulgarians, going forward into the new millennium.'

Arthur had no idea what this baffling gobbledygook meant, because it had been written for him, but what he did know was that he had missed an opportunity to tell Annabel about his future plans.

It was at this point the party folded up. When a very shifty looking character walked off with three gnomes under his arm, although it was eventually deemed to be perfectly legitimate, it was cause for some suspicion by both Lady Cumberpot and Dirty Macintosh, the presiding judges.

After some interrogation by Mick the security officer, it was discovered that this individual was in fact the French Ambassador. He had bought twenty raffle tickets to cheer up 'Ze Rosbeefs' when there was a lull in the ticket sales. Later he was heard to say in a very loud voice, 'Zis is just ze first tranche of an EU bailout for zis unhappy and impoverished nation.'

The German Ambassador left in hysterics, his American counterpart—who seemed exceedingly baffled by the whole matter—left un-amused, and the Italian Ambassador, draining his wineglass for the umpteenth time, shouted 'Bottoms up,' and lurched towards the exit.

On the whole the distribution was a great success; as was the Queen's Official Birthday Party itself, and most people went home happy. The main concern, however, was who would appear the following month at the inaugural friendship meeting between the Sofia Garden Gnomes Society and the British Embassy. Herodotus the gnome smiled in expectation, although a passing dog did hear a slight buzzing noise coming from his nether regions.

Nevertheless the overall signs looked good for the start of Great Britain's entry into a new technological age of intelligence-gathering and advanced sedition. The special mobile phones had been distributed, as were the gnomes of various dispositions, and all that now remained was to see what any future encrypted downloads might reveal.

Mr Andrey Antov was delighted with what he perceived to be the perfect outcome. That evening when he left the reception, he treated himself to two extra cakes en route to visiting his favourite restaurant for a health-giving low-calorie four-course meal. His smile told you everything.

Annabel had different plans however, and informed Sir Arthur that she would be leaving shortly for Watlington in order to arrange for the delivery of their new Range Rover, and to prepare for the forthcoming Henley Royal Regatta. She was also desperate to get together once more with Robin Caruthers, because she missed him terribly.

But it was equally important for her to get as far away as possible from Philip Filipov, and any insidious plans he had in mind for her. Annabel's instincts told her that they would not be good. How he had found out about her biological father was the real question? It was clear that despite his position as a presidential advisor, he was also a very smart man indeed.

HENLEY ROYAL REGATTA

Covering a period of some five days in July, there are many rowing heats at Henley, involving 500 crews from fifteen different countries. In rowing terms the event is generally regarded as the most prestigious regatta in existence, and to win puts a successful rower at the pinnacle of his or her sporting career; with far greater significance than even an Olympic gold medal might suggest. But, this is a very English view.

However, these accomplishments are mainly disregarded by the majority of visitors to the regatta, who are relentlessly preoccupied with the liberal consumption of Champagne, various types of Pimm's cocktails, and many other powerful alcoholic beverages. Dressed in their ill-fitting old school blazers with moth-eaten caps, frayed boaters, or bedecked in a groaning double-breasted blazer with old collage tie and Panama hat, the men resemble a nineteenth-century convention of Norfolk butchers on a seaside outing to Whitby.

And the women, well, they are all dressed for Ascot, which happens during the previous June, and so their expensive outfits can be worn twice. The general view of course is that they are all very English and extremely spiffy. But Henley Royal Regatta is also a place to exhibit one's wealth, and to be seen.

As they sit and guzzle their bubbles in total bliss, the results announced over the regatta tannoy system only occasionally invoke a murmur of interest from the gathering, when an old public school or university club is declared the winner. But these days it is the Russians and the Americans who seem to win everything. When these unwelcome results are declared, the average response is either total silence, or the occasional boo.

Then there are the incumbents of the various corporate entertainment venues that increasingly litter the banks of the Thames. They, and the majority of Phyllis Court members simply regard the presence of the Thames as an item of decoration, a lazy summer July backdrop for their determined and considerable gurgitation of food and beverages.

There are of course some exceptions to the rule, on this particular occasion one was Robin and Sarah Caruthers, and the other the Cumberpot family! Unbeknown to either Annabel or Robin, both had secretly made their family plans in the forlorn hope of enjoying an uncomplicated and relaxing Sunday afternoon watching the rowing, and sitting by the river.

James Cumberpot was busy helping out at the Stewards Enclosure with some of the other boys from Summerlake College. They were collecting tickets at the entrance and handing out programs to anyone who was vaguely interested in the rowing heats. Each day these programs are reprinted giving precise information about the day's races and the participants. Dressed in blue blazer and school tie, Summerlake boys ran in and out of the various enclosures carrying out errands, and generally being as useful as possible.

Sir Arthur and Lady Annabel had tickets for the Stewards Enclosure care of Mr Dent the Watlington architect. This included a pass for the Stewards' car park, where each member usually holds a jolly alfresco party. Homemade food is normally served up on camping or trestle tables, with the various guests reclined on a mixture of garden chairs and stools, and anything useful which they can easily fit into their cars. The rest have to sit on blankets or stand and balance plates and glasses in one hand, whilst waving a fork around in the other.

Annabel had spent the previous evening preparing their picnic by diligently frying four pounds of Cumberland sausages, and making piles of Marmite and cucumber sandwiches. These were her favourite, and she had purposely brought a large bottle of Branston Pickle to be served with the sausages which were to be eaten cold.

The poached salmon with mayonnaise was brought by the Dent family, together with various salads, and a very large trifle which Mrs Dent had thoroughly drenched in sherry, lashings of English custard—topped with fresh whipped cream—and finished off with a garland of red glace cherries. Annabel hoped that she would not be expected to eat any unusual or exotic dishes that day, just good old-fashioned English food.

Sir Arthur was pleased to be back by the Thames after all his years spent away in Foreign Service. He well remembered rowing for Beaumont at the Royal Regatta, or to be more accurate, coxing for their first eight. They had won all the heats in their section, but in the final, had lost to an enormous American crew from Boston. It was to be his last race, his ultimate moment of camaraderie, and his final moment of independence.

This year he had taken some early embassy leave to attend the regatta, to be near to his son James, who at eighteen years of age was fast becoming a young man.

'Did you bring the Rennies, Arthur?' Annabel barked as he drove towards Henley along the Fairmile. The traffic was packed and the going was very slow, but at 10 o'clock in the morning there was plenty of time.

The previous week Robin Caruthers had sat in the garden of The Rose and Thistle in Argyle Road which was only a few doors away from the half-way house. Des the Welsh landlord was very welcoming to Dan the hostel director, whom he regarded as a great asset to the community. His wife had experienced a nervous breakdown some years before, and he had marvelled at the devotion and patience of these practitioners.

Sipping a bitter shandy, Robin looked optimistic. 'Its Henley Regatta next week Dan, and I have had an invitation to meet some friends on Sunday in the Stewards Enclosure. Do you think that Sarah will be up to it? It's only for the afternoon, and they are very nice people.' Dan took a large gulp of his Courage Special Ale and thoughtfully rolled himself a third cigarette.

'Just be sure you can leave if she shows any signs of stress. As I said before, the smallest thing can set her back, especially if people keep probing her for information and answers.' But Robin knew that Norman Dent was a sensitive man, and his wife Naomi was famously understanding.

'It will just be the usual small talk, and I have already spoken about Sarah to the Dents, who I have incidentally known for a number of years, so they know what to expect.'

Robin understood that it was a big step for Sarah, and he also realized that one wrong word and it could affect her continuing treatment, which up until then had been largely successful.

However, the kindly Dent family had omitted one major piece of information. They had not mentioned the simultaneous invitation of Sir Arthur and Lady Cumberpot to the party. In her usual bullying fashion, Annabel had recently become rather demanding of her architect, and had presumed on him one afternoon whilst handing over some cash for the builders, together with a cheque for his professional services.

'Arthur and I would very much like to attend Henley Royal Regatta this year, and I heard from someone that you are a member of the Stewards, Mr Dent. As you know, my husband was a university rower, and my son in his final year at Summerlake College, and I thought it would be splendid if we could all meet up together; perhaps on the final Sunday?'

Architect Dent generally reserved his Henley activities for friends and family, but it also occurred to him that the inclusion of this distinguished couple might also help his professional interests if it could be properly managed.

Norman Dent also knew that his professional services had been recommended by Robin Caruthers to Lady Cumberpot, and so he assumed that they knew one another and that the regatta would be a welcome get-together. He was quite unaware of the private nature of Robin's relationship with Annabel Cumberpot, the cooling off which had recently occurred, and consequently saw no danger on the horizon. But kindness is not always rewarded that way.

Two hours later the Cumberpots finally passed over Henley Bridge. Arthur turned left past the Leander Club and onwards through the entrance to the Stewards. Presenting his invitation and car pass he was directed to the far end of the Stewards' car park, where they saw the welcoming figures of Norman and Naomi

Dent. They had kept a space free for the Cumberpots despite the attempted intrusion of nearby groups, as they expanded their numbers, camp chairs and tables. The Cumberpots climbed out of their new dark green Range Rover, and Annabel proceeded to introduce her husband to the Dents.

'This is my husband Sir Arthur,' she said waving in the general direction of her diminutive spouse, 'and you must be Mrs Dent?' Annabel had decided to take the initiative from the very first moment, something that Naomi Dent was uncomfortable with, since she was the hostess.

'Yes of course. How do you do, Sir Arthur, or shall I call you Arthur?' The ambassador felt rather out of place in his Kowloon stitched dark suit, but he had mistakenly left his double breasted blazer in Sofia. His florid countenance reflected a little uncertainty about how he wanted to be addressed, and because he was so used to meeting fawning sycophants, he was a little taken aback.

'Yes of course, that's my name; or the one I usually answer to.' His attempt at humour resulted in the first chortle of the day, and set the tone for the next two hours. It was now midday.

It was Norman Dent's theory that the first drink of the day should not be too strong, and so he mixed up his own concoction of Pimm's No 1, with lots of ice, and a considerable amount of lemonade with just a dash of angostura bitters. This was mixed up in a large glass jug with an assortment of cucumber apple, strawberries and a handful of fresh crushed mint. It was his job to mix and serve this concoction to the guests, whilst his wife Naomi dealt with the food. But the food could wait until later, and after the guests got to know one another better.

Arthur opened the back of the Range Rover and removed some padded folding garden chairs and set them out at the rear of the car. He also removed his favourite bottles of Han Krum white wine from Bulgaria, and a bottle of Dimple Haig whisky, which he carefully put aside on a small stool by the two chairs, together with some crystal glasses.

Norman Dent had brought an old-fashioned tin bath with great chunks of ice in it, which was already home to some wine bottles and tins of beer. Arthur placed his wine bottles with the rest.

'I see you are expecting quite a crowd to descend on you!' Sir Arthur looked amazed at the huge pile of booze. It was quite different from the previous week, and the Queen's Official Birthday Party at the Sofia Embassy.

'How many are you expecting, Norman?'

Norman laughed explaining that he had no idea, but that the Dents were always a very popular destination and therefore received plenty of visitors.

'There won't be much of that left by the time we all go home.' He smiled at the couple, and then as an afterthought, 'And if you're worried about drinking and driving, don't. The police are too busy directing traffic today, and if they breathalysed all the wobbly drivers on their way home, half the Government and the City of London would be banned from driving for the rest of their life!'

The Pimm's was cool and soothing and they all relaxed into chattering mode. Then another couple arrived, complaining about the traffic and the M4 motorway. He was a large burly man accompanied by a small woman who they assumed was his wife. Cuthbert Dent joined the group carrying a hamper, whilst Penny his wife carried two bottles of Krug Champagne, which she firmly held one under each arm.

'We have brought a rather good pate,' he announced to his parents, 'with loads of fresh baguette, stunning black olives, and some wonderful fresh butter.'

They seemed pleased that an element of sophistication was to be introduced into the feast, and promptly handed over their things to Naomi Dent, who swiftly put the Champagne on ice alongside the numerous other bottles and cans. Having been introduced, Cuthbert Dent was the first to speak.

'Aren't you the couple who bought that old manor house in Watlington? I think father has spoken about you recently.' Annabel produced her best expressionless smile, and then preceded to innumerate the many virtues of Orchard Manor. As she droned on it was clear that she believed that she occupied a very grand building indeed, and that architect Dent was in fact a heavily disguised reincarnation of Edwin Lutyens.

'I heard that it was falling to bits.' Cuthbert Dent was a simple soul, not given to understatement. 'We all thought it would end up as a block of nasty flats, so you did well to rescue it from oblivion. But it must have cost a bit surely?'

'Oh well, we left all those details in your father's capable hands,' she smiled her assurances, whilst wondering if they had been seriously turned over or tucked up by their generous host.

'Yes,' she continued, 'it has been quite a challenge, although we are nearly there now the garden is finished. We just need to buy some extra furniture, but the late Georgian period is not the easiest to find in the local antique shops. You see, the house really needs the right pieces in it in order to create the right effect. So really, that means visiting the auction houses in London or Oxford of course.'

Arthur thought that it was time he had his say, and blurted out, 'I personally think it will be in *Home and Gardens* one of these days. I have every confidence in my wife's choice of furnishings, but as long as I have my own study, a large whisky and a comfortable chair, I shall be quite happy!'

The chortling continued, and the Pimm's helped to blot out the possibility of rain, as clouds started to appear in the background obscuring the sun, and what seemed to be a perfect English summer's day.

'Where do you two live Cuthbert?' Annabel was getting into the *where and when* routine, whilst carefully steering away from any personal details if at all possible; just a few very broad brushstrokes.

'We live in Putney actually; Lacy Road, do you know it? It's not far from the Thames; where all those rowing clubs are by the river,' and as an afterthought, 'and quite close to the trains to.'

Neither she nor Arthur showed any immediate recognition. She hated London, despite her pretentions and talk of auction houses. And Arthur never admitted to any great knowledge of London, except to say he had once worked in Whitehall and been born many years ago somewhere south of the Thames.

'Oh really! And what exactly do you do in London, Cuthbert?' Annabel was trying to control the conversation away from money and her fiefdom in Watlington. 'Well, actually, I sell smells!' He started to laugh as he said it, as did his parents, but not his humourless inquisitor.

'I'm sorry, did you say you sell *smells*, Cuthbert? What does that mean exactly?'

'I have got a company that distributes those things that squirt scent into the air in restaurants, kitchens and their loo's. Some people find it quite refreshing, and I know my accountant does!'

The laughing continued, and a somewhat confused plastic smile reappeared on Annabel's face. Arthur on the other hand, had no idea what they were talking about and just laughed, hoping to get the point later, but it was one which had escaped him entirely.

When he asked Cuthbert's wife the same question, Penny Dent simply said that she was a print buyer for a West End design company.

'How interesting!' Arthur was glad to change the subject away from the somewhat confusing matter of smells. 'And what does that actually entail, Penny?'

Penny Dent filled up her tall glass of Pimm's for the second or was it third time, lit up a Benson and Hedges king-size cigarette, and then thought for a moment. 'Well, drinking mainly. I spend very long lunches with the contract printers, who try to get me pissed but can't! That's what I do most of the time.'

This was not a world that either of the Cumberpots had ever experienced, nor were they ever likely to. So they simultaneously smiled, chortled a bit, and then said in unison, 'Quite, absolutely, yes of course,' and left it at that.

In England this is what most people do at such events, particularly after imbibing a few strong drinks. They can frequently remember the questions though, but very few can recall the answers. What is important however is to look as though you understand precisely what's going on, and then to make astonishingly unrealistic laughing noises; similar to a barking dog, or a noise reminiscent of Basil Brush the TV fox! In fact, this might be the generic definition of the English at play.

To the Cumberpots, the Dent's daughter Louise Dent seemed by far the greater eccentric. She arrived on a psychedelic Vespa scooter, accompanied by someone who appeared to be a white Rastafarian. His name turned out to be Darren, and he came from Milton Keynes. It was unclear what these two had brought to the party, because no food or drinks were to be seen in their possession at all.

Annabel was loath to ask any searching questions, unless they received an honest answer. She was immediately concerned that James might be either abducted or turned into a drug addict. In her calcified middle-class mind, all she could rely on were a series of stereotypes and outrageously musty assumptions.

'And what do you do Louisa?' the astonished Arthur asked the black-clad Goth as she rolled herself a cigarette, despite wearing a pair of thin black lace mittens.

The faux London accent was straight to the point. 'Well Arthur, Darren and I both work for MI5. We have been attending a seminar this week in Cheltenham, buffing up on telecommunication products. It was as boring as hell actually.' Darren agreed but borrowing a blanket from Naomi, he suddenly stretched himself out on the ground and closed his eyes.

After this piece of unexpected information, Arthur was loath to mention anything about his personal job description. There might be some reference to a certain gnome in Sofia which would not fit very comfortably into their otherwise banal and anodyne conversation. The matter was embarrassing enough as it was, without it becoming a further topic for discussion.

Soon the races had started in earnest, and there were occasional cheers from the towpath, directing Arthur's attention to another time and the more youthful and exuberant part of his life. He wondered what had become of his son James who he was anxious to see after more than a year. And it was at this point that Sarah and Robin Caruthers walked into the picture.

'Ah! There you are Robin, we thought you weren't coming!' Norman Dent was pleased to see his old client and friend from Wallingford, 'And finally, the lovely Sarah! How very nice to see you again!'

Sarah looked very pretty in her wide brimmed sunhat and floral print dress, her white patent leather shoes with matching handbag. Despite her startling good looks, she seemed a little shy and reserved, which to the Dent family was only to be expected.

'How do you do?' The jovial face of Sir Arthur was proof alone that Sarah was indeed a very pretty girl, and according to him at least deserved plenty of attention. Annabel on the other hand glared at her with her father's eyes as if she was trying to destroy a hated and feared image.

'Yes of course,' she said, 'Robin has often spoken about you.'

It was hard to disguise her shock and angst, but with practiced composure the moment passed and Annabel managed a smile of sorts and said, 'How nice to meet you.'

'And Robin, of course you know Lady Annabel from the riding school, but I don't believe you have met her husband Sir Arthur. He has recently returned from Sofia where he is presently the British Ambassador.'

And then turning to Sarah, 'They have just purchased Orchard Manor in Watlington, I expect you remember the house. It lays back off the road on the right-hand side, next to the pub on the way in from Lewknor.'

The two innocent parties were Arthur and Sarah, although they got on like a house on fire. The two surprised parties, Annabel and Robin, simply glared at each other and kept as far apart as possible.

The Dent family saw that something was up, and so the guests somehow became polarized into two groups, settling at either end of the trestle table which Naomi Dent had unfolded. It was now covered with a large white paper tablecloth ready for the feast to begin.

First came the poached salmon which—still on the rack from the steamer—had been skinned, the pink cooked flesh revealed and was now decorated with parsley and little tomato roses. This was placed on a wooden board together with the silver fish knife and fork that would be used for serving. Next to this was a large sauce boat full of delicious homemade mayonnaise, a silver ladle, and finally large bowls of fresh vegetable salads, and an enormous dish of potato salad with fresh watercress.

After the shock of meeting Sarah, it took a while for Annabel to compose herself at least enough for her to remove her meagre offerings from the Range Rover. She put the Marmite and cucumber sandwiches and cold sausages onto two identical paper plates, and placed them next to the Pate de Foie Gras and a sumptuous looking English trifle.

'Oh good, you did some sausages. Well done Annabel; I have quite forgotten to do any this year, and I know the men like them because they don't need a plate, and it doesn't get in the way of their drinking either!'

Naomi Dent had catered for this very same event for thirty years. She went on, 'The main thing is to get them all eating before they start to collapse from all that alcohol.'

Meanwhile the segregation was becoming less noticeable, and despite her early shyness Sarah was having a jolly time talking to Darren and Louisa. Arthur was standing next to them, laughing his head off and enjoying every minute. Annabel was also attempting light conversation with Robin, but keeping to the subject of horses was quite difficult for any period of time.

However, Robin's success with the bookies at Royal Ascot during the previous month's event now became a useful subject on its own, and a bewildering prop to their withering conversation about horses.

'I did a Yankee double, put on a monkey and got back 1,260 quid, so it was a pretty good result, I thought; well, for an afternoon on the turf.'

This was a language that neither Naomi Dent nor Annabel could possibly comprehend, but Robin was trying his hardest to stay on friendly terms, to stay on the subject of horses, and not to be confronted by an obviously fuming Annabel. This was not the right time or place for any personal remarks, let alone any recriminations. But then the temptation became too much for Annabel.

'I see that your *wife* is looking remarkably well these days,' she announced, as the Dent family's attention was distracted by the arrangement of assorted food on the flimsy trestle table.

'Yes, I am pleased to say that she has vastly improved and is becoming much more confident.' Robin smiled awkwardly and then looking across at Naomi Dent he said, 'I think it's time that we all had something to eat, don't you Naomi?'

The pop of a champagne cork jolted everyone back to partial sobriety, followed closely by the welcoming rattle of knives and forks on plates. And it wasn't long before polite mutterings of approval began to occur, as thoughts turned exclusively to food.

Oddly enough, Annabel's sausages disappeared almost instantly while the Marmite and cucumber sandwiches remained untouched. Ignored by everyone, and curling up at the edges, they were curiously juxtaposed next to a large but empty jar of Branston Pickle.

Twenty minutes later James appeared on the scene. As he joined the group there was a distant clap of thunder, indicating a sudden change in the weather. He was happy to see his parents, although at first he only spotted his father who by then was becoming a little bit tipsy.

'Hello old boy,' Arthur said, grinning profusely from behind an alcohol induced florid face. He seemed very pleased to see his son James, and affectionately clasped his son's shoulder. 'Mummy and I wondered where you were,' he said grinning. The Henley charm school had clearly worked on his father, and instead of deferring to the authority of his mother Arthur steered his son towards the food.

'This is my son James and this is Mrs Dent who is our hostess today.' It seemed to James that nearly all the people at the party were getting extremely drunk with his father vying for first place.

'How do you do Mrs Dent? Sorry I'm late, but I couldn't find you, there are so many people here today.'

The accumulated chatter from the entire enclosure was becoming deafening, as the various groups became more animated whilst they gamely tried to speak above the tannoy announcements.

'I'm sorry, did you say that you are hungry? There isn't much left I'm afraid. But we do have plenty of sandwiches and a bit of trifle if you're famished.'

Dirty plates and empty bowls were everywhere, their remains congealing in what remained of the afternoon sun; the clouds darkening overhead largely remained unnoticed.

James viewed his mother's untouched plate of curly sandwiches with a sinking heart, knowing from experience whose hands had created them.

'Yes, that would be super,' he said politely, 'and if you

have got something to drink, that would be nice; it's been such a hot day and I have had to run around quite a bit.' Naomi Dent bent forward as though she was seeing two of James and squinted.

'You know, you should not drink alcohol at your age—it is very bad for you, James.'

As the hypocrisy of this ridiculous statement sunk in he started to laugh uncontrollably, and turning to his father he said, 'Oh sorry, I have just thought of something very funny that happened to me this morning Dad, I will tell you about it later!' And luckily his father believed him.

In the end he was forced to eat his mother's ghastly curly Marmite and cucumber sandwiches, which he washed down with the remains of the Pimm's, plus two cans of beer. Mrs Dent by this time had collapsed onto the grass and was fast asleep next to Darren, who had finally conked out for precisely the same reasons.

Afterwards it was agreed that a visit to the regatta would not be complete without a walk by the course. Arthur had read his program carefully, and was anxious to see Beaumont in their final race and to cheer them on, whilst leaving the recumbent Naomi Dent and Darren asleep on the grass.

Annabel said she was loath to join them, because her tummy was playing up rather badly, no doubt due to the two large helpings of English trifle she had consumed. Initially she had refused to eat it at all, but when it was presented to her by the Dents as a

Traditional English Trifle, it automatically became entirely within the strict ambit of her gastronomic preferences.

Robin also politely declined the invitation, claiming that since Annabel and he were busy discussing horse riding, that he would keep her company for half an hour or so.

'Arthur, did you bring the Rennies?' she barked at the disappearing figure of Sir Arthur, who timidly ran back clasping the indigestion tablets she required; and just as nimbly trotted back to his son and their newfound friends who were all on their way to the towpath. Sarah put her left arm through Sir Arthur's and her right arm through his son James', and they all marched off to the river laughing.

Without anyone realizing it, this was precisely what Annabel had intended; because she had a few pressing matters on her mind and needed to discuss them with Robin Caruthers. However, within the hour when the jolly group returned to the car park they found Robin sitting silently smoking a cigarette at one end of the trestle table, and Annabel sitting at the other end dolefully staring into space. Norman Dent could only guess at the reason, and thoughtfully suggested to Robin that maybe Sarah might like to leave shortly.

'No problems Robin, she is perfectly all right, but I think she is very tired! It has been an extremely long day for her,' and Robin agreed.

Walking over Henley Bridge together, they could see the entire length of the rowing course. It looked very beautiful, despite a sudden shower which erupted causing the crowds crossing the bridge to open an assortment of umbrellas, accompanied by various gasps and screeches.

Robin put his blazer around Sarah's shoulder to ward off the rain, and in so doing he pulled her close to him. He held her close all the way to Friday Street, where his old Land Rover was parked. As he turned left into the Reading Road, she smiled at him.

'Thanks for a wonderful day Robin; it was the first time I have laughed for a long time. It was great.' But she had eyes and she could see.

In contrast, Annabel had not enjoyed her day by the river one little bit, but for a very private reason. The Reading Road was very crowded and seemed rather dangerous with a large assortment of swerving and bouncing cars, but it was the return journey which they had fully expected. Norman Dent gave fair warning, and so it was easy to imagine the tossing of coins in the various car parks in Henley, and the arguments about who was fit enough to drive. Annabel did not want to drive, and sulked in the front passenger seat all the way to Summerlake College.

When they had originally looked around the school, it seemed a rather progressive and modern school. Of course it was quite unlike Croydon Grammar, which in the post-war environment had become seriously dog-eared. Now Arthur was curious to know more about the workings of the school and the living conditions experienced by the boarders.

As they entered James' school dormitory, a loud adult voice shouted out, 'Cumberpot, where the hell have you been?'

Arthur turned to the insolent perpetrator and replied, 'My name is Sir Arthur Cumberpot; are you talking to me young man?'

The shock was obvious. 'Oh no sir, I'm afraid I did not see you there. I am so terribly sorry.'

Was this explanation a comment on Arthur's diminutive stature, or were most parents invisible to the school housemasters? He would never know, but saying goodbye to his son he reserved a special scowl for this loud-mouthed master, who he left shouting at anybody and no-one in particular. Back in the car he found Annabel staring out of the window.

'How are you feeling dear?' he said with genuine concern. 'Do you think it was the trifle or the mayonnaise?' But he received no answer, just a grunt.

He went on, 'Did you enjoy it today? I did, especially the wife of that riding school chappie, what's his name? Rodger, or is it Robert? She seemed very nice to me, and very level headed.'

They drove back the long way to miss the Henley traffic, via Caversham Park Village on up through Nettlebed village, and then finally on to Watlington. As he climbed out of the Rover and the electric gate closed behind them, with Annabel's door keys clasped in his hand, Arthur made for the front door. Then, as if she existed in some debilitating time warp, Annabel finally shouted out from the car, 'Robin, his name is Robin bloody Caruthers!'

Back at the half-way house, Dan was there to greet the couple on their return, and taking Robin to one side, he asked how things had been and if Sarah was OK.

'Fine Dan; we all had a great time. There was one little incident with one of the guests, but I don't think Sarah noticed.'

They said their goodbyes, and with a first real sign of affection for years, Robin kissed his wife on the cheek. He smiled at her lovingly, told her that she had been wonderful and that everyone had enjoyed her company.

'I'll see you later in the week Sarah, but I have got to get back now and see to the horses.'

He waved at them both, the old Land Rover turned down Lorne Street, left onto the Oxford Road and then back to Wallingford.

Dan asked Sarah about her medicine, and wondered if she had drunk any alcohol. 'I didn't drink at all Dan, but the rest of them! You won't believe what they managed to pack away during the day. There were only ten of us altogether, but I counted over forty empty wine bottles when I left. I don't know how they do it! It's a mystery to me!'

CHAPTER TEN

WATLINGTON

WHEN THE CUMBERPOTS finally returned to Orchard Manor, Annabel complained of a headache, and decided to go to bed. By now the couple had reverted to an almost Victorian domestic arrangement, whereby they occupied separate bedrooms; Annabel's being the largest one, which was attached to her precisely designed dressing room and en suite bathroom.

On those rare occasions he was in Watlington Arthur slept in a slightly smaller bedroom overlooking the tennis club, which was conveniently next to the second bathroom. He rarely shared this bathroom with anyone else, because firstly no-one came to stay and secondly James was mainly away at school, and soon to go to university. James preferred to use the ground floor shower room on those occasions that he was at home. He occupied an even smaller bedroom situated at the front of the house, which overlooked the road.

So each to their own; it was a comfortable expedient for all three of them. Arthur also had sole use of a small room situated next to the kitchen, which he fondly referred to as his study, and where he experienced some semblance of privacy and reasonably long periods of peace and quiet. However, this was completely at the whim of his ceaselessly demanding wife.

During these few occasions when in England, and away from Bulgaria, Arthur found himself reduced to the status of errand boy and was often sent on shopping excursions into Watlington clutching one of Annabel's detailed shopping lists. His purchase of sausages from the local butcher was considered by many to be unusually prodigious, and the subsequent dietary implications became a matter for great speculation by some of the other customers in the town. It even reached the ears of Mr Griffith the estate agent. One day he spoke to farmer Grimmer, who then visited the Cumberpot home offering to fill their freezer with assorted lamb cuts from his local farm shop.

But Annabel was sceptical about the whole matter. 'It is very kind of you to come here, Mr Grimmer, but what you might not be aware of is my lifelong objection to consuming anything which is not wholesome and English. We do not sully our bodies with foreign muck and stick closely to the recipes and mores of Mrs Beaton and the practical advice of Fanny Craddock the TV cook, and her faithful husband Jonny. We will have none of that Galloping Gourmet rubbish, just well-prepared local dishes, especially sausage and mash.' Farmer Grimmer was amazed at her vehement rejection of his locally produced clover fed lamb and mutton.

'We also make pork or lamb sausages, Lady Cumberpot,' he muttered, 'but I thought that if I supplied you with a whole lamb, it might prove more convenient for you and your family, as well as being considerably cheaper.' Farmer Grimmer had also heard of Lady Cumberpot's odd views about food, and wondered if they might be pathological.

'Yes—well anyway—we haven't got a deep freeze, and I am not sure where I could put one even if I had one. But while you're here, perhaps you can tell me how much you charge for your sausages just in case we might need some?'

On the occasion of their return from Henley Regatta, whilst Annabel took to her bed, Arthur went and sat in his newly painted study and contemplated the day's events. He had very much enjoyed the company of the unorthodox Dent family, who showed little reverence for his diplomatic status and which had amused him greatly. He particularly loved the two spies—with their total disregard for convention—Cuthbert Dent who sold smells and even Penny his exceedingly thirsty wife.

But the creature that made the afternoon so memorable was the delicious Sarah, with her shyness and modesty. It was seldom that he was able to speak to someone so frankly and with such an open heart. She had somehow been able to comprehend his own small view of the world, something that reminded him of his devoted PA Edwina.

It was she who occupied much of his thoughts these days and had done so since James' holiday in Finland. After the many years they had known one another and worked together, they had obviously built up a good working relationship and consequently made a good team, but as he sat in his little home office he was perplexed. Was it Edwina's good humour and kindness that he missed, or could it be more than that?

This and many other matters had occupied his mind a lot recently, and it had been his intention to discuss these and other issues with his wife at the Queen's Official Birthday Party in Sofia. He wanted to tell her that he was quite content with their virtual separation, something which seemed to work despite the usual idle conjecture that would normally have accounted for her protracted absences.

It was now over two years since he had received his Knighthood in the New Year's Civil Honours List, and his appointment as Ambassador to Bulgaria. Consequently Arthur was more than happy with the course of events, and perfectly content to let his wife enjoy her newly found status amongst the inhabitants of Watlington. It was increasingly clear that the recently elevated Lady Cumberpot had finally achieved the personal distinction she had desperately craved for many years. Maybe this was Annabel's reward for standing by him, or even his for continuing to support her? After all, Croydon seemed to have disappeared off the radar screen, or had it?

It was the look of fear on her face that afternoon which dissuaded him from mentioning his present contentment, and his total acceptance of their on-going domestic arrangement. But what had frightened her so much? This was what was bugging him, and he dare not ask!

READING

As the months and years passed Sarah became more inured to life at the half-way house, amongst its many often bemused occasionally frightened residents. There were times when she too went running to Dan, pleading to be returned to the reassuring surroundings of the hospital, but these moments soon passed as she became used to her environment, and her newly found freedoms of both movement and expression.

The most important ingredient of her newly expanding world was a new Olympus camera which Robin had given her. This OM10 camera somehow gave her the freedom to roam the streets of Reading or to walk along the Thames in nearby Caversham. Looking at life through a single lens reflector focused her attention objectively, far away from the restrictions of her previously self-paralyzing existence, and the horrifyingly confused emotion it generated.

Dan was very supportive, and not only encouraged her to pursue this newly found interest, but he also invested in a small developer and an enlarger. These he purchased from an old friend who was a professional Reading photographer. Sarah kept this photographic equipment in a small hall cupboard in the basement, which also acted as an occasional dark room.

By now the relation between doctor and patient had moved on to a kind of guarded friendship and mutual respect. Even Dan could see that his patent had some obvious talent, which he nurtured with thoughts of future employment. Not only was he well aware that the people in his care needed hope, but that they would also need a job at some point.

For Sarah, the industrial revolution held a special interest as a subject matter. The many derelict buildings left to rot by the Kennet canal in Reading, the old mills and the crumbling locks with their leaking paddles, weirs and rusty hinges were all grist for Sarah's searching eye.

Robin was amazed by the change he saw in her, and he spent more and more time visiting Argyle Road. He also enjoyed many talks with Dan at the pub.

'How do you think she is progressing, Dan? She seems almost her old self to me,' and then as an afterthought, 'whatever that may mean!' Dan was less effusive than Robin expected.

'When you come here you see her on her best behaviour, Robin, but there have been times when she begged me to let her go back to the clinic. I of course said no because the whole point of the half-way house is to confront the patients—and remember that is what they are—with reality. They don't always like what they see, I'm afraid.'

Robin was silent for a while, and swilled the remains of his bitter shandy around his glass. 'I understand what you mean Dan, but I was hoping…'

Dan interrupted, 'I know what you are hoping for Robin, and I can see it plainly when you are with her during your visits, but it is too soon, old chap. My advice is to button it up if you can; which is my advice to her as well. I think it would be fair to describe your respective feelings at the moment as mutually exclusive, but—and it's a big but—the world does not turn on emotions but on practicalities as well!'

As he drove the old Land Rover along the Oxford Road, Robin's head was full of mixed feelings and contradictions. His mental picture of Sarah and the house in Argyle Road all seemed to become as one. He now saw her as a calm confident and attractive woman who was at peace in the surroundings of her comfortable room. A story heavily punctuated by the various black and white photographs, of Huntley and Palmer's 19th Century factory, Aldermaston lock on a winter's day, and the Island Bohemian Bowling Club on Fry's Island; the bar full of boozy old timers recounting the past and their many games of bowls.

These photographs and others, which now hung in neat wooden frames on the walls of her room, all seemed very normal to Robin; and so he was greatly perplexed by Dan's last statement to him about his feelings towards his wife Sarah, and any future they might still have together.

THE SOBRANIE SOFIA

From behind his desk in the Prime Minister's office King Gregory III stood up and smiled as the British Ambassador entered his rather dingy office in the parliament building. Shaking hands, he invited Sir Arthur to sit on the rather worn leather settee opposite a coffee table and two matching armchairs by a window which overlooked the Parliament Square. Sitting next to the diminutive Englishman, it reaffirmed his long-established custom of putting people at their ease by always talking to them on the same level.

'Well Sir Arthur, at last we have a chance for a chat together, away from the swanking and posing of the last few months. I for one, am enormously tired of these state occasions, and can't wait to return to my flower garden. My wife says that it is the only time I'm properly relaxed.'

The slight French inflection in his accent could not totally mask his English Public School education, or his stint at Cambridge University.

'Quite so Sir, and can I say how pleased we all are that you are here and that the election was so successful.'

'Hardly Sir Arthur, I only scraped home by a

smidgen, and I have had to indulge in a lot of political hanky-panky to put this present government together.'

'We were all behind you and so pleased when you won, and I know that our Royal Family is also happy about your success, but I expect you know about that from first hand. And if there is any way by which we can help you in the future, all you have to do is ask and the British Government will surely lend you its full support.'

Arthur was typically lower middle class with his worship of kings and his quite nauseating way of sucking up to any aristocrat or royal that came within fawning distance; a problem he also seemed to have with medical doctors and senior church clerics. Surely his Knighthood should have put paid to these sycophantic tendencies?

He of course had lost his common touch years ago. His habitual tendency to despise almost anybody he came into contact with during the course of his diplomatic duties was legion, except a king that is, but that was different! Gregory III frowned, leaving a kind of fretwork of lines on his forehead, and then looked almost angelically at the ceiling.

'There are two matters I hoped we could address today; one which you have already been discussing with the Norwegian Ambassador. I understand from Dr Lind that your country is greatly concerned about the unreasonable tariffs which my country enjoys on our export of white cheese. Of course the Greeks have had it in for us since the start of the accession talks.' Leaning back and stretching his legs, he put his hands behind his head.

'Mind you, they don't mind buying it from us for peanuts, and then selling it on as feta cheese; somewhat misleadingly marked *Made in Greece*. What they do, I understand, is to chop it up and then repackage it.'

Gazing at the British Ambassador he went on, 'They are of course our natural enemies, of that there is little doubt, although ex-King Dimitrios and I have enjoyed many a game of gin rummy together in the past and personally get on extremely well.'

'Another king, how wonderful!' Arthur's spirits rose, and although this interview had become a little too informal for Sir Arthur's taste, he was rather enjoying the intimacy of the conversation. 'I am sure Sir that this matter can be resolved in committee at the EU. I am told that the Germans have it in for the Greeks and the French are buying a cheese factory in Nova Zagora. So there is plainly no support for this matter, and all this angst is most likely just a bit of Greek mischief-making and their usual brinkmanship. They are born traders and frankly can't make anything worth buying. Well, not in my wife's opinion anyway.'

'How is your wife, Sir Arthur—Lady Annabel, I believe? I met her at your Queen's Official Birthday celebration. Quite amusingly she mistook me for the owner of a Casino in Sofia—a man called Don something or other! We had a long chat about horseracing, believing me to be a professional gambler.

She wanted to know what a Yankee Double was. I said it was probably Mickey Mouse and Donald Duck, but she didn't find it at all amusing and walked away in a huff.'

'I am so sorry, Sir, for my wife's behaviour; you must have found her rather rude, but she has been greatly under pressure recently organizing our new house in Watlington. She has had to do everything, while I have remained here in Sofia to attend to important diplomatic matters. I do apologize once more.'

'Think nothing of it, Sir Arthur, but it does bring me to my second point, which regrettably seems also to involve your wife. She may have developed an unhealthy association with a member of the President's cabinet—an old Communist warhorse called Philip Filipov. They were seen together in the Sheraton Hotel recently, which is something I thought you should know about.'

BRITISH EMBASSY, SOFIA

It was a sunny late afternoon, when Andrey Antov steered his rotund figure through the front gate of the Embassy, and into the immediate garden. Under his left arm he carried his favourite gnome which he called Rodney. Quite small but with a beaming smile, Rodney had been a boon companion during his trials and tribulations, especially during the dark days before the changes. With no friends to speak of, a hysterical wife and a troublesome daughter, Antov quite rightly felt that he had been dealt a bad hand of cards. It was only made bearable by the comprehensive collection of gnomes which remained in his possession after his humiliating departure from the Sofia Burial Service.

With rising spirits he strode up to Dirty Macintosh and, vigorously shaking him by the hand, he declared, 'Mr MacDonald, this is a very important day for us both, and it will I hope be a new beginning for British Bulgarian relations and evidence of all our very best intentions.'

Dirty looked at the bulging President of the Sofia Garden Gnomes Society (SGGS) with a certain disdain, and whilst ruing the antics he was forced to perform by MI6—in order to keep his job—he irritatingly replied, 'Macintosh is my name, Mr Angelov. MacDonald's make disgusting hamburgers! My name is the same as the waterproof coat!'

'My apologies, Mr Macintosh. I sometimes have problems with English names. And where is Mr Beamish, is he here this afternoon?' As he turned to inspect the filling scene, he saw the beaming pixie face of Ron Beamish coming towards him across the lawn.

'Hello Mr Antov!' He seemed almost pleased to see him. 'I'm so glad that you have arrived early, because you can now help me with all the introductions. There are more than forty people present here—eighty including their gnomes of course—so if you expect many more of your people to come I would like to know; the garden is getting very full of guests, and their gnomes as well of course,' he said cheerily.

The fat man cast his eyes around the crowded garden recognizing the familiar faces of his fellow society members, but he was very puzzled by many of the others who were there, because as non-members they seemed strangely out of place. Most of his members were characters, academics and artists, philosophers and writers. They had fallen in love with the idea of gnomenclature, as a harmless pastime, and an expression of their own peaceful aspirations.

Apart from the two British diplomats and his familiar SGGS members, there now seemed to be an equal number of suits with sunglasses milling around the garden, hugging various gnomes whilst nervously sending text messages on their mobiles phones. The French Ambassador was also there, with his three gnomes, in his usual state of euphoria, as were a number of rumpled and bleary eyed businessmen all of whom had been winners in the now famous Queen's Birthday raffle.

Herodotus, the British Embassy gnome, on the other hand stood patiently in the corner of the garden staring at the assembled guests with a look which could only be described as superior. He seemed to come from a different gnome genre, far more upper class than the little grinning plaster halfwits who were being introduced to one another by all and sundry. Although the suits did look a little sheepish as they attempted to emulate the antics of the experienced SGGS members, they took heart when they saw the ease by which both they and their gnomes communicated with one another.

'How is Krassy?' one member asked of another. Holding his gnome close to one ear his eyes flicked from side to side as if in deep concentration. 'He said he is very well thank you, asks me to thank your gnome Vency for his concern, and offers him his kind regards in return.'

The owner of Vency the gnome then held him to his left ear, finally relaying the message that he was pleased to see his friend Krassy after all this time, and that they should get together more often. These antics were repeated throughout the garden by all the eager participants, until the egg mayonnaise sandwiches arrived together with a few bottles of cheap Bulgarian plonk.

At this point all the gnomes were left together in the corner of the garden alongside the smirking Herodotus—who seemed to remain above the whole occasion and quite frankly impervious to their presence—whilst their proud owners mingled enthusiastically, passionately discussing the salient virtues of their respective gnomes, and how they had changed their lives. Then came the speeches.

First to speak was from the inflated figure of Andrey Antov, President of SGGS. With a smile which could only be described as angelic he regaled the assembled crowd with plaudits and congratulations.

'I can't tell you how happy this first meeting of the Anglo-Bulgarian gnome appreciation group has made me. For many years I have painstakingly supported the presence of a friendly gnome in every home. They are such cheery chaps, and take up so very little of our precious time to look after. And now that the British Embassy has seen fit to support our cause, I am bound to say that the future of our bi-lateral relationship is assured for many years to come, which of course is greatly due to our little friends the gnomes themselves.

'Although our numbers are small, it is due to the imagination and resolve of Ambassador Sir Arthur Cumberpot and his own private gnome—called I believe Herodotus—that our numbers are due to swell. The winners of the raffle—held at the Official Queen's Birthday Party—are all therefore cordially invited to join the SGGS, at no cost I might add, to enjoy the support of our knowledgeable members and to help develop a national interest in the ownership of gnomes throughout the country of Bulgaria.'

The jovial figure then turned to his hosts with considerable deference and asked them to say a few words, whereupon Dirty Macintosh confidently addressed the thinning crowd:

'Dear friends or dare I say gnome lovers. The British Ambassador—who was unable to attend this evening due to pressing diplomatic commitments—has asked me to extend his good wishes to Mr Antov the SGGS and his membership, and to say that he is firmly behind the Anglo-Bulgarian gnome appreciation group and their future activities. He also wished me to inform you all that—subject to clement weather conditions prevailing—he is pleased to invite you all to attend an Embassy garden reception each month, in support of the SGGS and their burgeoning membership. We thank you all for being here, and we look forward to seeing you again later next month.'

Although a few people clapped, by this time the garden was practically empty. What was unnerving however was that a number of garden gnomes had been left behind and were to be seen standing shoulder to shoulder with Herodotus in the corner of the garden.

'How many have been left?' Dirty asked Ron with a sinking feeling.

'Only five so far, but three I know belong to the French Ambassador who went home early. He said he had a previous engagement, and left with tears in his eyes, heaving with uncontrolled laughter.'

Ron was not as concerned as Dirty, because he knew that every bona fide spy had left with their personal gnome firmly tucked underneath one arm.

'It's all that riff raff from the Irish pub.' Ron was quite adamant. 'I heard locally that there might have been some breakages too, and I was also told that some of the winners could not work out where their gnomes had actually come from in the first place, when they finally woke up the following morning.'

Dirty was equally amused. 'I saw that two of the gnomes left have been stuck together with superglue and duct tape, and all their bells are missing!' The last part left Ron and Dirty in stitches, as they finished off the cheap plonk and egg sandwiches in their office.

The following day however was very crucial to them

all, as Ron decoded the encrypted messages left in Herodotus' memory bank which had been downloaded to the embassy computer that morning. This was going to be the acid test. They had received ten messages as expected, although two of them were strangely garbled, and one which was altogether stranger than the rest.

That afternoon they all met in the secrets room at the embassy to discuss their first tranche of messages and their various implications. Causing as much distress as enlightenment, this day would not be an easy one for any of them, particularly Sir Arthur.

WALLINGFORD

Robin and Sharon continued to run the riding school as usual. Members of staff got on well together, and were loyal to him in every way. When he wasn't there, due to his frequent visits to Reading, Sharon enthusiastically took the reins and kept the business running smoothly. When he was there, he also found time to make some improvements to the house which he had neglected for quite a while.

Norman Dent was very helpful, and with his canny eye was able to make suggestions which were constructive and mostly inexpensive. Although he enjoyed spending clients' money on frivolous and luxurious things, he also knew how to be frugal as well.

Robin was grateful to him and had recently remarked, 'Sarah seems to be getting better by the week.

Dan the psychotherapist in charge of the half-way house in Reading says she is not ready to leave yet but that it won't be long.'

Norman Dent was of the same mind as Dan. 'Don't get your hopes up too soon, Robin, there is a lot of adjustment still to go. I know how you feel but take it gently, and don't go rushing into anything. Let things happen naturally.'

It seemed that despite his isolation, Robin still had some good friends he could rely on, but that did not solve the problem of Annabel Cumberpot. She was someone who could destroy his embryonic plans completely, especially if Sarah were to get wind of their relationship.

When she phoned, Annabel tried very hard to seem rather matter of fact about his mysterious absences. 'Oh! I never go to Reading or Newbury for that matter,' and 'what was the weather like there, it's been raining here?' These and other inane questions disguised a burning need to know the truth.

Was it another woman, or had he just gone off her? She really could not care less about his mundane daily routine, but she hoped that her questions passed for genuine concern when the fundamental questions could never really be asked.

His was a similar dilemma, because although it was convenient to meet her from time to time, it was not appropriate to discuss the slowly developing circumstances surrounding his newly found feelings for his wife Sarah. To tell Annabel that she was only his *Bit on the Side*, would let all hell loose and probably wreck his business as well as his extremely vulnerable marriage to Sarah. He knew that there was no greater demon than a woman scorned, especially a woman like Annabel. But the question was how to let her down lightly?

He had always kept her at some degree of arm's length and had never really let her fully into his life, but that might not be the way she saw it. Although she came from a fractured family background with a traitorous father and a phony family history, who could tell the extremes she might go to in getting even with him? Clearly jealous and considerably demanding as a person, she might go for broke and destroy everything around her, including her marriage to Sir Arthur and the parenting of James, her poor neglected son. His mind boggled.

But he had to face the facts. When Annabel came along for the second time, he was only looking for a squeeze and not a serious relationship. For many years he had nursed Sarah from crisis to crisis and when she was finally hospitalized, his life had changed dramatically.

Sarah's years of screaming and shouting, unfounded accusations and the gradual evaporation of most of his friends, were instantly replaced by silence and calm. It felt as if he had been let out of some grotesque prison, and free to live his life with impunity away from the daily abuse, there would be a slim chance for some personal happiness.

It was not long before Robin learned to live for himself, to carry out his daily tasks, to develop his business, and occasionally to meet some of the locals down at the pub. This was all well and good, but then quite suddenly a feeling of loneliness set in!

The sun still shone, and the world seemed full of its usual sounds and colours. People were kind and he in turn was helpful and sometimes even generous. But there was now a kind of languor inhibiting him, and no matter how hard he worked or how exhausted he became it was always there. Then along came his old flame Annabel.

He well remembered their few months together as students, and how she was neither sensitive nor particularly romantic. Although she studied an intellectually demanding course at Oxford, in common with many of her contemporaries, she was neither particularly intellectual nor imaginative for that matter. But she fitted in with his student world: the Jazz clubs, the parties, and of course the long lingering evenings by the Thames.

He even remembered how little they spoke then, and how clichéd her views were; students have very little original thought. Had he been asked to describe it, he would have said that their relationship was fun-loving monosyllabic and hedonistic; because there was very little real empathy, and little evidence of compassion for others.

He was kicking off of the gloomy remnants of the Second World War, and his parents' very dull and conservative world. When his parents talked, they talked about the relatives who had died in the war, and the rising costs of living. He wanted music and dancing, pretty girls and a little bit of hope. He didn't want what they had.

He had finally ended up with Annabel, her secrecy, her mystery and of course her bloody father. It was all too much for him at the time, and with the benefit of hindsight he now realized that it was probably wise to have dumped her when he did, although it must have appeared very old fashioned by the standards of the time.

To break off his relationship with her because of her father's treachery, simply confirmed that he also shared his parents' pre-war standards and prejudices whatever he might have thought. But as always there had been plenty more fish in the sea, and as he zipped around Oxford in his red MG Midget, this thought quickly became a reality!

SOFIA

To Sir Arthur the Secrets Room always smelt of garlic. The ventilation was very poor, and over the years the incumbents having become addicted to the local food, tended to project their tainted aromas around the room. Sir Arthur on the other hand had been at home that day, having lunch with his wife, and consuming slightly burnt Cumberland sausages with mashed potato and brown sauce.

Annabel's aversion to foreign food was beginning to affect his waistband as well as his patience. In some ways he longed for her to go home, so he could visit the Chinese restaurant at the Slavyanska Hotel or even the Mexhana restaurant at the Nicky Hotel. Annabel was due to go back to England shortly, whereupon he could return once more to a semi bachelor existence.

'Well, how did yesterday's farce go then?' he sneeringly remarked to the assembled staff. 'Did the gnomes enjoy themselves at the reception?'

The superior look on his face created a mirror vision in Dirty's mind. He was finding it increasingly more difficult to tell the British Ambassador and Herodotus the gnome apart, they looked so similar!

'Actually Sir, it went quite well. There were all the SGGS muppets, all ten of the spies—mostly in black suits with Rayban sunglasses—and the rumpled remains of the Irish pub, fresh from an afternoon's drinking. Thankfully many of them will never return, although the thought of a free drink will be very tempting to them no doubt.'

'I see, so it was a total shambles then!' There was no room in the Ambassador's mind for any kind of success, and he simply hoped to have vacated his present diplomatic post before the Bulgarian secret service moved in.

'What about the downloads; whatever you call them, was there anything there that might invoke some interest from your beloved MI6, Macintosh?'

Ron Beamish interjected, 'We received ten messages actually Sir, although to be fair, one of them was an extended grocery list which appeared to have been sent by mistake. We are just checking on who the intended recipient is as we speak. You never know it might have been some sort of secret code.'

'You mean it might have been a grocery list, or an almighty balls-up by Benefon or the fault of the local telephone provider, even one which you might similarly never know about? Or do you think that the word *potato* might perhaps refer to a secret rocket silo?' Arthur's mind boggled as he thought through the hocus-pocus he had to contend with.

It was like trying to fit the bits of a jigsaw puzzle together without a picture to follow, and then coming up with arbitrary conclusions. 'Well, what about the rest then, and how did—what's his name—Herodotus the gnome perform?' His sarcasm was scathing. 'Did he enjoy the reception, or did he get drunk like the rest of them?'

'Well Ambassador, of the ten informers all their phones worked perfectly, according to our computer, and all the downloads were made flawlessly as well. All ten phones are in perfect working order, as is the Wi-Max unit called Herodotus, which is situated in the front garden of the Embassy.'

Both Dirty and Ron were very keen to confirm that the technical side of this MI6 ruse was working well and according to plan, so, ignoring the Ambassador's sarcasm, they continued with their report.

'Apart from the shopping list, the other nine encrypted messages have been de-encrypted, but say little more than to confirm that their users were present at the reception, and to wish the British Embassy and SGGS good luck in the future. There were no secret reports made; indeed one of their number asked if we had some secrets which they should know about. Needless to say we have switched off that particular phone for the time being, and we will be interviewing the phone user in due course.'

'So it is just the shopping list then?' Sir Arthur's rhetorical question had the effect of précising the whole gruelling project into just a few words. 'And, what's the next step, Macintosh, I'm dying to know?'

'We will just have to wait for the telephone company to tell us who the intended recipient of the shopping list is, in case they are of a suspicious nature, known criminals, or indeed local interior ministry operatives. We should know tomorrow if we are lucky.'

'Fine. Well, let me know who it is and we will try to get to the bottom of it then.'

Finally the meeting was over and the ambassador left the building to walk around the block.

Savouring the polluted air of Moskovska Street Sir Arthur took a very deep breath. 'Bloody garlic,' he muttered, 'why can't I have some?'

Returning once more to his office and the important matter of Bulgarian white cheese, Sir Arthur asked Edwina if she would bring him a cup of tea, but for the sake of the British economy with only one biscuit.

'You have no idea how much drivel these spooks come out with, Edwina. I reckon they make most of it up as they go along, and think we are silly enough to believe them!'

The Petit Beurre biscuit was surreptitiously dipped into the Tetley's tea and the world of diplomacy returned to normal. Edwina sat opposite the ambassador and smiled at him admiringly.

THE SHERATON HOTEL, SOFIA

Annabel Cumberpot dismissed the embassy driver and with a look of considerable purpose, passed through the swing doors and strode into the hotel reception area. Announcing her presence in a loud voice, the receptionist scurried from behind the hotel desk quite ignoring a garrulous American who was in the process of questioning various items on his bill.

'But I didn't have peas with my stake,' he announced to the vacant desk before him, then turning he saw the receptionist bobbing and smiling before a large Englishwoman with staring blue eyes.

'Hey lady, she was dealing with me before you!'

Annabel's gimlet eyes turned to meet his with a look of utter contempt, as she wondered how anybody wearing a Hawaiian shirt might occupy a moment of her time.

'Mind your own business and shut up,' she said. 'I don't know what is happening to this hotel, accommodating riff raff like you? I'm afraid it is really going to the dogs; so just sit down and be quite!'

The spluttering American did exactly as he was told, although; clutching some American banknotes in his hand, he was pleased to see the reassuring face of George Washington smiling at him. Taking a nearby seat as instructed he proclaimed, 'Damned limy's, who the hell do they think they are?'

It was an event put on by The International Woman's Club, and Annabel was due to hand over an Embassy cheque for 500 USD to the committee of *Paws for Thought*. It was the proceeds from the raffle held the month before.

'You are a little early, Lady Cumberpot I'm afraid, because the reception does not start until midday. May I suggest that you wait in the lounge and I will arrange for some coffee to be sent to your table?'

Annabel thought for a moment and, turning to the girl and with an expressionless face, she nodded and strode purposefully into the crowded room and looked for an empty table. There were none, so she decided to sit at a table where an elegant grey haired man was busy reading a copy of *The Duma*. Asking him in English if he objected, he casually waved his hand towards the vacant chair and continued to read his newspaper.

Counting the days before her return to Watlington, there were some pressing matters she had to attend to other than making encouraging speeches to a room full of dog obsessed loonies, whose organizers seemed to her to be altogether menopausal.

For example, she had to order some groceries for her husband the Ambassador, which she generally sent by text message for the sake of accuracy. Mr Andrews the English grocer in Sofia—in common with many at the time, was not online—and so this new innovation was a very convenient time-saving expedient. In the past she had tried to phone in her order, and in the confusion she generally got someone else's stuff delivered which then had to be sent back. This way Mr Andrews dealt with the order himself directly and not his useless staff.

Taking out her written speech, she placed her Benefon mobile on the table together with the silver pencil given to her many years before by Robin Caruthers. It seemed she had some thirty minutes to spend, and if nothing else, she liked to make a good speech, despite the nonsense it represented. Who cared a damn about a load of mangy mongrels anyway? But as the shopping list grew in her mind, she decided to make some notes on the back of her prepared speech, prior to her final text message.

1 x Marmite
10 x Tins of Heinz tomato soup
12 x Tins of Heinz baked beans
1 x Large Jar of Branston pickle
1 x Bottle of Daddy's sauce
5 x Kilos of Cumberland sausages
6 x Kilos smoked bacon
4 x Bisto gravy mix—beef

4 x Bisto gravy mix—chicken

2 x Kilos white sugar

The list went on a bit but was interrupted by the arrival of her filter coffee together with a little jug of milk, a bowl of sugar and a ginger biscuit.

'Please accept this with the compliments of the management, Lady Cumberpot. I have been told to tell you that the reception will start in thirty minutes, if you don't mind waiting?'

As the waiter disappeared, the grey haired man folded up his newspaper and in so doing smiled at Annabel Cumberpot.

'Lady Cumberpot, this is an unexpected pleasure, how nice to see you!' The friendly face opposite seemed very cordial and relaxed.

'I'm sorry, do I know you?' Annabel looked a little perplexed as she inspected the older man before her. 'Have we met before somewhere? I'm sorry, I don't remember your face; can you remind me?'

'I'm sorry, of course, my name is Philip Filipov. We met at your Queens's official birthday celebration a while ago. I was with my wife Ksenia and we spoke about your father.'

The ambassador's wife's face became ashen and her composure suddenly ebbed away. Quite unexpectedly she had been confronted by the worst thing she could possibly imagine—the truth! Her hands started to shake and as a result she knocked over her coffee cup and milk jug, which spilled over the table, the ginger biscuit and the sugar bowl falling to the floor.

'I'm sorry, I can't have this conversation,' she said, smartly rising to her feet. 'I am afraid that I must go immediately,' she blurted out.

The waiter cleared the debris from the table, wiped the surface clean with a cloth, and then picked up the rolling sugar bowl and a crushed ginger biscuit. Annabel removed her Benefon and silver pencil, grabbed her prepared speech, depositing them into her commodious handbag. She then strode off without uttering another word.

Philip Filipov, bemused by the whole incident, watched her vanishing figure as it swiftly exited the room and made for the lift. He then picked up the copy of *The Duma* newspaper, his Benefon mobile phone, shook his head in bafflement and finally left the hotel with a smile on his face.

But the whole incident, no matter how innocent it appeared to be, would be cause for great concern amongst the intelligence communities of both countries, leaving compelling evidence behind which could only be described as highly suspicious.

CHAPTER ELEVEN

THE EMBASSY SECRETS ROOM, SOFIA

IT TURNED OUT to be rather a sombre meeting, and one which everyone would remember for many years to come. Sir Arthur had lost his disdainful expression and looked a little pasty that afternoon as certain suspicions were revealed.

'It seems that an attempt was made to send this grocery order by text message to Mr Andrews, the English Grocer in Sofia. As you may know, he now advertises this service in his weekly circular as being the most reliable way to order things. The poor man is trying to keep up to date with modern technology, but mainly because his staff make rather too many mistakes. You know how these Bulgarian workers are these days; a bit short on details.' Dirty Macintosh was getting round to his usual spate of speculative thinking.

'The message we received seems to have come from the Benefon mobile phone of a Mr Philip Filipov. He is one of our more important informers, and holds an important post within the President's Cabinet as his security advisor.'

While these revelations were being revealed, Ron Beamish stuck to his IT job function, leaving Dirty Macintosh to do all the talking. But quite suddenly, Beamish stood up, politely excused himself, and walked out of the secrets room leaving the two of them together.

After he had gone, Macintosh smiled. 'He doesn't need to know any more than that Sir, because I'm afraid there is just a little more to it than I have divulged so far—none of which is for his ears—and involves a discussion we must unfortunately hold together absolutely privately!' Dirty Macintosh looked at his boss with a look of considerable regret as he moved on to the next point on the agenda.

'Both the telephone company and Mr Andrews believe that the text message that was sent to him from Mr Filipov's phone might well have come from your wife, Lady Cumberpot.' The silence was deafening as the truth emerged. The ambassador moved from side to side as if in deep thought, finally exploding and attacking the table with his fist.

He shouted, 'Are you saying that my wife is a spy—I mean a real one? What are you trying to say, Macintosh; spit it out man? I need to know the whole truth!'

'No, not at this stage Sir, I am only relating to you what I know so far. I'm sure that there is a rational explanation, and I am sure that there has been some mistake, but stranger things have happened in the past and we need to be cautious. Maybe she is being blackmailed?' Dirty Macintosh retreated into himself whilst the Ambassador spluttered and came out with unintelligible half sentences.

'I mean… I can't believe… It's not possible… It's unimaginable… There must be some mistake!'

The look of abandonment caused by her implied treachery seemed to annihilate his whole being, and left him staring at the wall open-mouthed. The dribble which had accumulated in the corner of his mouth dripped onto the table, at which point the Ambassador quite unexpectedly burst into tears.

Dirty Macintosh was not entirely surprised. 'There-there, Sir Arthur, we don't have the whole picture yet. It is all supposition at the moment; just a possibility, we don't have any real proof. It is just an unexplained piece of evidence possibly involving your wife, that's all!'

The Embassy spook was regrettably rather enjoying this moment, and amazed to see how quickly his pompous boss had disintegrated before his eyes. It was proof, however, that he was not only unreliable but had no objectivity either. Whether Macintosh would mention his views to his Masters in London at some point was another matter, but he would not do so for the time being!

THE PODLY PITTA, SOFIA

Lady Annabel Cumberpot explained her one and only clandestine meeting with Philip Filipov by telling her husband that she was lunching with the 'doggie ladies.' It could have been true, despite the fact that she thought them to be half mad, but it occurred to her that even they might conceivably need reassurance from some sort of authority figure, and so of course he believed her.

Since the handing over of 500 quid to the *Paws for Thought* charity, she had occasionally been seen by others in this enlightened capacity, therefore making it a plausible lie. Suddenly she was thinking like her father and she knew it!

Aimlessly walking down Moskovska Street into the city centre, she stopped from time to time to look at the overpriced trash for sale in the shoe and dress shops, most of which were used for laundering money by the more established up and coming gangsters. Their paid for girlfriends sat there each day, ignoring any customers as they self-indulgently painted their nails, held inane conversations on their mobiles, or just sat there smoking slim-line cigarettes and drinking coffee.

When she got to Papa on the corner of Slavakov Square she stopped from time to time, and glanced at the occasional bookstall. She was looking for some good secondhand books in English. Those she came across were mainly pot boilers, but she did manage to find an unusual early English copy of *Thirty Clocks* by Vita Sackville West which she bought for two Leva.

Taking out a small pack of pre-paid tickets, she pushed her way onto the crowded and rickety yellow tram which was to deliver her to her first ever clandestine meeting in Sofia. She inserted a ticket into the ticket punch machine on the cabin wall, and carefully observing the three puncture marks in the ticket she found a seat next to a sad looking pensioner. Having an authentic ticket would save her from a fine if she were to be caught by the Municipal ticket inspectors who occasionally lurked incognito amongst the passengers. On this particular occasion she was not prepared for a noisy fracas.

Rattling and swaying along Graf Ignatiev Street, the tram turned right and then left again up the incline to Journalists Square, where most of the people got off. The old tram then shuddered and ground its way into the forest of Borova Gora, where it stopped at a little picturesque tram station amongst the trees, the romantic reverie of some long forgotten hero of socialism. When she got off the tram, she sat for a while on the station bench in order to consider her position.

She needed to befriend Mr Filipov somehow, not only because he was a threat to her anonymity, but because she was also desperate to know more about her father; her real father, the shadow of whom had haunted her childhood and her entire family for most of her life.

An elderly uniformed policeman had quite suddenly stopped her outside the British Embassy the previous day and had slipped her a note before swiftly disappearing into the crowd. It was from the man who she now feared the most.

Dear Lady Cumberpot,

I am very sorry if I caused you displeasure when we last met at the Sheraton Hotel, and I also hope that I wasn't responsible for any unwarranted distress on your part. It was not my intention, because I had no idea that you would be there, let alone sitting at the same table as me. This much should be perfectly clear.

However I believe we have got a common problem, because we appear to have one another's mobile phones, and for reasons I cannot easily explain, this might well place you in some personal danger.

Therefore, I respectfully suggest a meeting tomorrow at the Podly Pitta restaurant by the forest in Borova Gora for some lunch. I apologize for all this subterfuge, and hope that this will bring an end to this matter. Perhaps 2pm would be convenient? I will wait for you.

Respectfully yours,
Philip Filipov.

Annabel walked along the path through the woods, marvelling at the quietness which was sporadically interrupted by birdsong. When she got to the end of the forest pathway, she immediately turned left into the entrance of the old restaurant. An elderly waiter then swiftly ushered her into a dingy corner booth where her nemesis was waiting for her, holding a glass of red wine in his hand.

'Ah! There you are Lady Cumberpot, I was afraid you couldn't make it! Would you care for a glass of wine? I assure you that this is the best Melnik I have had for many years—well, at least since the changes.'

A tall and distinguished figure, Filipov was the nearest one might come to a Bulgarian gentleman; charming and attentive to Lady Annabel, he was able finally to get her to relax a little.

'I mean you no harm Lady Annabel; I just had to gain your attention.'

In her usual offhand manner she replied, 'Well Mr Filipot, of course I am interested to know why I have been summoned here?'

As the story about the phones unfolded she could see how the transfer might have been inadvertently made, when she hurriedly stood up after tipping over her coffee in the Sheraton Hotel.

'If you look at the phone you have with you, in the contact or address section, you will see a list of about thirty numbers, with all the names in Cyrillic script. In the same section in the one which I now have in my possession, there only appear to be three saved numbers. One I believe is for your husband's private office in Sofia, another for a man called Norman Dent, and finally somebody called Robin Caruthers; both in the UK. That's all I had to go on and so that and our unfortunate accident with the coffee is my reason for being here today.' Filipov poured her a glass of the dark red wine.

Annabel reached into her handbag and produced an identical Benefon, which appeared to be either switched off or in need of charging. 'I am sorry, I think it needs charging again. I always forget to do it because I have only recently got the damn thing. It was a present from the telephone company.'

Filipov continued, 'If you inspect this Benefon mobile you will see that what I have said is absolutely correct, and of course you can have it checked by the English telephone company if you wish. But it proves that in your haste to escape my presence the other day, we picked up one another's telephones by mistake. Lady Cumberpot, it is as simple as that!'

It did seem hopelessly true, and Annabel meekly handed over the phone to Filipov, who carefully returned the identical one he was holding. To be sure it worked properly, she promptly made a call to Norman Dent and was immediately reassured by his affable greeting, thereby proving that Filipov had been truthful with her.

'Ah! Norman, I am just phoning to see if those plants have arrived yet, the ones for the patio?'

Norman Dent didn't have a clue what she was talking about, and simply replied, 'What plants are those, Annabel? I don't know anything about any plants.'

Smiling at Philip Filipov she replied, 'I am Sorry Norman, something has just cropped up and I have got to go now. I will phone you later, sorry,' and then she ended her call.

'I believe you now Mr Filipot, and thank you for your help. I hope your phone works OK and hasn't been compromised in any way. I assure you that it has been in my bag all along and nobody has had access to it except me, so please don't have any concerns.' Then as an afterthought, 'Did anyone phone me by the way?'

'Not to my knowledge, Lady Cumberpot, because when I noticed the mistake, I immediately switched it off.'

She sipped her glass of Melnik and seemed to relax. Turning to more mundane matters she went on, 'I hate the damn thing anyway, because you cannot use it in the UK, and so there is no point in taking it home. I am seriously considering getting a cell phone from the other Bulgarian telephone company Tel-Net, which I can apparently use anywhere in Europe.' She took a further sip from her glass of wine, turned on a plastic smile, and then putting her glass down, she sat back and folded her arms.

'So, how well did you know my father then?'

Her penetrating look brought back some old memories to Philip Filipov, as he recounted the meetings which he had in a former life with the Hero of The Soviet Union, her father General Kilbey.

THE EMBASSY SECRETS ROOM

The following afternoon Sir Arthur admitted to Dirty

Macintosh that his was not the first warning concerning his wife's meeting with Filipov. He apologized for his burst of emotion, and admitted that he had already been warned by King Gregory III during an earlier meeting with him in the Prime Minister's office. He reluctantly explained.

'I am afraid that my recent behaviour is due to my bottling the whole thing up, Macintosh! You see I was desperately hoping that it would go away, prove to be untrue and consequently be forgotten. I'm very sorry.'

The day before, when the embassy spook told him of his wife's connection with the text message grocery order, he was finally able to put two and two together and to realize the truth. He was absolutely gutted. His wife was now genuinely under suspicion, which was unbelievable!

'It is actually a little more serious than we expected Sir, because she was also seen talking to him again yesterday, which makes things even worse for her, and consequently for you as well.' Macintosh stared at his boss, resigned to the fact that they were now all either under scrutiny, or victims of an enormous conspiracy.

He continued, 'I have no idea what the next move is Sir, but I do think that you need to have a private word with your wife, to see if we have any further grounds for concern.'

Sir Arthur's eyes nearly popped out of his head with this last remark, and once again his mouth opened in dribbling bewilderment. 'I say Macintosh,' he blabbered, 'is this really happening, or am I dreaming?'

The spook looked very downcast, and then suddenly his face brightened, and said as an afterthought, 'By the way Sir, Mr Andrews wants to know if you still want that grocery order? Apparently he is running short of baked beans!'

Sir Arthur dolefully left the secrets room with Dirty at his side. The embassy security officer who had been lurking in the corridor eyed the two departing figures suspiciously, and then firmly locked the door behind them.

'*Very unusual for just the two of them to be in there alone; there must be something important going on,*' he thought to himself as he counted the packets of pork scratchings and potato crisps in the embassy bar.

WATLINGTON

When Lady Annabel returned to Orchard Manor, it was with the proviso that she stayed there permanently. She was told to leave her phone behind, but the most disconcerting event occurred on her arrival at Heathrow.

Walking through the *Nothing to Declare* section at customs, she was firmly directed into an empty and rather featureless room by one of the female officers. There she was hand searched, and all her bags were opened and inspected in minute detail. 'You can't do this to me,' she announced loudly, 'I am a British diplomat's wife and I have a diplomatic pass—how dare you do this! I shall complain to the Foreign Office immediately. Who is in charge here?'

The senior duty officer, realizing that a serious error might have occurred, carefully inspected his day book and also the office computer. But, he was adamant, 'I am very sorry Lady Cumberpot, but our instructions are quite clear and we have carried them out as directed. I apologize for any inconvenience it has caused you, but we are only doing our duty.'

Annabel's parting remark was, 'Yes, and for how much longer I wonder?' But it was a cheap shot, and she knew it. Although it made her angrier than ever, it was just a further humiliation to add to her recent and distasteful experiences in Sofia.

For the first time ever her husband had shouted at her. He accused her of being a foreign spy whilst using her position as the ambassador's wife to indulge in her treacherous activities.

She could not believe what had been said! After years of marital domination, it was inexcusable that her diminutive husband should address her in such a manner. Summoning up her usual hubris she addressed him with considerable scorn.

'Listen to me you little twerp, all that happened was that our phones got mixed up at the Sheraton when I was there the other day with the doggy ladies. So I had to meet him again in order to swap them back again. Is that too hard for you to understand, Arthur?'

Her haughtiness only served to annoy her husband

even more. 'Swap, swap? I know what you have been swapping, Annabel. You have been swapping your country's secrets. That's what you have been swapping, just like your bloody father did! I should have known better; what a fool I have been!'

The silence was deafening as she took in what he said, and what it implied. It was at that very moment she knew their marriage was finished. When Dirty Macintosh handed her a one-way ticket to London on the next British Airways flight the following morning, and then personally escorted her onto the plane at Sofia Airport, she at last understood how far things had gone without her realizing that anything was actually wrong.

During the journey home, Annabel had plenty of time to consider her position, and to calculate how compromised her personal situation really was. But she also knew that the only sets of keys to Orchard Manor were safely lodged in her handbag. Picking up the home phone on her return, she dialled a local number.

'Ah! Mr Grimmer, there you are. I have been reconsidering matters, and I think I will take you up on your kind offer of a whole sheep, but I would be greatly obliged if you would also provide me with a bench freezer.' She went on, 'Yes, I have found some extra space in a little room adjoining the kitchen. No, everything is fine thank you, but I don't much feel like shopping at the moment, because very shortly I shall be going back to Oxford University as a researcher.'

Farmer Grimmer smiled to himself and said that it

would be his great pleasure to supply her Ladyship, assuring her of his most devoted attention at all times and that her delivery would take place the following day.

Pleased with her decision, Annabel Cumberpot finally remarked, 'Thank you. That will do splendidly Mr Grimmer.' And then as an afterthought, 'Oh yes! Can I also have five kilos of your homemade pork sausages too? I am told locally that they are very good indeed.'

READING

'I am sorry Dan, but I am afraid that I no longer love him. It is as simple as that. I know you will think I am wicked, but remember we have been apart for many years, and I don't believe it is possible to rekindle my old feelings for him. They have all slowly disappeared over time, and now it's too late. You see, these days I only really see him as a dear friend!'

Dan looked at his patient with deep concern because of this most unexpected revelation. He imagined that her return to Wallingford was a given; at some point at least, especially considering the chemistry which appeared to exist outwardly between them. But looks can be misleading.

But even though their relationship was to be a platonic one from her point of view, he well knew from his most recent conversation that Robin's burgeoning feelings towards her were quite different. Oddly he felt equally concerned for both of them, although he had to keep reminding himself that he should be exclusively concerned about his patient's welfare, and her only.

If Robin knew what Dan had just heard, would Robin continue his support for Sarah? Conversely, could Sarah be able to remain stable without Robin's help and support? Dan attempts at mollifying Sarah had an air of desperation.

'It is very early days Sarah, but maybe you should try and get to know him again; it has been quite a while. Think of him as someone you have recently met; that might change your view of him.' But there was little more to be said. Suddenly the moment was disrupted with the clanking of a tea trolley and a cheerful invitation to elevenses, as Flo the housekeeper liked to call it.

'Out of your rooms you lazy gits!' she shouted. 'It's tea time and I've got beds to make!'

One by one the patients, who were not working that day, assembled in the television room and sipped their tea. Smiling at a shy looking man, Flo asked caringly, 'Would you like some sugar in your tea, Duck?' Nodding his head he shyly said that he would. Then leaving her trolley to one side she announced, 'The rest of you lazy gits can help yourselves if you want some more, because I've got a lot of work to do this morning.'

It was as though the patients were relearning their basic social skills. Helping one another to a further 'cuppa' with the inevitable ginger nut biscuit seemed to be a particular challenge to many and their eyes seldom met. Maybe it was a desperate need to hide their inner demons, the ones which they carried around like great bags of cement?

Standing in the centre of the group Sarah's presence seemed not only attractive but very reassuring, as they went through the daily litany of questions starting with, 'How do you feel today?'

Some complained of headaches, others of bad stomachs, but most admitted that they felt just a little bit depressed. As they mingled, it was clear that they had all decided to help one another and were now going through a transitional stage from being just a patient to being part of a mutual support group. Somehow it had become plain to them that few would survive the half-way house unless they worked as a team, and to help one another release the hobgoblins which constantly accompanied them in their solitary world.

In Sarah's case, the demon she found most hard to dispel was her total lack of feelings for anyone except herself. During her years at the hospital something had changed inside her—something that would inevitably inhibit any future personal relationships, because she had become cold and self-obsessed. This was the true reason behind her revelation to Dan.

Although she was quite prepared to continue her secret charade with Robin for the time being, she knew it to be a simple matter of survival rather than any genuine feeling of love. Unfortunately for Robin, the truth would have to wait.

THE SECRETS ROOM, SOFIA

'As you know Sir Arthur, I have now had to report this incident to my masters and typically their response is to batten down the hatches so to speak, until we know more about this incident.'

Macintosh was enjoying his lead in the present conversation, mainly due to the numerous occasions when he was forced to listen to the Ambassador's angry retorts and over-simplistic remarks.

'Quite so Macintosh, quite so,' the ambassador timidly agreed, 'and the gnome thingy; what is happening there?'

Macintosh looked at the compliant face of his boss with relish, hoping that this would remain his future state of mind; although it was obvious that either the state of mind or the ambassador himself would shortly disappear. If it was true that Lady Cumberpot was the last of the 'cold war' spies, then he was fully aware that both he and Sir Arthur would surely be in for the diplomatic chop.

'They have quite rightly suggested that we continue our Herodotus program as though nothing has happened.' Ned Macintosh realized that his masters were generally apathetic but was aware that HMG traditionally maintained certain reservations.

'They pointed out that they are reluctant to make any hasty decisions, and told me that they need to investigate matters more fully at their end. Also Sir, they seemed to know very little about Lady Cumberpot, other than you both met at university and absolutely nothing about her family.' He shrugged his shoulders. 'That is all I am able to tell you Sir. They said that they will make a few discrete enquiries, and will let me know. Meanwhile they suggest that you take a few days off somewhere nice and warm, and well—to be perfectly honest they also used the expression *discrete* on four separate occasions—and to let things take their course!'

They both sat and looked at each other in glum silence until it was interrupted by a tapping at the door. Dirty opened it and saw the excited figure of Ron Beamish waving a piece of paper at him.

'We have got our first real massage, Dirty. It's from one of our informers, and I think it's important.'

WALLINGFORD

Sharon was enjoying herself, sitting in the riding school office and staring out of the window. The weather was changing, autumn was getting nearer, and it was time to tidy up the riding school, to rake up the leaves and to have the first delicious bonfire of the season. She loved the smell of the burning leaves and watching the steamy smoke drift into the clear blue sky. She also liked to watch the European Red Kites effortlessly circling like gliders around the thermals as the warm air rose and sent them skyward.

But today she was in charge of the office. Her boss

Robin was away on business for the day, and so it represented a well-earned rest from her normally arduous tasks around the stables. The weather was becoming chilly and it occurred to her that it was almost time to turn on the central heating, and for Robin to order some more fuel oil for the furnace.

Christine the other groom was helping the groundsman to collect the leaves. She was driving the old Zetor farm tractor which in turn pulled a big four-wheeled farm cart. The groundsman was throwing plastic bags full of leaves onto the back of the trailer, which she then took to the rear paddock and emptied in a heap onto the smouldering bonfire. Sharon shivered, put on her winter body warmer and then hugged herself to keep herself warm.

She didn't notice him at first, but when he got nearer she could see that he was an older man wearing a crumpled raincoat. As he approached the entrance to the main building, she observed that he was getting a bit thin on top and that he frequently combed what little hair that remained over his bald head. When the breeze blew it seemed to streak out behind him like a horse's tail.

Carefully rearranging and combing it back into place, he slowly walked into the industrial building and stood looking at the arena, and then, slipping his comb into a side pocket, he turned and looked at Sharon.

'Can I help you Sir? If you're from the council or something, Mr Caruthers is away today, and there is only me here.'

'Hello,' he said chirpily. 'My name is Edgar Tobin. I am doing some market research on behalf of the *Wallingford Mercury*, your local paper,' he said smiling. 'I am a researcher with John Butterfield & Co., in Reading.' He handed her a business card. 'And who are you, my dear.'

'I am Sharon; Sharon Woods. I work for Mr Caruthers as his assistant, and I'm also his head groom. Perhaps I can help you... er, Mr Tobin.' His card looked expensive, and he looked quite posh to Sharon. It was his constant twitching which slightly unnerved her, despite his soft educated voice.

'Ah! Good Sharon, then I'll talk to you if that's OK. I'm not interrupting anything am I? You must tell me if I am, and I'll come back some other time.

'Although,' he leafed through what she imagined was his diary, and turned one page backwards and forwards a couple of times, 'I won't be back hereabouts for a few weeks, so if you can help me now I would be very grateful to you, Sharon.'

He had a nice even smile, and Sharon imagined that he must have been quite handsome when he was younger, although it was a pity about the twitch which seemed to travel all the way down the right side of his face.

'No problem Mr Tobin, we aren't very busy today because the schools are back, and most people have finished their holidays and have returned to work. We are just tidying up the riding school annat and burning all the leaves. Autumn is here again!' She smiled and gave a shrug. She was an open and happy girl, and wanted to help. 'What do you want to know, Mr Tobin?'

'Well, the *Wallingford Mercury* is thinking of doing a weekly article about local business, and it came to my attention that your riding school would make a good centrespread. You know, with the horses in the paddock, people doing dressage, and youngsters jumping on their ponies.'

'Oh, Mr Caruthers would be gobsmacked if that happened! He is such a nice man and works so hard to make his stables successful, and needs all the publicity he can get.'

'Well, we must see what we can do Sharon, and of course there will be plenty of opportunities for you to be in the photographs, and the *Mercury* reporter will probably want a little quote from you!'

'Well, if there is anything I can do to help, Mr Tobin, I'm sure Mr Caruthers won't mind." Her kindly smile showed a genuine willingness to help her employer.

Edgar Tobin went on, 'Is it possible you could take me round the stables? I would like to make a note of everything I see so I have the whole picture in mind.' His charming smile was interrupted by an involuntary twitch, but Sharon was far too preoccupied with the pending publicity campaign to notice.

Half an hour later the viewing was complete, and they returned to the office smiling and laughing. 'That was very interesting Sharon and I hope I didn't take up too much of your time?'

'Oh no, Mr Tobin, it was a pleasure to be able to help you, I am sure. Mr Caruthers will be pleased when I tell him about your visit.' She was very happy with her performance, and hoped that Robin would be proud of her when he returned.

'There are just a few final questions, if you don't mind, about your customers—or should I say your pupils? What sort of people come here during the year and how would you describe them, Sharon?'

Sharon had never been asked such questions before, and sitting in her boss's chair she smiled with a look of some embarrassment on her face as she thought what her answer might be.

'Well Mr Tobin, I suppose the answer is all sorts in fact. We have all ages really; from little mites to grownups, and even some oldies too. We try to help children with disabilities and have a special day for them once a month, but we also have our stars—people who compete in competitions—and our riders come from all walks of life, rich and poor. The one thing we don't get involved in is fox hunting. Mr Caruthers is adamant about that.'

Edgar Tobin faithfully wrote down all that was said in his notebook, turning over the page as he ran out of space whilst offering an interim smile and the occasional twitch. When her account had been faithfully recorded, Tobin sat and sucked his pencil, and paused as though he was dreaming up a final question.

'Do you get any posh people here Sharon? And—

how can I put it?—does anyone get up your nose?' He summoned up a big twitch-less grin and then went on, 'Well, you know what I mean don't you? Some people can be such a pain at times, can't they?'

As they both chuckled away, a picture of Lady Annabel Cumberpot found its way into Sharon's mind and she nodded in total agreement.

'Well, Mr Tobin, there is one customer I can't abide. She is a diplomat's wife and she thinks she's the cat's whiskers, I can tell you. Rude—you have never heard anything like it; treats all us staff like peasants, and generally acts like Lady-Muck."

'What do you mean? She tries to be what she is not, Sharon?' Tobin looked at her with growing interest as the story unfolded.

'Well, she is one actually—a certain Lady Cumberpot—and what makes me laugh is that she actually thinks that Mr Caruthers fancies her! Unbelievable; although I imagine there might have been some hanky-panky between the two of them in the past.'

'Don't tell me he has been bonking her!' Tobin's mouth fell open in disbelief.

Sharon nodded her head, giggled, and gave him a knowing look. 'Anyway, these days I have to answer the phone in case it's her, and tell her that he is not in. She's a horror, Mr Tobin, and we can't wait to see the back of her; I mean all of us!"

They both sat there laughing, and finally Edgar Tobin put his notepad into the pocket of his scruffy raincoat and got up to go.

'But that's between you and me, Mr Tobin,' Sharon added. 'Don't tell Mr Caruthers I said anything, will you?'

The man in the scruffy raincoat smiled and promised Sharon faithfully that he would not tell Mr Caruthers anything about the last part of their conversation, and then he shook her hand, thanked her for all her help and quietly left.

As it turned out, this was the only truthful thing he had said all morning, and he was never heard of again. When Robin Caruthers returned that evening, Sharon was full of the visit and talked of two-page spread in the *Wallingford Mercury*.

The next day Robin rang John Butterfield & Co., in Reading, but the phone was disconnected, and later he contacted the editor of the *Mercury* who he vaguely knew. But there was no indication that the man Edgar Tobin had ever existed, and the editor denied that any such proposal had ever been made by his newspaper. Robin Caruthers very sensibly said nothing to Sharon, but his suspicion had been aroused; and what was more, he was convinced he knew who was behind it.

ALEXANDROPOULIS

Sir Arthur stretched his aching limbs, closed his eyes, and let the warmth of the sun penetrate his pallid body. In the last few days he had been drained of all his usual self confidence and the energy that went with it. He felt quite defeated by the brazen activities of his wife, and shattered by the implications of her actions and her possible betrayal.

When he had finally come to his senses, he turned to his only remaining confidant at the embassy, and it was she who offered the Ambassador the opportunity to escape from Sofia and a chance to consider his choices. Now his mind was focused he carefully went through his options. Should he resign, and what could the future possibly hold for him? These questions and more began to occupy his waking hours.

Edwina could only feel compassion for her boss, and watched with pain the sudden withering of a man who she had known for so many years. Whatever they said about Sir Arthur in the service, he had always been cheerful and accommodating with his staff, despite being occasionally a little short tempered and over simplistic.

He had always been kind to her, and she in turn had tried hard to help him to fulfil his duties throughout his career. She was always there to catch the occasional loose ball, or to plug up the omissions and errors that he occasionally made.

She put his condition down to his pompous wife, and the way she terrorized and humiliated him. The poor man had no life of his own, and little if any peace and quiet. His son James had become alienated from him, he had no friends, and was dominated by his wife; both within the Embassy and no doubt at home too. Well anyway, it was time for this to change and for her to help him to get through this present outrage.

Edwina always liked Greece but not the islands, and tried to keep well away from the well-trodden path and the oafish behaviour of most British tourists who descended on Greece during the summer months. In Alexandropoulis she was known as the Englishwoman, which said a lot about how geographically removed she was from the holiday spots of Corfu and Mykonos. That was why she had bought herself the small two-bedroomed flat.

Situated in nearby Nea Hili and overlooking the Aegean, with views over an almost deserted sandy beach, the apartment block stood beside a beautiful seafood restaurant. Next to a little fishing harbour, this was a place for Greeks, and was where she felt at home.

It was also well away from the embassy in Sofia, and about as far as she could get from the confines of the village of Theale in Berkshire where she was born on the Benyon estate. Edwina Prothero was a Grammar schoolgirl who had made good. As the daughter of a tenant farming family she had broken the country code and moved to London as soon as she could.

What had attracted her to the Foreign Service was the thought of travel. What had actually occurred was that she had unwittingly dogged the steps of Arthur Cumberpot, by following him from appointment to appointment. This journey had begun in Nassau, and had continued throughout his diplomatic career to when he finally ended up in Sofia with his much coveted knighthood. She was one of only a few people who believed that he deserved to be honoured in this way, and was thoroughly proud of his achievements, many of which she had been a part.

Now that he seemed to be broken and dejected, it was high time for her to demonstrate her belief in him, if not some genuine affection! Sir Arthur seemed grateful for her simple offer, and a chance to unwind in the sun. Overlooking the deep blue sea, Edwina Prothero's roof terrace seemed unusually silent, warm, and extremely safe.

HAMBLEDON

Lionel Pergamon sat in his roomy library. He was of an age when any interruption to his daily routine was to be considered outrageous. In his early eighties, he was content to spend the day with his books and newspapers. Occasionally this calmness would be interrupted by a telephone call from a London antique chess set dealer, rear book dealer or a fellow collector, but generally each day was much the same as any other.

Although he would never claim to be much of a chess player, he was the proud owner of many rare Staunton chess sets and a number of exotic oriental and Asian box sets, together with their intricate and unusual chess boards. These were now distributed amongst the leather-bound volumes and the first editions he had accumulated over the years. His library was the world he lived in, one with few interruptions either from his elderly wife Susan or their daily help.

He was however, passionate about the occasional game of backgammon which he frequently played with his close friend Garry Kaufman. The retired university mathematician proved to be a worthy opponent for the aging publisher, and over the years had been seen to leave the secluded riverside mansion with the sound of coins jingling in his pocket. They were due to play that morning, and it was nearly eleven o'clock.

Due to an unfortunate car accident in East Germany in the 1950's Pergamon had become a tad disabled and had therefore been obliged to join the family publishing house in his mid-twenties. The security services were sorry to see him go, but the accident forced him to choose the quill in order to earn a living, as opposed to practicing the art of deception. He was unashamedly a very successful publisher.

His kindly face disguised his shrewd demeanour, and his memory, although failing with many mundane daily issues, was able to recall with considerable clarity the events of the past. His friend, turned mortal enemy, still occupied moments of thought during his day, as did the unrelenting incredulity which followed his defection. Jim Kilbey was by no means a forgotten man.

As to Jim Kilbey's daughter Annabel, a creature who in the past had been a considerable problem to the now aging intellectual, it seemed that his unwritten obligations to her father would never end. He had kept his word. He had taken the orphan under his wing, renamed her, and given her the best childhood that a childless family could give.

He had concealed her true identity and managed the secret monthly government payments with discretion. The prevailing logic at the time was that anything that Jim Kilbey had represented and whatever he left in his wake should disappear forever.

Since her marriage to Arthur Cumberpot and the birth of James, the devils from the past had grown old with him, together with all his shadowy ex- colleagues who had helped him to obscure the truth. Lionel Pergamon was aware that most of them were now dead and so therefore was their secret, but he was wise enough to realize that history had a habit of repeating itself.

The front doorbell rang, and expecting to see the smiling face of Garry Kaufman, instead before him was an odd looking man in a scruffy mackintosh. 'Good morning Sir. My name is Adrian Throades, and I am a building inspector from Thames Valley Council. I wonder if I might have a word.'

His officious bearing seemed to confirm his credentials, and the old man ushered him into a small sitting room which overlooked the manicured lawn which ran down to the river Thames. 'How can I help you, Mr Throades? I'm sorry but I was expecting someone else, so if we could keep this short.'

He noticed the twitch first. It seemed to start with a wink, and then progress down the man's face, until it ended up with a slight movement of the lower jaw. What hair that remained, hung dolefully like a rat's tail over one eye, which encouraged him to sweep it back periodically. This action had become part of a well-orchestrated routine.

Handing the old man a business card from his pocket, Throades looked around the room with interest, taking in some silver framed photographs that were displayed on the sofa table next to the fireplace. 'Is that your family Sir?' he asked with interest. 'I see you have a daughter about the same age as mine! She is mad about riding too.' The coloured photo was of a much younger man with a teenage girl wearing jodhpurs and a hacking jacket.

'Yes, that's my daughter Annabel,' he smiled, and then said, 'That was a few years ago.' The man perched on a club chair in the corner of the room and opened up a plastic clipboard. He then announced the purpose of his visit.

'I am sorry to tell you that we have received a complaint from a neighbour that you have recently erected a fence by the river which may affect people's right to walk the length of the towpath. According to an 18th Century statute owners are compelled to recognize a way-leave along this stretch of the Thames, and in erecting a fence you have inadvertently broken one of our local bylaws.'

Twitching with new vigour he continued, 'I don't know if you are aware Sir, but under the new Green Pasture Act 1995, as a Council we are obliged to enforce this statute in compliance with the aforementioned Act, and in due course to take legal proceedings against you.'

He sat back and stared at Lionel Pergamon, looking for some visible reaction. But, what happened next was quite a surprise.

'Nice try whoever you are, but you haven't done your homework have you?' The old man started to laugh. 'You nearly had me there!' And rising from his seat, he turned and looked through the window. 'Just ask me what you want, and then fuck off will you.'

'I don't know what you mean Sir, I have every right to be here on Council business, prior to issuing a summons for you to appear at the local Magistrate's Court; you surely don't want to go there, do you?'

'I am a Magistrate you clown, and you are a low grade spook with a junior John Bull printing outfit. What the hell do you want?'

The man, realizing that his ruse had not succeeded, was left with two choices; to stay or to go. 'It's about your daughter Sir. There has been an incident in Sofia, and there is a possibility that it might involve espionage. I have been sent to investigate.'

'Well, why didn't you say so? I used to work for your firm many years ago; surely you knew that? What the hell has happened to the service? It used to be the best in the world.'

What annoyed the old man was not the intrusion, the attempted deception or the total waste of his time; it was the insult to his intelligence. The idiotic local Council pretence, the gobbledegook Green Pasture Act and finally the threat of court was extremely amateur and very annoying.

'You Burk, don't you realize that river banks are the sole remit of the Thames Water Authority? Do your homework next time; whatever your bloody name is, before somebody works you over. You can tell that to those establishment morons who pull your strings in London!'

The man in the rumpled mackintosh twitched and finally closed his plastic folder. 'If you could help fill in some of her background Sir, it may help to alleviate some of the suspicion. You see, she has been seen consorting with a known spy and has apparently exchanged information with him.'

READING

Annabel Cumberpot rapped on the door of the half-way house; she was very angry and impatient. When Flo answered the door, she was surprised to see this large woman glaring at her. "Yes, can I help you Duck?"

'My name is Lady Cumberpot, and I have come here to see Mrs Sarah Caruthers; is she in?'

Flo was hesitant. She had no idea who this woman was, and was reluctant to reply in any case, and not until she knew the purpose of her visit.

"I am afraid this is a medical establishment, and we do not receive visitors unless they have made an official appointment. Perhaps you can tell me what your visit is about?'

Annabel was not about to give any reasons to

anyone, especially to someone who appeared to be a servant—judging by the green house coat—and who was unlikely to give any information away simply out of sheer stubbornness.

'Do you have someone here in authority? I am not going to discuss anything with you, so kindly tell them who I am and that I wish to speak to them,' and as an afterthought she added, 'Now!'

'Well now!' Flo was equally adamant, 'I am afraid that the director is in town on business, and there is no one here with any authority except me, and my answer is the same as before! You need to make an official appointment, and that is that!'

Closing the door somewhat abruptly in the face of Annabel Cumberpot, Flo was heard to mutter loudly, 'Toffee nosed bitch, who the hell does she think she is?'—leaving the agitated figure of Annabel seething on the doorstep.

But Annabel was not to be put off so easily, and sat in the Range Rover which was parked nearby and waited for someone else to come out of the building. After a while she spotted a young man leaving from the front entrance. Carefully closing the door behind him, he turned and made his way past the parked car on his way to the Oxford Road. As the shambling figure passed by, Annabel lowered the window and stuck her head out.

'I say, do you know where I can find Sarah Caruthers today? I've got something for her.'

The young man looked surprisingly distressed at her

question. With his eyes firmly glued to the pavement he managed to say, 'She has gone to Caversham,' pointing vaguely in the direction of the river. 'She told me that she is taking photos of the swans.' Then, without a further word the strange young man retreated around the corner into Lorne Street.

'Thank you very much,' she shouted after him, but there was no reply. She started the car, drove past the shambling figure, turned right into the Oxford Road and finally down Chatham Street towards the Caversham turn. When she got to the Thames she parked her car at the Crown Plaza Hotel and then walked across Cavasham Bridge.

Looking to her right, there were just the usual river boats moored along the river bank, but there was no sign of Sarah. Crossing the road, she then looked to her left at the lush green meadow which occupies that part of the Thames.

The young man had been right—she could see Sarah's figure further along by the Thames Path on this upper reach of the river. Kneeling by the river bank, she was studying a small group of swans through the viewfinder of her camera.

The large white birds were chattering to each other, whilst keeping an eye on their young signets and making sure they avoided the many pleasure boats and cruisers which navigated this stretch of the river. Many river craft ignored the four knot speed limit, and so it was no longer a place of peace and tranquillity.

Climbing down the steps to the river, Annabel now found herself by the towpath and on the same level as Sarah, whose stooping figure she could easily recognize in the distance. Totally absorbed with her photography, Sarah did not see Annabel approaching until she was practically upon her. Looking up in surprise, she smiled, 'Hello Annabel, what on earth are you doing here?'

'I thought we might have a little talk about Robin,' she said without a shred of emotion. 'I think that it is time we did, under the circumstances; don't you agree?'

She casually looked up and down the river with little interest at the passing boats, and then turned to Sarah saying, 'Well! Do you agree or don't you?'

Sarah was not a doormat, despite her delicate condition, nor was she used to being spoken to in this way. 'Sorry Annabel, I think that you had better explain yourself a little more fully, don't you? What exactly do you want and what are you doing here?'

By this time the swans had moved on and the signets were playing by the river bank some yards away. Sarah got to her feet and put the cap on her zoom lens, and switched off the power. It was time to put a new film into the camera anyway, and to get back to the dark room at the half-way house.

'As you know, Robin and I have been seeing one another while you have been away; although I think that the word "seeing" is somewhat of an understatement, and it is time for him to make a choice between you or me.'

Once more the silence was deafening, and as Sarah

tried gamely to form some intelligible words, all she managed to do was to splutter in exasperation.

'What did you say? Make a choice between you and me? How did you come to that conclusion?'

Annabel gave Sarah one of her more practiced withering looks. To Annabel it was clear that the temperamental Sarah was totally unsuited to a man of Robin's stature or for his station in life.

'It is obvious that since you have been away in the loony bin, very little of what has happened between Robin and me has got through to you.'

Her contempt for this very pretty but ordinary girl was reaching levels which even Annabel was unused to, and the poison continued to to drip cruelly from her lips.

'What can you honestly give a man like that Sarah?' she continued. 'Nothing! He doesn't need you, he needs someone who will support him, help him with his business, mix in with the county set, and put the riding school on the map. He needs someone like me.'

Sarah started to laugh, and in so doing Annabel clenched her fists as though she was going to strike her.

'You're such a bloody fool Annabel,' she replied. 'You haven't got it, have you? Apart from the fact that he clearly doesn't want anything more to do with you he can't have me either, you silly cow, because I simply don't want to be married to him anymore. Surely you can see that Annabel? Or are you blind?'

'What do you mean I am blind? I saw you both together at Henley Regatta, and he was all over you. You can't pull the wool over my eyes, Sarah Caruthers, it was as clear as day!' The unremitting stare and the clenched fists were beginning to unnerve Sarah, who was still teetering on the edge of reason.

What kind of woman could treat her this way, knowing how fragile and vulnerable she was? She had been warned by Dan not to get involved in any aggression or argument and to keep well away from people such as Annabel. In her desperation she knew that all she could do now was to get back to the half-way house in the hope that Dan would give her something to calm her down.

She could feel the gradual numbing beginning inside her head, as great waves of depression enveloped her mind and the creeping horror that went with it. Was it time for her to return to the Hospital, because she hadn't felt this bad for a very long time?

Turning away, Sarah gasped and then grabbing her things together she ran towards the bridge and the nearest telephone box. As she did so Annabel shouted after her:

'Got the message now, have you? You're finished! Do you hear me, you're finished.' Smiling to herself, she watched the retreating figure running up the steps next to the bridge in what seemed a total panic.

'*Won't see her again in a hurry,*' she thought to herself. Believing that she was now the only competitor left in the race for Robin's affections, and despite the rapidly lengthening odds, at least now she had an outside chance of regaining his undivided attention, if she used her guile and kept her head.

CHAPTER TWELVE

ALEXANDROPOULIS

ARTHUR could hardly believe that so much peace could be found in such a remote part of Greece. From the roof terrace he was able to watch the morning SAOS ferry ply its way towards the island of Samothraki. It was one of very few ships to be seen each day.

So far that week he'd spent most of his time on Edwina's roof terrace, sitting on a sun lounger gazing out to sea. Later during the night, he stared at the plate sized stars which spread across the deep dark Aegean sky. It was supposed to help him fathom out his uncertain future.

Small fishing boats could be seen on the horizon during the day, which came closer to shore as night approached, their little electric lights suspended over the side to attract the fish.

These same boats would return home in the early morning, bearing the fruits of their long lining, assuring the local beachside restaurants of sufficient fish for the day with which to feed their eager customers. Tired fishermen would then slip their boats, and drink Ouzo or little Greek coffees at the beach bars, before going home to sleep.

Industrial trawlers were depleting the fish stocks. The locals blamed it on the Turks who lived in European Turkey or Turkish Trace, a mysterious country which existed on the other side of the Evros estuary just a few kilometres away.

The kitchen was well stocked and the little freezer full of familiar foods, including smoked bacon and Cumberland sausages. Arthur decided for reasons of his own to forgo the sausages, and tucked into a large plate of bacon and eggs. It was a pleasure for him to cook for himself and even to wash up afterwards.

When he had put the breakfast things away in the kitchen, he wandered down to the beach café to take his coffee and to enjoy a large slice of the locally made baklava. Wandering back up the slope to the apartment an hour later, he saw Edwina coming towards him waving. The joyous smile on her face was the most welcoming he had seen for a long time, and his face too broke into an uncontrollable grin.

'Hello! I didn't realize you would be coming so early, I expected you this evening.' It was Friday and the Embassy closed at midday for the long weekend.

'I took the morning off and started from Sofia at seven this morning,' she said as if slightly out of breath, 'because the roads are much less crowded at that time of the morning. The problems start when you get past Plovdiv, and you are back on those horrible B-roads. Turkish lorry drivers are so dangerous!'

He could see the red diplomatic number plate on her Ford Escort where it was parked in the street. He had flown to Athens by Olympic Air from Sofia earlier that week, followed by an internal flight to Alexandropoulis airport. It had been all so easy.

'I thought I would leave my car here for you to drive, and then go back by air. It makes things a lot better for you Arthur and I really don't want to do that drive again for a while.' She looked a bit bleary eyed and he suggested a drink in the nearby bar.

'How are you feeling Arthur?'

She looked at him with different eyes now; no longer as the compliant PA but more a willing friend. Arthur had not quite got past the trauma of Annabel's deception, and still felt greatly peeved by the way she had disgraced him.

'Oh well Edwina! I am still very upset about events, but I have begun to feel my old self again. It is as though—and don't laugh,' he sipped his beer and then sat for a moment staring at it, 'it's as though I am a young man again!' He looked at her with slightly tearful eyes and she put her hand on his and smiled.

'You have been in fight or flight mode for some while now Arthur. You simply haven't realized how destructive your life has become. It seems that everyone wants a part of you, and none of them will let you have any peace.'

Arthur nodded, held her hand in his for a moment, and then smiled. 'I should have done this years ago!' Edwina looked at him and put her other hand on his arm.

'Yes, I agree Arthur, and you would have been very welcome to come and stay at any time!'

The little apartment was a bit untidy when they returned with her luggage, and a few things she had brought with her from the Metro supermarket in Sofia. But in minutes the flat was back to normal, as she went round the sitting room plumping up cushions and neatly placing magazines and newspapers on the sitting room coffee table.

Edwina put her belongings into the second bedroom, and then went into the bathroom and placed her toothbrush into a glass on the mirror shelf. It did not seem to be out of place next to his toothbrush, a metaphor which did not exactly escape either of them.

Finally, they agreed that they would go into town for a good lunch at the Kalamakia Restaurant and to walk around the port. It was time to have a long chat and they had a lot to discuss.

WATLINGTON

Annabel was furious. She did not mind being at home on her own out of choice, but to be sent home and put under virtual house arrest was too much for her. It seemed to her that her whole life was to be blighted by the disloyalty and incompetence of others, plus a good measure of serendipity.

Filipov had been very clear when he said that Jim Kilbey seemed to have little or no remorse for his actions in the past, nor the consequences. It was then that she had asked him the burning questions about her paternal father, those which had puzzled her all her life.

In the end much of what he said had not surprised her. Her real father hadn't mentioned his English past or his family to the young Philip Filipov at all, other than complimenting his eldest son John, who he spoke of as if he were some sort of affable drinking companion. Sitting in the Podly Pitta Annabel had finally asked him if her father might have loved her. Filipov's reply was simple and to the point.

'My dear Lady Cumberpot, your father was a psychopath. People like him have no remorse and very few feelings. You must stop thinking of him as an English gentleman, and start seeing him as a rogue!'

The look of disappointment was clearly written on her face as he casually moved his forefinger from side to side in order to emphasize his point. He continued in an almost schoolmasterly fashion.

'I have known many people like him during my life, and they all have one thing in common. They are constantly trying to prove how clever they are, and expect others around them to be honest and trustworthy when they themselves are certainly not. Also, people somehow forget that defectors are rarely seen as more than criminals in their own society. Although outwardly regarded as heroes—on their arrival in some political Valhalla of their choice—their life from then onwards is pitted by distrust and hate. That, Lady Cumberpot, is their true reward.'

She returned to the Embassy that afternoon in some confusion. It was hard for her to accept that her presence on earth was of no interest to anyone except herself. Surely someone must love her, or have loved her in the past?

The following day coincidence and chance successfully completed the circle, and the consequent suspicion and innuendo had finally choked the last vestiges of duty and allegiance from her very being. What happened from now on would be about her, and she alone.

Back home in Orchard Manor and surrounded by twenty years of memorabilia from a life spent in the diplomatic service, most of the photographs on display were of groups of long forgotten politicians and leaders.

There were very few pictures of close family, and only one had been taken of Arthur and her together. It was when they'd visited Buckingham Palace to receive his honour from the Queen two years before.

There were no photos of Lionel Pergamon and only one with James, taken by Norman Dent at Henley Regatta. It was a group photo, and in it were the smiling faces of the entire Dent family, Arthur James and her, with Robin and Sarah Caruthers standing to one side. Arthur had insisted that it should be framed because, as he explained to her, it represented a very happy day in his life. What she did not divulge was that it had been one of the worst in hers! Looking at it made her even angrier.

'Papa, I'm in trouble—you have got to help me!'

Lionel Pergamon was not surprised at her phone call, and had in fact been expecting it for some days.

THE SECRETS ROOM, SOFIA

In the absence of Sir Arthur, it was incumbent upon Dirty Macintosh and Colin the First Secretary to hold the reins. It would have been a somewhat uneventful task in the normal run of events, were it not for the possibility of an internal security crisis. It was also strange that Herodotus the gnome had all of a sudden started to receive a number of revealing messages.

Consequently, Ron Beamish had been kept quite busy, ever since receiving a devastating message from Philip Filipov the day before the Ambassador's departure to Greece.

When it had been decrypted Beamish had chosen to give it directly to Macintosh his superior officer, who in turn had kept it to himself. The Ambassador didn't matter now his position was untenable, which automatically put Dirty into the limelight with his murky masters in London. The message was short and sweet.

'Items successfully swapped. LC informed of KGB connection. Secrets are secure. Business as usual.'

It was as simple as that. The question was how to

interpret this text message? In the end it was something that Macintosh felt should be better left to his masters in London.

As it was they chose to go down the path of conspiracy, and left the details to their researchers—or failed fiction writers—to put the puzzle together and to analyse the evidence. Sir Hilton Cotteslow, Dirty's boss in London, seemed rather blasé about the whole affair when he explained his present position and how he intended to proceed.

'Well Macintosh, it is rather like doing a jigsaw puzzle where you don't have a picture to follow. Any fool can fit the edges or the surround together, but it takes a very creative mind to fill in the bits in the middle. Fortunately, in this case there are not too many pieces to fit together and the picture itself cannot be too complicated.'

WALLINGFORD

The office of Norman Dent & Partners was the final destination for Inspector Peter Squinty—Retired, because as far as he was concerned his investigation was practically complete. An experienced policeman, he had been seconded to the security services some years before, from what had then been known as Special Branch.

Although a perfectly good investigator, there had unfortunately been some complaints about a gradually developing nervous tic, one that had rapidly progressed into a significant twitch which many found a little unnerving.

After a while his condition had got to the point where a combination of these fully developed nervous mannerisms had become orchestrated into a kind of silent opus, one which kept many unwitting interviewees completely spellbound. Consequently his curious antics had now become a part of his interviewing technique, and so it was that he entered the stylish office of Norman Dent.

Tracy Booth was curious to know who the nervous man was, but after a short explanation and the presentation of a card, she picked up the office phone and spoke to her boss. She then ushered their visitor into the private office, and as she did so, he shook hands and announced himself.

'How do you do, my name is Julian Noakes, and I am the property correspondent for *Country Squire Magazine.*'

He took off his shabby raincoat and placed it over the back of the office chair, sat down and then removed a notebook from his jacket pocket.

'We are doing an article about manor houses in this part of the Home Counties, and our readers are very keen to know who is presently moving into the area and how easy it is to get planning permission for building alterations and additions.'

He reached into his inside pocket and produced a

business card. In so doing an involuntary but minor twitch invaded his countenance, somewhat dissipating his insincere smile. On receiving the glossy and embossed business card the first thing Norman Dent noticed was the smart address in Regent Street, London. It would seem that he had finally been acknowledged, and that a lifetime spent in provincial architecture had not been in vain.

'Mr Noakes, I can assure you that it would be a pleasure to assist such an important magazine as yours, although it would be helpful if you could prepare some written questions for me so I can think them over carefully.'

His professional smile covered up any qualms he felt about an impending interview. Noakes removed a slim diary from his pocket, and opening it he inspected it carefully, turning one page back and forth two or three times.

'I see that I will shortly be going away for two weeks to Somerset, and I was hoping to get this article in our next edition!'

He looked up at Norman Dent and brushed the few strands of hair he still possessed over his fast protruding cranium. This was followed by a full twitch, and a sniff.

'I wonder, is it possible to have a few words with you now? Then I will get my secretary Nora to send you a letter with some questions later on today. You see it's a monthly magazine Mr Dent and I am afraid that my life is all about deadlines.' The logic of his last remark sank in, and Norman Dent did not want to lose this valuable opportunity.

'Can we say thirty minutes, Mr Noakes? Will that be enough time for you? I am rather busy today.'

Whilst Norman Dent was in the process of deciding which of his more interesting projects he could publicize in this important glossy magazine, prevarication seemed his best weapon of choice.

'Yes of course, Mr Dent. Now briefly I am told that you specialize in alterations and additions to historical houses. Do you ever new-build anything?' Noakes' question suggested certain knowledge of architecture.

'In the past I have built the odd industrial building, like the one at our local riding school here in Wallingford. But generally I concentrate on listed buildings and buildings of historical interest. That is my true forte!'

Julian Noakes AKA Inspector Peter Squinty—Retired, took down every detail, concentrating on every word as if they were made of gold.

'And if you could briefly outline some of your more recent projects Mr Dent, it would be helpful, particularly one I heard of in Watlington. Mr Griffith the local estate agent, who I believe you know, told me that you were employed as architect on Orchard Manor, which in fact is partly why I am here."

A convulsion of major proportions seemed to shoot down one side of his face, making his bottom jaw jut out, followed by a sniff, the nervous rearrangement of his hair, and finally a cough.

Uncontrollably wrinkling his nose, he finally continued, 'He told me that he was the selling agent, and that you were employed by the owner to carry out some extensive renovations there. Tell me about that project? Our readers would be most interested.'

Inspector Peter Squinty's report to his masters was far more detailed and analytical than one might imagine, because despite his trenchantly nervous disposition, he was a very observant man.

SHEPHERDS BUSH, LONDON

The old Amstrad computer was on its last legs when Inspector Squinty finally put his thoughts on paper. Generally his investigation into the affairs of Lady Annabel Cumberpot had been fairly uneventful, except in the case of Lionel Pergamon, who had surprised him with his responses and his contempt for the way in which he had been approached.

It was not entirely his fault that Pergamon had called his bluff, which was mainly due to his master's apparent ignorance about the history of Lionel Pergamon himself. During his briefing at Vauxhall Cross in London, no mention was made of the fact that Lionel Pergamon had been a friend in the past, or the fact that Annabel his daughter had been adopted. Perhaps Pergamon was right when he said that the present secret service was in a shambles.

To Whom it May Concern—Vauxhall Cross London.
A report on Lady Annabel Cumberpot—a British Subject.

Lady Cumberpot appears to be a typical Englishwoman who enjoys living in an historical building called Orchard Manor House, which is situated in the small town of Watlington in Oxfordshire. She enjoys some country pursuits but is mainly interested in her home, the improvement, modernization, and the furnishing of Orchard Manor with expensive antiques. In Watlington, she tends to keep herself to herself.

She and Sir Arthur have a son James, who has recently left his Public school. He was a boarder at Summerlake College which is on the Reading Road near Sonning Village. For over a year he has been at Leeds University, studying Politics and Geography. He rarely goes home to Watlington, preferring to stay with his grandparents who some while ago moved to Ashford Hill in Hampshire.

Mr Norris Cumberpot—Sir Arthur's father—has a comfortable three-bedroomed cottage there, with a small workshop, which is where he makes pottery objects and occasional sculptures. Both he and his wife have been retired for some years.

As the wife of a British diplomat, Lady Cumberpot seems to spend little time with her husband, preferring to pass her days in her Watlington home. According to the local postmistress, she hardly ever visits the local shops and relies on telephone deliveries for groceries and any other household needs she might have.

She has a cleaning woman called Doris, who travels from the village of Lewknor which is a few miles away, but these days her visits are few and far between. The garden is attended by a local man who I could not identify.

According to Mr Norman Dent, who was the Cumberpot's architect during the extensive renovation work, Lady Cumberpot was a very difficult client prone to argument and summery decisions. From our conversation at his office in Wallingford it seems that they all had a great falling out after a picnic at Henley Regatta the previous year.

Apparently Mr Dent invited an old client and his wife to attend his riverside party, who it appears Lady Cumberpot did not like. During the afternoon an unpleasant argument took place and the three Cumberpots left early, apparently to return their teenage son James to his boarding school. The client in question is a Mr Robin Caruthers.

Afterwards, Lady Cumberpot convinced Mr

Dent that the whole incident was caused by a misunderstanding about a horse she was considering buying from Mr Caruthers, and so Mr Dent consequently thought no more about it.

I visited the riding school in question, and it turns out that Lady Cumberpot has been having some sort of an affair with the proprietor—the said Mr Robin Caruthers—which according to his head groom Sharon Woods was at an end, despite Lady Cumberpot's constant visits and phone calls. Miss Woods told me that these phone calls were a regular occurrence and a constant irritation to her employer, who no longer wished to have anything more to do with Lady Cumberpot.

I also discovered that Mr Caruthers has a wife, who is currently in what is referred to these days as a 'Half-Way House.' This is a euphemism for a low security clinic for the mentally ill. She has recently been moved there from the Fair Mile Hospital in Wallingford, where she has been receiving in-house treatment for a number of years under a certain Dr Coates. I believe that Mr Caruthers visits this woman regularly.

I have also spoken to the local Watlington estate agent, a Mr Griffith, and both he and the local publican agree that Lady Cumberpot is a rather nasty woman, arrogant and bullying, who treats all about her with contempt. This is also the general view. Now we move on to Mr Lionel Pergamon.

This interview was very difficult for me. There are many reasons why, one of which was that I underestimated his intelligence. When I finally regained his confidence, it appears that in the past he was one of us! It seems that he worked for the firm during the latter part of the Second World War and was also involved early on in the Cold War.

He is in his mid-eighties now and walks with a pronounced limp, which he told me was the result of a car crash he had in East Germany in the 1950's! He knew exactly what I was, told me that my cover story was absurd, and said I was a low grade stringer working for MI5. Well he was right about that!

He made it clear that his past service should have been known to you, and that if not, it proved that the Service was going to the dogs. I told him that I was just a humble investigator, and that he should talk to someone in authority at Vauxhall Cross if he had a particular gripe. Meanwhile he mellowed and described his daughter Annabel to me.

He said that she was a high spirited buxom girl when she was young, and that she had been adopted by Pergamon and his wife Susan when she was a little girl. He said that she had been offered for adoption when she was three years old, and that nothing much was known about her true parents.

I was told that she had attended Roedean Junior and then Senior Schools and had taken a First at Oxford where she studied History of Art. It was at Oxford that she met Sir Arthur, where they were fellow students, and that they had married soon after graduation.

He told me that she was tough and stubborn, took her own council; was not a natural academic, and enjoyed sports especially horse riding.

This is all that is known about Lady Cumberpot, her history and her lifestyle. The Cumberpots seem to have few friends; neighbours are never invited for dinner parties, and finally it seems that she practically occupies Orchard Manor on her own.

Sir Arthur stays for a few days each month and at Christmas and Easter, with their son James. When she is not there, it is because there is an important diplomatic occasion which she is obliged to attend in Sofia.

It is clear that she was with him when he was received at Buckingham Palace for his investiture, but generally she keeps away as much as possible.

In conclusion

I do not understand why an obviously high ranking retired MI6 officer would have told me such a simple story with so few details. Surely a man like Lionel Pergamon would have been interested in his adopted daughter's real parents. He would have known from the birth certificate who the real parents were, so why is this such a mystery?

When I spoke to Doris the maid, she told me that she was the next door neighbor to the Cumberpots in Lewknor for many years when they lived there. (I was pretending to be an historian at the time, who was researching the Lewknor Parish records.)

All she was able to tell me was that Mrs Cumberpot—as she was known then—had an older brother called John who came to visit her from time to time. This does not fit in with Mr Pergamon's story of an 'only' adopted daughter, and obviously leads me to believe that we might have been misled by him. Possibly it involves a very old case which you may have overlooked?

I hope that this report is helpful, and that it will give your researchers something to ponder on in the forthcoming days.

Signed.

Inspector. Peter D. Squinty—Retired.

READING

When Sarah returned to the half-way house she was severely agitated and in need of sedation. Dan realized that she had been under some duress and gave her two Mogodon tablets to relax her and to calm her down. After two hours' sleep, she awoke and Flo made her a cup of tea.

When he returned, Billy—the nervous young man— told Flo about a woman who had spoken to him from her car, asking the whereabouts of Sarah. Putting two and two together it was evident from his description of her that it had been Lady Cumberpot. Flo took Dan to one side and explained about that morning's visit, and what had been said.

'You did exactly the right thing Flo, so don't worry yourself. The most important matter now is to make sure Sarah is OK, and to look after her.' Dan was very fond of Flo and respected her good nature and common sense.

'She was a very unpleasant woman Dan, but I managed to put her in her place,' she said laughing. 'I left her fuming on the doorstep, and slammed the door in her face. I rather enjoyed that!'

Meanwhile Sarah had started to cry uncontrollably, which Dan recognized as a good sign. It let vent to her anger and frustration; her fear and self-hate would have to wait for another time.

'It was that bloody woman from the Regatta I told

you about. She was the one who argued with Robin, after he had introduced me to her and her husband. He said that it involved a horse, but I knew it went much deeper than that.'

Her eyes were swollen and her face was white with anguish, as she recounted her meeting that morning with Annabel Cumberpot. 'You cannot begin to imagine the arrogance and contempt she had for me; it was almost as though she was addressing some sort of medieval surf, who needed to be scourged for stealing a rabbit.'

Dan could only assume that he had been kept totally in the dark by Robin about the intervening years between Sarah having been sectioned, and the most recent events. He liked Robin Caruthers, and would have done almost anything to put Sarah and him back together. But he knew that only she was his immediate responsibility, and the one person he solely had to protect from the rather grubby and disappointing outside world.

'Have you told Robin about your feelings, Sarah?' Dan remembered their fleeting conversation a few days before. 'Under the circumstances, don't you feel it would be wise to get a few things straight with him, especially your feelings towards him?'

'I know he has been very attentive and helpful since I came here, and he knows that I will always be grateful to him, but whatever feelings we had for each other in the past, for me at least, are no longer there. Dan, I don't feel anything for anyone anymore, don't you see?'

She felt dead inside when it came to her feelings, but that morning's experience had destroyed her self-confidence as well, and she had now become extremely confused.

'Would you like me to have a quiet word with Robin? He has always trusted me in the past, and I think you need someone to break the news to him gently.' Dan understood that after Annabel's tirade there was a lot of explaining to do.

Dan believed what was important to Sarah was the continued support from her husband, in order to help her back into a normal life and a balanced frame of mind.

'I can't deal with it now Dan, I am exhausted, depressed and I feel quite horribly bruised.' What to most people would be an unhappy experience, to a recovering mental patient, the day's event was devastating.

'Yes, I think it would be better if we both put our cards on the table, Dan. I cannot go on with any more deception no matter how mild it may be. You see, I never want to hurt Robin, and it seems that I have always been a burden to him in one way or another.'

Dan made the call, and that afternoon they met in the garden of the Rose and Thistle for what turned out to be a devastating conversation. When he explained to Robin what had happened that day he was fuming, and with uncontrolled anger he smashed his beer mug against the garden wall.

'That fucking bitch! I can't believe that she would do this to Sarah—she knows Sarah has been ill.'

Apologizing to Des the pub landlord, who came out to see what all the commotion was about, Dan explained that Robin had received some bad news. Assuming him to be one of Dan's patients, Des just calmly tidied up the broken glass and emptied it into the dustbin.

"You can't speak to Sarah at the moment Robin, but she has asked me to talk to you because right now she is having difficulty in explaining anything at all, let alone her feelings.'

It was a hard struggle for Dan to get to the point, but Robin was wise enough to realize that there was a back-story, and it was not just a matter of bloody Annabel's appalling behaviour.

Dan continued, 'Sarah has asked me to tell you that since her treatment and hospitalization she has changed. It is not that unusual Robin, because many patients have the same problem. But it is a change which has made her cold and unresponsive. She admits that she is mainly concerned with herself these days, and finds it difficult to relate to others, except as some sort of opponent. We doctors call it Paranoid Narcissism.'

In order to let Robin digest Dan's last homily he had the good grace to leave for a moment to replace Robin's pint of Courage Best Bitter and one for himself. On returning from the bar and taking a long swig from his own pint glass, he went on.

'When she was originally confined she had all the symptoms of Paranoid Schizophrenia, but this has burnt itself out over time due to the treatment she has received, and of course her on-going medication. But it has left her a little dead inside; if you forgive the expression, despite her outward appearance which we both know is very attractive.'

'What are you trying to tell me Dan? This is becoming a nightmare, and I really cannot deal with all this physcobabble! I'm sorry, Dan. Please, just give me the facts.'

'Sarah does not love you anymore, and only sees you as a friend. She is frightened that you will go away and leave her in the lurch, with no one to turn to. She seems more worried about hurting you than anything else. She said that she is not in the least upset about your apparent relationship with this Cumberpot woman, and has always assumed that you would meet someone else. Ten years is a very long time Robin, and you are human after all!'

Sarah was his wife, and despite the unfortunate circumstances in which they now found themselves, at least Robin now knew the truth. She was dependent upon him and he was responsible for her. What was difficult for him was to reconcile his feelings for her and his increasing abomination of Annabel.

After today he could only think of Annabel Cumberpot as a dangerous and predatory woman. It only served to underscore his now historical view of her when they were fellow students at Oxford.

'My God,' he thought, 'now the sins of the father have been truly visited on the daughter!'

VAUXHALL CROSS, LONDON

Sir Hilton Cotteslow spun the report round on his desk like a windmill, stopping it with his forefinger, as it once more became the right way up and readable.

'So what in your opinion is this chap Inspector Squinty like? Is he reliable, Max?' It all seemed such a bore when he had so many more important things to ponder. Commander Kintbury shrugged his shoulders and looked at the ceiling.

'He has been in the firm for years, and although he can be a little odd at times, he gets the work done quickly and has a sound analytical approach.'

Sir Hilton went on, 'I mean, who is this bloody woman anyway? You told me that she was the wife of a second-rate ambassador to a coconut republic on the Black Sea. Surely Max, you are only sent to somewhere like Bulgaria if you have done something seriously wrong in the first place?'

Max Kintbury was equally puzzled. 'All I know about Bulgaria is the assassination of a BBC hack called Georgi Markov on London Bridge. He was poisoned with a ricin pellet from a special umbrella in 1978. And I don't really know if they do anything important there, except make a few forklift trucks, and of course there is a thriving sex trade.'

'They do make quite a good drop of wine though. I remember that Churchill used to drink Bulgarian

Merlot and Melnik, and it was nothing but the best for our Winston!'

Sir Hilton read the concluding part of Inspector Squinty's report, and then instructed his assistant Antonia to search the files for a Mr Lionel Pergamon.

'I seem to remember reading about someone called Pergamon who worked in Istanbul just after the war Max. Wasn't Jim Kilbey there too? I think he was running things from our Consular section. There was also something called Operation Valuable, when we sent all those unfortunate agents into Albania. Of course they were all rounded up and shot but that was exclusively due to Kilbey. Bit of a bastard really; but still, he was one of us.'

He got up from his desk and walked to the window. Looking over the Thames it reminded him of why he had joined the service in the first place. Unlike Kilbey, it was because he belonged. Looking at a passing bendy-bus as it crossed Vauxhall Bridge, he turned to his assistant Commander Kintbury.

'That's right Max; Pergamon was his legman as I recall. When everything went pear shaped he was sent back to Blighty and Kilbey went on to Washington. Don't know what happened after that; might be worth a poke about. What do you think Max?'

'Well Sir, our man Macintosh in Sofia thinks that there is enough evidence to connect this Cumberpot woman to this Philip Filipov. I discovered that he was at one time the Minister in Charge of the Bulgarian

Embassy here in Kensington. You may remember he was put in as a replacement when that state of the art RAF flying helmet went walkies from the Farnborough Air Show. Filipov had to grovel on the embassy steps— I remember watching it on the box and it was hilarious. The Met finally nicked the bloke who did it, and because he was not a recognized diplomat we locked him up for five years; job done!'

Sir Hilton lit a small Cuban cigar. 'Isn't Macintosh the knob head who's testing out that bloody electronic gnome? What are we calling it now? Oh yes, Operation Herodotus! Apparently our little problem with the Cumberpot woman stems from that.'

Blowing a thin puff of cigar smoke out of one side of his mouth, Sir Hilton considered the possibilities.

'Perhaps we should confiscate her passport for the time being, although if she is a spy, she probably has a drawer full of dodgy passports anyway. Maybe we ought to bring her in for questioning or at the very least do over her home? I am told that there are a lot of burglaries in Oxfordshire at this time of the year!'

CHAPTER THIRTEEN

READING

SARAH CARUTHERS seemed to come to terms very quickly with the reality of her situation. Sitting in the sunny bay window of her ground floor bed-sit, Dan was prompted to question his patient more aggressively than ever before.

'Sarah, do you feel cold and uncaring?'

'Yes, I do at this moment.'

'Have you ever really been in love?'

'No.'

'Do you think that you could ever be in love with someone?'

'No.'

'Then what is your reason for living?'

'To survive!'

The blackness of her world frightened Dan and was a place he never wanted to enter. He realized that if he did, that it would be almost impossible to escape.

By now Sarah was trapped in a spiral of negative

thought and self-destruction. And with her self-esteem crumbling fast, Dan could see that she was rapidly approaching a significant danger point with her illness.

'Will you be all right if I leave you on your own?'

Dan was concerned about her historical threats of suicide, and his experience told him that if repeated too often, it occasionally came true.

'I will be downstairs in my apartment if you need me Sarah, I have got a lot of paperwork to do, and you know how it is? So just tap on the door if you need me.'

'Don't worry Dan; I will get over it in time. It came at a bad moment for me, that's all, and you don't meet hideous creatures like Annabel Cumberpot every day. Do you Dan? I sincerely hope not!'

WALLINGFORD

The weather was getting winterish and Robin shivered as he sat behind his desk in the riding school office. But it was the chill he felt in his heart that was overwhelming. Realizing that his private life and his business had finally collided, it had left him emotionally devastated and angry.

OK, so he had an affair with a married woman, but what was so unusual about that? He'd been living on his own for years, working bloody hard building up his business and expanded the riding stables.

He wasn't a monk, and most men would have been just as frustrated as he was under the circumstances.

What was he supposed to do? It was intended to be such a simple and convenient arrangement. She was a married woman, practically estranged from her husband, who was having an affair with a virtually unattached male. It seemed the perfect relationship for them both at the time, and one which was supposed to go nowhere; she knew it and so did he. What the hell had gone wrong?

'Listen to me you horrible bitch, why are you trying to destroy Sarah? She has just come out of hospital, and you know very well how fragile she is at the moment. You might have done untold damage to her. Her doctor has told me that she is completely distraught. What the fuck do you think you are doing?'

'Well Robin, I have tried to phone you on a number of occasions and you have refused to speak to me. I had to get your attention somehow. What do you expect?'

'My attention, my attention? You are a married woman, Annabel. Not only that but you are married to senior British diplomat for crying out loud, with a young son at university. What the hell do you think you are playing at? Are you blind? What on earth did you imagine could come out of our sordid little affair? It is finished, Annabel, it is totally finished, surely even you can see that? What are you looking for Annabel, revenge?'

'Yes, now you mention it, that is exactly what I am looking for, Robin! How kind of you to speak to me in this way.' The tone of her voice had a disturbing quality.

She went on, 'You have managed to crystallize my thoughts perfectly Robin, and I will be absolutely delighted to see you suffer in any way possible. Goodbye Robin!'

Robin wrote to Sarah:

My Dear Sarah,

I am writing to you today because Dan quite rightly has told me that you need to be on your own for a while. He also told me that you were worried that I will no longer wish to support you due to some recent revelations about your feelings towards me. Let me say straight away, that nothing has changed and although I am understandably disappointed, I will remain steadfast—not just because you are my wife—but because of the feelings we have shared in the past and because of the friendship we can now have.

Annabel Cumberpot turned out to be a truly malicious and unscrupulous woman, and has now started to threaten me as well. What she did was unforgivable, and it may be just the tip of the iceberg as far as she is concerned.

I realize now that she is like that with practically everyone, including Arthur her silly husband, and her poor son James who we met at Henley. Lord knows what will happen to him if they split up, which seems inevitable to me.

Meanwhile, whatever you might need you just have to ask me, or send a message through Dan. And don't worry, Sarah, I will not let you down.

Robin.

If he reread his letter to Sarah once, he must have done so a hundred times. Sitting rigidly at his desk he tried to remember the good days amongst the many bad ones that occurred when Sarah was becoming irrational and abusive.

During their ten years of marriage, they had only really been together for three, and out of that it was only the first year which he remembered with any joy. The rest was a blur, and probably best forgotten. What would happen to them both in the future was anybody's guess.

THE PRIME MINISTER'S OFFICE, SOFIA

Gregory III was more a king than a Prime Minister, and very determined not to have his throne usurped. Very foolish politicians imagined that they could manage him somehow, when the opposite was in fact true. He had spent his whole life in a diffused royal limelight, and whilst fighting for survival in the business world, his resolve had been mostly tested when dealing with the press as they continually tried to push their way into his inner sanctum.

His present objective was to rid himself of certain individuals who surrounded the current President and even some who had been actually appointed to the President's Cabinet. Many were from the old regime and on record as saying that the citizens of Bulgaria had little appetite for kings and never would. Well, he would see about that.

They continually neutralized most of the more innovative changes needed to put Bulgaria back once more on its feet, and very few of the Acts approved by Parliament were agreed to by the President. He used his veto to delay everything, and Gregory III realized that his 800 days were swiftly running out.

The old guard enjoyed special privileges which went far beyond their luxury villas and comfortable pensions. Vast business loans were agreed by the Swiss and Austrian Banks to purchase many of the factories and enterprises, none of which were supported by any realistic business studies. The privatization process, which was an inviolate part of the constitution, was now being cherry picked by a new raft of entrepreneurs who seemed to have appeared from nowhere. Who were they?

They were the educated first lieutenants of the old brigade, now wearing smart expensive suits. Educated at Harvard and Oxbridge, they confidently came into the Bulgarian business arena with the same shiny toys and gizmos as their Western counterparts. And who did they appoint as directors and consultants to these newly privatized companies? The very people who had surrounded the old Dictator in the old days!

And where did all these loans originate? They emanated from the very banks which harboured the countless millions which had been secreted away in numbered bank accounts in Switzerland and Austria, by the old regime itself. Now these millions were being surreptitiously repatriated after a fifty-year holiday abroad, plus a considerable amount of added bank interest.

What Gregory ideally needed was a huge scandal involving certain members of the old Bolshevik coterie who now surrounded the current President. Because he knew it would surely be followed by very firm rebukes from The European Union, and of course the ever-present USA.

Generally referred to as the World's only superpower, it would surely be possible to use them to dislodge certain members of the Bulgarian *Red Bourgeoisie*, by evoking the wrath and outrage of the American President whilst encouraging the current US Ambassador to address the press with his usual bluntness and candour. That is why he personally wrote to the American Ambassador.

> *Excellency,*
>
> *It has come to my attention that all is not well with our internal security; not I might add due to the Russians and Chinese who will always remain a de-facto on-going threat, but from a friendly source far closer to home.*

It seems that The British Ambassador's wife, Lady Cumberpot, has been seen in the company of one of our more renowned Cold War spies, who is now part of our current President's Cabinet. This has apparently happened on a number of occasions; leading my Minister of the Interior to believe that there may be some risk to our NATO alliance should this be allowed to continue.

Since there remains a somewhat ambivalent trust between your good selves and the British intelligence services, I thought that I would address the matter to you rather than to continue any meaningful discussions with the British Ambassador himself.

In the past I have warned him of our suspicions, but predictably he has chosen to ignore my caution. I hope that you can handle this information with your customary discretion, as the facts are not totally clear to me yet, nor the extent and degree of the threat.

Yours sincerely,
Gregory III
Prime Minister of the Republic of Bulgaria.

The American Ambassador overreacted, in the usual American way, and instead of passing the buck to his local security chief, he chose to communicate directly with the State Department in Washington, who then in turn sent an internal memo to the CIA chief on the local European desk.

He consequently advised the State Department to take the matter up at ministerial level with the British Foreign Office in London, and the American Ambassador in the UK was duly dispatched. The British Foreign Secretary Sid Hay was baffled by the whole matter, and therefore passed it on to Sir Hilton Cotteslow at MI6.

Sir Hilton was heard to comment, 'Bloody hell Max, this is becoming really silly! What the fuck is going on in Bulgaria, I would love to know?'

ALEXANDROPOULIS

They sat together on the sand. He held her hand in his and was perfectly content. It was October, but the sun was still hot. A few people were happily swimming in the dark blue sea and then lying beneath the bullrush shelters which are a permanent feature of beach life in Greece. Edwina rubbed sun cream on Arthur's slight shoulders and he in turn smeared cream on Edwina's ramrod straight back.

To all intents and purposes they were an established middle-aged couple taking a late holiday, or a last minute travel deal. They could have come for any reason or from any part of Britain, by the casual way in which they guarded their privacy and kept to themselves. They seemed used to each other, and however simple a task they carelessly worked as a team.

'Arthur, I spoke to Mr Macintosh this morning, and he very gently suggested that we stay here a bit longer. He said that he is attending all the diplomatic receptions on your behalf, although he says he is sick to death of them.' She rubbed some cream on Arthur's arm.

'He is quite a nice guy, when you get to know him Arthur, and I think that he is just as hurt and worried as we are. So, a few more days Arthur, eh?'

'A few more days Edwina? A few more years more like! I can't tell you how much better I feel being here with you in Greece. I never want to leave, it's simply heaven. I haven't experienced so much peace and quiet for ages!'

ORCHARD MANOR HOUSE, WATLINGTON

Annabel realized that she had lost Robin for good. The rest? Well, she didn't feel too bad about losing Arthur which was inevitable under the circumstances. With James she felt some responsibility, but however much she tried it was difficult for her to picture a world where she was not the centre of attention.

What was more annoying was the fact that her luck was changing and she seemed no longer in control of events, something which had never happened before. She sat at the kitchen table and wrote down all the plusses on one side of a sheet of writing paper, and all the minuses on the other. It was rather like an audit carried out on a lifetime spent in self-indulgence and acquisition.

First of all there was the house itself which she reckoned must be worth twice as much as they initially paid, bearing in mind all the alterations and improvements. Then there was the antique furniture which she had amassed over the intervening years. Even Orchard manor was beginning to look like an overstocked antique shop, although exclusively in the Regency style. The value of these furnishings would surely amount to a considerable sum on their own account.

Although the family bank accounts were in joint names, her own personal bank account had the largest balance in it, as did her account with The Malmsbury Building Society. Her Access credit card was paid up, as were her American Express and Optima cards, and lastly her Iceland Frozen Food card. Together with this, she also had a lot of unused Air Miles.

And, she must not forget the collection of stamps and gold coins that her stepfather Lionel Pergamon, knowing her acquisitive nature, had helped her to assemble over the years. This collection must be worth a few bob too.

To sum it all up, she realized that she had more than enough resources to live on for quite some time. Together with this she had possession of the house, and as the mother of a nineteen-year-old university student who also lived at the manor house, she could stay there with impunity. So generally speaking, Arthur was stuffed.

English law was absolutely clear about such matters as her continued use of the matrimonial home, of alimony and child support. Should a divorce occur in the near future, which she not only anticipated but expected to win hands down—with or without Robin Caruthers—she believed her position was very tenable indeed.

On the minus side, she had to deal with the local gossips, the scandal and finally a legal jungle which would have to be traversed with enormous care. She knew that there were snakes in the jungle, and that she would have to be mindful of where she trod; other than on other people's feelings of course, which were of little interest to her.

The little room next to the kitchen, once known as Arthur's study, was now used for storage. The desk had become home to boxes of tined food, and piles of old newspapers tied up in bundles together with a vast number of *House and Gardens* magazines. There were also a number of lidless glass jars, various broken picture frames, and James' old bicycle.

In the corner was a very large white bench freezer which was next to a small fridge. It was where Arthur kept his precious bottles of Han Krum Bulgarian dry white wine and various assorted cans of beer. Surprisingly Annabel was teetotal, and showed little interest in such things.

She opened the bench freezer with her key and looked at the contents. She could see that she was getting short of Mr Grimmer's clover-fed spring lamb, although there were still plenty of her favourite homemade Cumberland pork sausages. She removed six fat frozen sausages, and then closed the lid with a bang, locking it as she did so.

She put the key in the top drawer of the desk, and opened the door of the microwave which was perched on top of the little fridge. While she defrosted the sausages, she searched inside one of the boxes, where she found a tin of Heinz baked beans, and a large packet of potato mix.

Taking the tin and the packet into the kitchen she sat at the table contemplating her list, to see if she had left anything out from her financial appraisal, but she was suitably satisfied with her present position. Hearing the ding of the microwave, she went once more into the little room, took out the rotating glass plate and brought her supper into the kitchen ready for cooking.

First she made sure there was enough water in the electric kettle before turning it on, ready to rehydrate the potato mix. Then checking that the oil-fired Aga cooker was hot enough to fry the sausages, she took a heavy wrought iron frying pan from the rack, put it on the front plate, and then placed the six sausages in it together with some cooking oil.

While they slowly cooked she returned to the kitchen table, carrying a large bottle of tomato sauce, some pepper and salt, sat down and continued to inspect her list of figures. It seemed that they had become rather rich in the last few years, which made her pout her lips in a grotesque and cunning way. The question was how she could keep it all?

The side door to the garden terrace was locked, and the house seemed very secure to her. She had managed to dissuade both James and Arthur from getting a dog, due to their peripatetic existence, but in truth she was rarely in Sofia or elsewhere for that matter. So the only addition to the family had been a large black cat called Tommy, and he came and went as he pleased. The sausages sizzled on the stove and the kettle came to the boil and switched itself off.

'Perhaps I could let some rooms out as well,' she thought. 'There are still a number of RAF officers in Benson looking for somewhere to stay.' But with this thought she suddenly became appalled as she pictured herself as a drudge slaving away in the kitchen. No, that was not for her.

She heard a slight noise outside on the terrace. Unlocking the door she turned on the terrace lights, but saw no sign of anyone, except Tommy the cat who was wandering about aimlessly. Back once more in the kitchen, she left the terrace door partly open for the cat to enter.

He liked to sit by the Aga cooker during the evening, which she also found agreeable because he kept her company. Hearing what she thought was the sound of the terrace door as it opened, she said in a loud and rather pompous voice, 'Tommy, is that you?'

WALLINGFORD

Robin Caruthers had spent his lunchtime in the town at the Partridge Inn. He wasn't drunk, just a little bit squiffy. Chris the Irish landlord had been a friend for some time, and between serving drinks to other customers at the bar he enjoyed talking with Robin especially about horses; his background in Ireland having been a farm near Bishopstown in County Cork.

'Ah well,' he would say, 'at least I'm not on the shovel!'

Today had been different, and Robin was forced to admit to his friend that he was rather disenchanted with the opposite sex.

'Not that bloody Annabel woman is it I hope, Robin?' He shook his head and wiped the bar down with a look of disdain on his face. 'That's a fearsome woman, Robin; surely you could find some normal lass from around about that is better suited?' He pulled a pint of Morlands Old Speckled Hen and placed it on the beer mat. 'What about that Sharon girl that works for you? She's a comely one and no mistake.' But Robin seemed engrossed with slurping down his favourite bitter.

'You can't fraternize with the staff, Chris, it's not done. In any case I have never even considered Sharon as a possible squeeze.' Thoughtfully taking a gulp from his pint, 'Well, I mean, she's too…!' Robin was lost for words. Chris smilingly butted in.

'You mean nice, don't you Robin? She is too bloody nice! That's what you really mean Robin, don't you?'

Swallowing the last bit of bitter, Robin looked at his friend in surprise. 'Actually, I suppose you could be right, I have never thought of her that way!

WATLINGTON

Inspector Squinty's instructions were very simple. He was to watch Orchard Manor in order to determine an opportunity for an MI5 team to safely break in. They needed a reasonable amount of time to do the job, because this was to be a highly secret mission. Leaving the house sterile with no signs of it having been minutely searched, it also had to appear that it was a sloppy break-in by a local burglar.

The service employs a number of specialists either from the SAS, or occasionally directly through the Prison Service. Good burglars are seldom caught and convicted, but those that are can occasionally be recruited with the promise of early parole.

Together with these operatives come a group of specialist cleaners, whose job is to leave a perfect crime scene for the local Police to discover and to subsequently botch up. They in turn pursue their normal enquiries, but with a nod and a wink from the intelligence service, they find it hard to discover either enough evidence or even a culprit.

If they do find a suspect—which has rarely happened in such cases—the Crown Persecution Service is lent on by the Home Office in order to dissuade them from prosecution, generally for lack of sufficient evidence.

This way a burglar's reputation remains intact; they remain at liberty and are well paid for the services they provide into the bargain. Everyone is happy including the local newspaper, which glories in an orgy of uncontrolled conjecture. No one is caught, the insurance company is forced to pay up and the incident is soon forgotten.

Inspector Peter Squinty—Retired, felt a little uncomfortable in the cab of the Series IIA Land Rover Defender pickup truck, but mainly because the windows kept on steaming up. He also rather resented having to wear green wellington boots and a Barbour Jacket both of which he associated with the somewhat pretentious Fulham Farmers in London. He felt more at home in his aging raincoat which he wore during all the seasons; the emotional cocoon in which he habitually lived.

He was well aware that his compulsive disorders and twitches were increasing by the day, but a few more years in the service would mean a generous cash payment, and the opportunity to relax. He looked forward one day to a time when he would be able not only to tell the truth, but to make some genuine friends. Thirty years of deceiving people had left its mark.

Looking through his binoculars he was able to see Orchard Manor in its entirety, and with clear vision. Parked behind a hedge in the adjacent farmyard, he managed to blend in with an array of forlorn and rusting bits of agricultural equipment that the local farmer was reluctant to dump. Armed with a large thermos flask of tea, and a tin full of corned beef sandwiches with Branston Pickle, he had spent the last few days in total isolation.

The first few days had proved fairly normal, with the figure of Lady Cumberpot seen looking through various windows, and occasionally wandering around the garden. It seemed that she rarely went out, judging by the dark green Range Rover which remained a permanent feature in the driveway.

Inspector Squinty's task was to watch the goings on at Orchard Manor from eight o'clock in the morning until eight at night, after which time it was arranged by London for the local police to keep an eye on the property during their night-time patrols, and to report any movement or changes in circumstances to him in the morning.

For this purpose he had been supplied with a heavy brick sized mobile phone, which he kept in the breast pocket of his Barbour Jacket. By this means it was also possible for his masters to keep track of him and his activities.

On the fifth day there was no movement to be seen at Orchard Manor at all. Although the Range Rover was still parked in the driveway, no lights had been switched on or off in the house for three days, and when he tried the doorbell, there was no answer on the intercom implying that nobody was in.

According to the Oxford Police, the BT security alarm had not been activated, and according to the local telephone exchange there had been no phone calls either made or received for the last three days. With blank windows and no sign of Lady Cumberpot, it was decided to do the job that night.

'Is five ready Sir? I think it is a go.' Peter Squinty twitched with anticipation.

'She must have slipped out late a few nights ago, although the plod hasn't noticed anything, but then what do you expect? She must have been picked up by a friend or colleague, because the Range Rover is still in the drive. Also there is no sign of Doris or the gardener. The Cumberpot woman recently told the local postmistress that she didn't really need them anymore. Apparently they come only occasionally when she phones them which isn't that often.'

Commander Max Kintbury was left to deal with the details of the mission. 'Yes, it sounds like a go doesn't it? What time is good for you, Inspector? It better be after midnight surely?'

'Absolutely Sir! By that time of night Watlington is as dead as a dodo. All the shops are closed until at least eight o'clock in the morning which is when the newsagent opens for business. It's like a ghost town up until then.' The crackling mobile was running out of charge.

'I'm ready my end, Sir, and parking for a couple of our vehicles won't be a big problem. They can park in the next door farmyard where I am now. No one hardly ever comes here anyway, and definitely not at that time of night.'

'OK, we will make it tonight. You will be the coordinator, and a Captain Stafford will be the CO for tonight's escapade. Oh, and Inspector Squinty, make sure you have your pistol with you, just in case!'

At last his mission would soon to be over, all of which meant that he would shortly be able to enjoy a few quiet evenings at home with his family. They were becoming strangers to him, and he with them.

'I will await your orders then Sir, and let you know if there are any significant changes.'

READING

The half-way house now seemed bleak, and her room depressing. The colour had somehow begun to seep away from her surroundings and even her black and white photographs now looked sepia and characterless. She sat on her bed and read and reread Robin's letter to her, each time causing her to weep over the same sentence.

'I will remain steadfast—not because you are my wife—but because of the feelings we might have shared in the past and because of the friendship we can now have.'

He had accepted the truth. Robin as usual was being noble and honest; the qualities she had first seen in him before her final nightmare had begun, and now he was offering his friendship in consolation. She didn't deserve it and she knew it. Perhaps the horrible Annabel was right and she was not good enough for him. But then, neither was Annabel.

VAUXHALL CROSS, LONDON

Dirty Macintosh was surprised at his summons to visit London; he was also pleased for the opportunity to redeem his flagging reputation within the service, and to put his own version of the truth on the table. Sir Hilton and his sidekick Max Kintbury were not as nonplussed as he expected.

'You see Macintosh, to us this is all in a day's work, and inevitably all these problems are here to be solved! The main thing is for us to understand what the implications are and to be able to gauge the threat to our national security. Because it now seems that the Americans are also interested in this Cumberpot woman, and are asking us some very hard questions indeed.'

'If I may speak freely Sir, don't you think that this matter is getting a little bit out of hand? After all, as far as I can see no damage has been done to the Herodotus Project which continues to spawn some useful background information about our future EU partner.'

'Would that were so.' A serious look appeared on the

sun-tanned countenance of the enigmatic Sir Hilton. 'You see, some background information has only recently surfaced from the past, and it is now clear that this woman's history is not as squeaky clean as one might have hoped, and nor is her identity.'

Picturing the somewhat fuller figure of Annabel Cumberpot it was hard for Macintosh to visualize her in any guise other than as a bully and a consummate manipulator. People like her usually came in small packages and were generally to be avoided, but it was hard to ignore the Cumberpot woman, who either pushed one around or spat out venom instead.

'Surely she is just a horrible creature Sir, I mean I don't know anyone who likes her, which is something which seems to matter very little to her I might add.'

'She was adopted, Macintosh, and although that is not an important issue, it is her natural father who is. She happens to be the youngest daughter of Britain's greatest traitor, Jim Kilbey. Susan and Lionel Pergamon are her adopting parents. They adopted her when she was three years old when her mother died. Since then it turns out that she has been the subject of a security blackout. Even Pergamon was one of us in the past.'

'But she cannot be under suspicion because of that alone; after all, she was just a baby when all that stuff happened, and totally innocent. Pergamon gave her a home and brought her up to be middle class educated and socially acceptable, which she undoubtedly is. Surely the sins of the father do not come into it?'

'I would agree with you, Macintosh, but now that the Americans are involved you can see how this whole matter has been brought up an extra notch or two. It is no longer a purely domestic issue, and as you yourself have intimated, there are increasing grounds for serious doubt.'

'So what do you want me to do Sir?'

'Just keep on doing things as usual and of course keep me posted on the Herodotus Project. As to Sir Arthur, I suggest you put out a local press release saying that he has recently suffered from a bout of Meningitis and is recuperating at a nursing home in Greece. I think that should be sufficient for the time being. And Macintosh, I want you to keep this buttoned up, because we don't want to get Sir Arthur's son James involved, and the least he knows the better.'

CHAPTER FOURTEEN

WATLINGTON

MAX KINTBURY gave the go-ahead at 1 a.m. The Special Service Land Rover Defender was duly tucked in behind Inspector Squinty's old Series 11a pickup in the farmyard. The van carrying the searchers and the cleaners was hidden in an adjacent field and covered by copious amounts of camouflage netting. No pedestrians had been seen by Inspector Squinty for over an hour, and only two passing cars. One was the local plod doing his rounds and the other a local drunk on his way home from a party. Neither had stopped nor noticed anything.

Captain Stafford easily got over the back wall of Orchard Manor, which he approached from the local tennis club that backed onto the manor garden. In total there were three in his team including an SAS Sergeant on secondment from The Ulster Rifles, and a jemmy man recently released from the Scrubs.

The jemmy man had his own set of tools, while the Sergeant carried some sophisticated surveillance equipment including an endoscope, which could be attached to a small laptop if need be, in order to inconspicuously inspect the interior of the property.

He also had a number of small listening devices which he was able to connect to the windows. In the form of small arrows, these powerful microphones were attached to the glass by a rubber suction cap and fired from a small crossbow with a pistol grip. Huddled on the terrace the three men waited patiently while the Ulsterman listened for any tell-tale signs of movement inside the building. Believing the house to be unoccupied, the jemmy man was set to work.

Unclear if the front door was double locked or not, it was decided to enter via the rear door from the terrace. Using a small battery operated drill, the professional thief made a small hole in the door frame where he assumed the tongue of the lock was situated. He then pushed a thin metal gimlet through the aperture. By moving this around, he was able to trip the lock and the door swung open.

As he did so Tommy the cat came hissing though the gap, running up the jemmy man's arm, clawing its way over his shoulder, and giving all three men an unexpected fright. Having regained his composure, Captain Stafford carefully edged his way through the door.

Without a light on in the room, he had to rely on his night vision goggles to see his way, and holding a Glock 17 pistol at his side he finally stepped into the main room. What he then saw was quite unexpected.

'Inspector Squinty,' the Captain radioed the controller, 'we have found a stiff here in the kitchen. From what I can see it appears to be a rather large lady; about forty-something who is lying on the kitchen floor. It looks to me like she has been slotted, and some days ago judging by her condition. Can we have some instructions please?'

When the Inspector passed on the message, Commander Kintbury was gobsmacked. This was the last thing he expected to have to deal with on the moonlight shift at the factory, and especially with no boss there to give him some creative ideas.

It had once hung in the entrance hall of Downing Street during the premiership of Harold Wilson. Depicting an old mill in Salford, Kintbury gazed with certain resentment at the hugely valuable W. S. Lowry painting which hung on the wall in front of his desk. One day he would have a proper window of his own to look through at the outside world, with no bloody matchstick men to divert his attention. But now he had a corpse on his hands.

'Are you sure that it is Lady Cumberpot, Inspector? You had better go and have a good look for yourself, if you don't mind, because you know what she looks like and we don't want to make any mistakes at this stage.'

Inspector Squinty—Retired, climbed out of his old Land Rover, only to discover that his legs had gone to sleep. He stood there rubbing them, trying to get some feeling back, and wondered if, with all his years of surveillance, his muscles had begun to atrophy. Slipping an old Webley .32 Mark IV revolver into his Barbour jacket pocket, he stumbled across the road like a drunken man. Soon he would have to start going to his trendy local gym in Shepherds Bush Road, to try and get fit again.

The searchers had already covered up all the windows with black plastic sheeting, and were busy at work inspecting the upstairs rooms of Orchard Manor. This meant that with the doors closed none of the electric lights could be seen from the outside.

Turning on the florescent kitchen lights and spotlights, the Inspector could clearly see the body of Lady Cumberpot. She was sprawled on the floor next to the kitchen table. Removing the telephonic brick once more from his breast pocket, he dialled his boss in London.

'Yes, it's definitely her Sir, no doubt about that. Captain Stafford was right, it seems, she has been stabbed from behind. I don't suppose she knew who her assailant was and there is absolutely no sign of any struggle. But I am not a regular policeman or a forensic expert, and if you need to know more I will require some further instructions from you.'

Someone had thoughtfully moved a large frying pan from the stove. Whatever food that had been cooking in it had by now been eaten by the black cat which had given all three men such a shock when it ran off. So that and the murder itself were the only genuine signs of intrusion.

The body was beginning to settle and rigor mortis had long since dissipated, meaning that some three days had elapsed since the murder. Allowing for the heat in the kitchen, mainly due to the Aga cooker, this would approximately coincide with his surveillance report and his conclusions so far. Inspector Squinty was not that kind of policeman, but he knew enough from his past experience to make certain minor judgments concerning the cause of death.

A tomato sauce bottle, an unopened can of baked beans and a new packet of potato mix were on the kitchen table, together with some pepper and salt. Also on the table was a biro pen, and a list which appeared to be of various property assets, antique furnishings and bank balances. To the casual eye they would have seemed of no particular interest, but to Squinty they appeared to be specific financial details drawn up prior to the late Lady Cumberpot's demise. It might well have been a final assessment of her assets. After all, if she was planning to leave the country for good she would need plenty of cash to cover her expenses. Unnoticed by the others present, he slipped this information into his Barbour Jacket breast pocket, and once more he removed his chunky mobile phone.

'I think she was about to do a runner Sir! It seems she was adding up all her assets. Now I ask you, what sort of person would do such a thing unless they were about to flee the country?'

Max Kintbury was as bewildered as ever, and had

few if any inspired ideas. 'Is there anywhere we could hide the body, Inspector? I don't mean permanently—although that is always a possibility—but for just a few more days before the local plod gets involved. That way we can finish the search, tidy up and leave as though nothing ever happened. We can't afford to have any clues left hanging around, absolutely no evidence that we have been there, and hopefully no body either. That would be a perfect solution, and would keep us well out of the picture for the time being!'

Captain Stafford was dying for a cigarette, as were his crew who were all hoping to get back to London before morning. He and the Sergeant to the Hyde Park barracks, and the jemmy man back to his home and loving family in Peckham.

'Do you have any idea where we could store her body for a few days?'

Peter Squinty walked around the house looking for suitable cupboards and old trunks, but nothing seemed to be appropriate. For a start he did not want to leave any unnecessary evidence of blood spills or movement of a body, because it would imply that there were a number of people present at the time of the murder.

'What about the freezer Guv?'

The jemmy man from Peckham had been looking around for some memento to steal, and had been poking around in Sir Arthur's office looking for hidden treasure. He was a recognized thief after all was said and done.

'She would fit in their nicely Guv, and we would all be well gone before anyone twigged! Whoever finds her might think she is a Raspberry Whopper!' They all laughed except Inspector Squinty who still believed death should be treated with dignity.

'Bloody thing won't open; I bet it's all iced up,' said the Ulsterman fumbling with the lid whilst rocking the freezer backwards and forwards. The jemmy man looked through the desk drawers and produced a small chrome key.

'You got to know where to look Paddy! There is a key here which looks about right if you ask me. Remember I used to be a locksmith, didn't I, or have you forgotten that?'

Inserting the small key into the freezer lock it effortlessly turned and at once the lid miraculously sprung open. The jemmy man laughed. 'There you are Paddy, and now you won't have to break the bloody thing open, will you?'

The Ulsterman and the Captain somewhat reluctantly picked up the corpse of Lady Cumberpot, and carefully placed her into the bench freezer. The jemmy man reverently draped some of the sausages across her inert body, turned the thermostat up to maximum and then closed the lid with a bang.

'That should do the trick,' he said with a smile. 'Can we all go home now Guv, I think we have done enough for one day, don't you?'

He relocked the freezer chest and placed the small

key back in the desk drawer. The cleaners carefully removed the disposable black overalls that the threesome had each been wearing, their rubber gloves, the plastic overshoes, balaclavas the masks and plastic goggles. They put these into a separate bag which they would burn at the crematorium in Ealing the following morning. Leaving the way that they had come, the specialist team would never be seen together again, and their escapade in Watlington would soon be forgotten.

Having finished their search of the upper floor of Orchard Manor, the team now moved down to the ground floor. As they did the expert cleaners went to work in the upper part of the house, leaving not a single trace of the recent inspection.

Not only did they clean all the surfaces, but they expertly repaired any damage which might have occurred during the removal of floorboards and various wall panels. Cleaning their way down the stairs, they announced that the upper part of the house was now sterile.

There was nothing which might support any of the convenient conspiracy theories, and there was no evidence of subversion or intrigue to be found in the five bedchambers and two bathrooms. Two of the bedrooms were obviously not used as such, but were crammed full of antique furniture, various oil paintings, objects d'art and certain items of historical interest.

It was clear that the three bedrooms in use were occupied specifically by Lady Cumberpot, Sir Arthur, and their son James. Although it seemed odd that the couple did not cohabit and appeared to have separate bedrooms, the search team was not there to determine the state of the Cumberpots' marriage but to look for clues.

In the dead woman's dressing room there were a considerable number of expensive clothes and draws full of giant knickers and braziers. There was also evidence of her horse riding activities, and in one cupboard they found riding boots, jodhpurs, hacking jackets, and a blue Barbour jacket. This plus a number of riding hats and whips, was evidence that she was either a dedicated equestrian or an accomplished pervert. Other than that there were no safes in the upper part, no strongboxes and no locked cupboards, and very little left to inspect bar the enormous number of cosmetic products and palliatives which littered the deceased's dressing room and bathroom.

The ground floor of Orchard Manor proved more fruitful, and the search team took their time photographing not only the contents but photocopying the correspondence too. It seemed that Sir Arthur in common with many men kept most of his correspondence at work; other than letters to Summerlake College, Leeds University, or to various trades people who the Cumberpots obviously paid by Bank Cheque on a regular basis.

So Sir Arthur's affairs were quite commonplace, and Inspector Squinty suspected that he carried out most of his private business from his diplomat's chair in Sofia.

But Lady Annabel was quite a different matter, and her effects were far more revealing. In her private drawers were documents going back to her days at Oxford, and even before. They were all carefully filed away in arch lever files of various colours, minutely detailing her entire life.

Then there were the dairies which she had diligently kept, in which she expressed her most private thoughts. These were carefully duplicated on the small photocopier the searchers had brought with them, and the results carefully stored in a large canvas bag. This was then removed from the property to be sent for analysis in London.

When they had finished the ground floor search, it left the cleaners free to finish their expert work, leaving the house exactly as it was when they had first arrived; although there were one or two exceptions. Firstly there wasn't a body on the kitchen floor, and secondly there were no signs of any bloodstains or forensic evidence left for the police to follow. In fact, other than the unfortunate incumbent residing the freezer, there were no signs of any recent occupation at all. The house was completely sterile.

The back door was finally shut tight, the small drill hole in the door frame was puttied and painted, and as dawn approached the remaining figures crept surreptitiously out of Orchard Manor and back to their day jobs in London.

Inspector Peter Squinty—Retired, could now look

forward to a week's rest, and Tommy the cat would in future have to look elsewhere for his breakfast. And the murder weapon; it was nowhere to be seen!

READING

Sarah Caruthers realized that she could no longer live in Reading because she was retreating once more into the blackness from which she had so recently escaped. The punishment that Annabel Cumberpot had so viciously administered now played remorselessly on her mind, and it seemed that there was no solution to her dilemma other than to return to the Fair Mile Hospital, and to continue her treatment under Dr Coates.

As far as she knew she was still under the protection of the hospital authorities. If she insisted, they would be forced to let her return as an in-patient and that would be an end to the whole matter. Everyone would be better off if she went back; including Robin and Dan, and it would also free up her room at the hostel for someone new.

'Have you discussed this with Robin?' Dan was feeling crushed with disappointment and failure. 'You were doing so well Sarah, getting your confidence back, and starting to do things for yourself. Why not have a chat with him? I am sure he will understand.'

'Dan, I am feeling so depressed and ill at the moment, all I need is to go somewhere safe. I need the routine of hospital life and to be amongst people who can help me.

I don't want to get back into the suicidal state I was in a few years ago. Please permit me go back Dan!'

'I thought you were getting over the shock. You must realize that the world is stuffed full of people like Annabel Cumberpot. I know people like her can be poison to sensitive souls like you Sarah, and the many others who find themselves in your predicament, but you have to learn to deal with them somehow.' Dan took her hand in his and squeezed it affectionately. 'All I can do is to advise you to keep away from them. You see her kind of aggression is not only pointless but destructive. In the end people like her have no friends at all to speak of, and without friends I am afraid we have little or nothing in this world.' But Sarah was determined to go.

'I have packed my case and I'm ready whenever they say. Please tell Robin that I am sorry, and tell him that I will be thinking of him and looking forwards to seeing him again shortly; in a month or so when I am feeling better.'

Her tears were not those of self-pity nor were they about a deep-set emotion. From her disquiet it seemed to Dan that she was in a great hurry to leave, which was something that he could only put down to fear. What was she so frightened of, he wondered?

Dan spoke to Dr Coates who grudgingly confirmed that he was prepared to receive Sarah back at his clinic that day. 'I will need to reassess her Dan. I can't just let her back whenever she feels like it. This isn't a bloody health spa where you can come and go as you please!'

Coates was annoyed by failure, and in the past would have put money on Sarah finding her feet and going back to a normal life in the community. He went on, 'She is a very canny patient Dan, and although she has had considerable problems in the past, she is very intelligent and plays the part of someone inflicted extremely well when it suites her; a little too well at times!'

They were all sorry to see her go from the half-way house. This was especially true of Flo who had done so much to encourage Sarah during her stay, and of course Dan who wanted her to find a new life through photography.

'I don't know what I can do with your darkroom while you are gone Sarah; not to use it would be such a crime.' The very shy man came out of his room, muttered something inaudible, shook her by the hand and then disappeared back into his private domain.

Dan said, 'I will phone Robin in the morning to tell him what has happened, and no doubt he will bring all your remaining things up to you at the hospital this week sometime. You must keep up your photography Sarah and remember the darkroom is always here when you need it.' The hospital car arrived driven by a burly orderly, and then it was time to say goodbye to Argyle Road. Sarah was very pleased to go.

'Thanks for everything Dan, and do give my love to your wife. You have both been so kind to me, and I have been such a problem to you all.' Then she was gone.

Later that week the despondent figure of Robin

Caruthers knocked on the door of the half-way house, and Flo took him downstairs to Dan's flat where he was waiting.

'What can I say Robin, we all did our best but it was obviously not good enough.' He went into the under-stairs kitchen and returned carrying a hot mug of tea. 'Here you are Robin, and I have put a little something extra in it to cheer you up!'

'Well Dan, I can't help feeling that this is entirely my fault. I will never forgive myself. I should have kept my libido more under control and stayed well clear of that bloody Cumberpot woman. I knew her when we were students at Oxford, but she was not like she is now, she was very different. It was my mistake; it was far too easy to slip back into the past. I'm so sorry and I have no idea how I can make all this up to dear Sarah.'

'You don't have to Robin. This wasn't your fault, it was Serendipity. If it had not been that Cumberpot woman it would have been someone else or somewhere else, and much the same thing would have happened despite all your misgivings. That's what life is like, isn't it?'

The large ground floor studio flat looked much the same to Robin as before; the framed black and white photos were still on the wall, and although the room had been cleaned and the bed made by Flo, he could still smell the scent of Sarah and the feeling of her continued presence overwhelmed him. But now she had finally gone, and for him at least, it would probably be forever.

Piled on the dressing table were the rest of Sarah's

things, desolately announcing her departure from the half-way house. The OM 10 Olympus camera was in its black leather case, next to the Western light metre in its little brown sheath. Then there were the magazines and books about photographers: Ray Man, David Bailey, and Terry O'Neill, and art books containing glossy copies of paintings by David Hockney, Lucian Freud and Francis Bacon. Glorifying the eighties, they represented a visual account of a very large chunk of both Robin and Sarah's history, together and apart, both in sorrow but with occasional happiness.

Having put all her belongings into a large canvas holdall, all that was left on the dressing table was a mysterious set of car keys and a sharp kitchen knife. Placing the car keys on the reception desk by the entrance, Robin asked Flo what to do with the knife.

'Don't worry Duck, I'll put it back in the kitchen drawer where it belongs. And don't you worry about Sarah; she is much better off where she is now and you can always see her when she gets a little better. Meanwhile, just get on with your life Robin, and everything will be fine. Ta-ta Duck and God bless!'

The trip home to Wallingford was full of nostalgic thoughts, with many memories of sunny days and happy holidays floating through his mind. It was strange how the blackness which represented most of their time together had simply evaporated from his recollection, now Sarah's departure from the real world had become a reality. His real world and his reality that is, would no longer be quite the same now that he was faced with the prospect of protracted loneliness, with little hope and a possible future scandal as well.

Driving through the entrance gates of the Wallingford riding school he could see that darker days were upon him and winter was fast approaching. It would soon fill his life with colourless views, a true reflection of his colourless existence.

As for Annabel, there remained very little to be said. He foresaw that she would one day succumb to the very same poison she had so casually administered to anyone who came near her, and for that he would shed no tears.

SHEPHERDS BUSH, LONDON

Inspector Peter Squinty—Retired, finally sat back in his comfortable office chair and stared at his aging Amstrad. He was exhausted due to the excessive demands made on him by the Cumberpot case, and the damage it had inflicted upon his health. Too much time spent watching had made all his bones ache, and the chill he had developed sitting in a draughty Land Rover was beginning to make him cough. Tipping strong tea down his sore throat had its therapeutic effects, but generally his condition would only improve with some early nights, an aspirin or two, and a warm sustaining environment.

Due to the bizarre outcome of the Watlington operation, he would now have to write a lengthy official report to his bosses at Vauxhall Bridge. But unbeknown to him, they in turn would have to report to the Foreign Secretary, who would then speak to the American Ambassador. This information would be transferred to Washington, the final leg of the journey being back to Sofia, and with typical American reservations omissions and errors, to the Bulgarian Prime Minister, King Gregory III himself!

A final report on Lady Annabel Cumberpot—a British Subject.

Top Secret.

Due to the unusual circumstances surrounding the case of the wife of the British Ambassador to Bulgaria, and her unexpected death, I think it wise that I take you carefully through the events as they occurred.

As you are aware our team entered upon Orchard Manor House at approximately 1.15 AM gaining entrance through a patio door situated on the adjoining terrace. This was easily achieved due to the fact that the door had only been closed to and not double locked as we supposed. Our operative easily pushed back the tongue of the Yale lock, giving immediate access to the ground floor kitchen area through which an SAS officer cautiously entered. The shock for us all was finding the body of the Cumberpot woman lying on the kitchen floor, where she had no doubt been for some time.

The cause of death by our observation was a stab wound to the back, which judging by the limited amount of blood spilled, had penetrated her heart, so her death was probably instantaneous. I am not a pathologist and nor were any members of the SAS team, but as experienced soldiers they reckoned that the death blow was probably delivered by a professional killer, one who was used to stealth tactics and surprise.

Having gained entrance to the house, the question was how we were to proceed. Even though the situation had changed dramatically, it did not deter us from achieving our original objective which was to search the house for any evidence that would connect the Cumberpot woman with certain alleged espionage activities. Consequently the search team went ahead with a minute inspection of the upper part of the building while we considered what to do with an unexplained corpse.

To have contacted the local Police about an apparent murder at this stage, would have created a furore which would have wreaked havoc on our clandestine operation, and the attendant publicity and press reports alone *would have reflected very badly on the service. So it was agreed by us all, with the support of Commander Kintbury at HQ, to create a false delay in the discovery of the deceased whilst we completed our original task. Consequently it was decided to place her body in a rather large bench freezer which we discovered in an adjoining room next to the kitchen. This freezer unit was the ideal size for such a purpose, and it is where the body of the late Lady Cumberpot presently resides.*

Having searched the entire abode, various items of interest were found which were exclusively attributable to the Cumberpot woman. Sir Arthur Cumberpot does not feature in this report, because it is clear that due to his infrequent visits to the Watlington property and the little time he spent there, his presence is hardly discernable, and his private bedroom is the only place where his few effects can be found; likewise his son James. Therefore, we concentrated our efforts on the ground floor area where the deceased spent much of her time.

Having removed the body to the freezer, it then became incumbent upon the cleaners to mop up any evidence of foul play in the kitchen, which they have achieved with remarkable success. It is my view that very little evidence of a murder remains, meaning that the whereabouts of Lady Cumberpot will continue to be a mystery for some time to come, and the local Police will consequently be totally baffled if or when the body is finally discovered.

As to any evidence pertaining to the Cumberpot woman's intentions before her untimely death, it is evident that she was intending to disappear from the scene—not in the way that actually transpired—but due to a somewhat detailed account which I found of her present financial position, it is obvious that she had considerable resources available to her for such an event to take place.

Fortunately for us, her plans were cut short by her untimely death at the hands of a professional assassin, and we will all be spared the spectacle of a humiliating and public trial. Having made photocopies of all the potential incriminating documents, the search team handed over the premises to our experienced cleaning operatives, and the door is now closed on the whole issue. It is anticipated that nothing remains in the house pertaining to our involvement, and that it is now a totally sterile environment.

Finally, I called Doris today—she is the late Lady Cumberpot's occasional domestic help— and informed her that there was a large black cat meowing at the front door of Orchard Manor, which looked half starved. She said that she would go round later this week to see what the problem was because apparently she still retains a key to the property and can let herself into the house.

Inspector Peter Squinty—Retired.

VAUXHALL CROSS LONDON

Sir Hilton Cotteslow decided to keep the information concerning Lady Cumberpot's demise exclusively within the intelligence community, leaving Sir Arthur to be made aware of her death only when her body was finally discovered. There was no telling how long this would take, because even if Doris had access to the house, there were no guarantees that she would delve into the freezer! Sir Hilton could leave all such speculation to chance, and watch with interest for any details which might appear in the newspapers.

Meanwhile it was suggested to Foreign Secretary Sid Hay that an acting British Ambassador should be sent to Sofia to take the reins, and to exclusively devote their time to damage control. It was suggested that Sir Arthur should be officially informed of his temporary suspension on full pay, whilst matters were formally put to rest. No mention was to be made of any secret activities or discoveries and it was intended that Sir Arthur should remain firmly and totally in the dark whilst these investigations continued.

'I thought it turned out rather well Sir.' Max

Kintbury had not blotted his copybook after all. 'I must say that man Squinty is a very good organizer; it's a pity about the twitch!'

'He has been with us a long time; must be due for retirement soon, and I assure you that it will be a great loss to the service when he goes.'

'I thought that these old Cold War veterans went on forever, and that age didn't matter anymore?'

'It doesn't much, but that is because most of them are illegals and are paid offshore. It unfortunately means they can't enjoy our famous inflation-free Civil Service pension as such, and are stuck with the rotten UK old age pension which is rubbish unless they pay into it themselves to top it up.'

'How are we going to play this one Sir? The evidence we have received from Inspector Squinty is very circumstantial, isn't it?' Max wondered out loud. Gazing at the matchstick men, he clutched his internal telephone firmly to his right ear. 'I mean, someone will have to lean on plod if I am not mistaken. They cannot be allowed to cause a stink, and we definitely do not want a public autopsy either. I suppose there must be a tame Coroner around somewhere? Surely we don't want a repeat of the Dr Kilroy affair!'

It seemed to be a scenario mainly about covering their tracks, and thoroughly distancing themselves from what might be construed by some as an extrajudicial killing, and a death which was not their responsibility in the first place.

Wriggle opportunities were looming on the horizon everywhere, but without the continuity of knowing when and where events would occur, it was a very abstract puzzle which was far too fluid for Commander Kintbury to comprehend, or for Sir Hilton to manipulate.

WATLINGTON

Doris let herself into the side door using her duplicate key, and wondered why it was not double locked. Looking around the kitchen it occurred to her that Lady Cumberpot might have decided to employ another domestic help without telling her. The place was spotless, as was the dining room and the commodious sitting room too. She had never seen anything like it before during all her years with the Cumberpot family with their haphazard domestic routines and wholly impractical nature.

She called out, 'Lady Cumberpot! Are you at home? I saw the Range Rover outside. Hello, are you there, Madam?'

Doris ran up the stairs and knocked on Annabel Cumberpot's bedroom door, and once again shouted, 'Hello, are you there Madam?' But no one answered.

Doris could not imagine why the house was so perfect, and she went from room to room only to see further evidence of spotless order. The bathrooms seemed totally unused and by the time she returned to the kitchen area her mind was spinning with all sorts of theories. Then she heard the scratching on the terrace door. Carefully opening it, she saw the tiny black figure of Tommy the cat which freaked her out as he bolted through the door and made for a clean but quite empty food dish by the Aga cooker.

Doris felt the cooker which seemed quite warm. It had a heavy frying pan left to one side. Turning round, she was surprised to see an unopened tin of Heinz baked beans and a new packet of dehydrated potato flakes. They were placed on the highly polished surface of the large rectory kitchen table which occupied the centre of the room. She had never seen such a shine before, and in common with the rest of the house, it all seemed unbelievably bizarre to her as if she was in someone else's home altogether.

Opening the cupboard under the sink, she found Tommy's Pedigree cat food, and put some in his dish. Taking a bowl from the sideboard, she filled it with water and placed it next to the cat food which was being rapidly consumed. Walking into the sitting room, she casually looked at the answer phone, but there were no messages on it. Picking up the receiver she dialled a short number and waited for an answer.

When she eventually got through she said quite calmly, 'Is that the Police? I would like to report a missing person.'

Ten minutes later there was a knock at the front door, and standing there was the roly-poly figure of the local police constable. With a friendly grin on his face he asked, 'Are you Doris? I believe you rang. How can we help you?'

After making a statement to the Police, Doris asked to be excused and leaving the side door key with the local Constable, who had now been joined by a young WPC, she caught the next bus back to Lewknor swearing never to enter the house in Watlington ever again.

Three days later WPC Milligan, on finding the little chrome key to the freezer chest in the desk drawer, made the horrifying discovery of the corpse of Lady Annabel Cumberpot.

Draped in Cumberland pork sausages and as stiff as a Raspberry Whopper, it was the beginning of a major local police enquiry that would never be forgotten, thereby putting Watlington on the map forever.

THE BRITISH EMBASSY, SOFIA

Dirty Macintosh was unhappy with the outcome, because he felt somehow that Sir Arthur had been unfairly treated. He was not directly responsible for his wife's behaviour, a woman quite rightly regarded by the FO as a loose cannon. Had he known, it was why Sir Arthur had been posted to Bulgaria in the first place. In their wisdom they had not only seen his wife Annabel as a threat, but as a punishment as well.

Dirty Macintosh also realized that time was running

out for him too, and he sensibly chose to quit while he was ahead. He expressed his reason for leaving with considerable passion, by revealing a spiritual side to his nature which had hitherto remained an anathema to people in his line of work.

He made it clear that he was enrolling himself into a theological collage, after which he would be seeking a future position as an Anglican Pastor. He had been accepted by his old Alma Mata and would be attending Wycliffe Hall, Oxford, the following year. John Mitchell, the new Embassy Charge de Affair, seemed sorry to see him go.

'I know that there has been some turmoil of late at the embassy but in my opinion Macintosh, you handled yourself very well under the circumstances. It isn't every day that an ambassador's wife is accused of espionage.'

Dirty had held the embassy fort for over two months, and that was enough for him. He now dreamed of a future where he was no longer expected to attend any more dreary diplomatic receptions. He was sick and tired of the many asinine diplomats, their devotees and hangers on, the turgid conversations, and finally the egg mayonnaise sandwiches. Whoever thought that being a diplomat was a glamorous occupation needed their head examined. Janis his wife, who was also the embassy doctor, was equally fed up.

'Let's bugger off Ned; I'm sick of these wallies. I really cannot imagine what good they really do in this world. I want to be a proper doctor, darling. I am sick of treating the expat Brits. If they haven't got the clap or cirrhosis of the liver, they are bonking their secretaries and dumping their wives. I have to deal with all that Ned, and then, having looked up their bottoms a few times, I am supposed to shake hands with them at a drinks party. Why can't I have some normal patients for a change?'

'I have resigned Jan as we agreed, and now all I have to do is to tidy up the Herodotus project, make sure my replacement knows how to operate all the bells and whistles, and then its Oxford here we come!'

It sounded so simple when put like that, but even while he said it there was a huge question mark gradually appearing over the next few months. Ron Beamish, ever anxious to indulge in embassy gossip, had heard rumours about Sir Arthur.

'I hear he has got the chop, Dirty! Is it something to do with the ghastly Annabel?' His pixie face was full of glee. 'I know she wasn't here much, but *not at all* sounds considerably better!'

Dirty Macintosh was counting the days before he left. 'What is happening with Herodotus Ron, he seems to be very active?' It recently appeared that the Herodotus Project was actually working very well. 'Is there any more news from Mr Filipov? I would particularly like to monitor his communications; he is after all an important source of information.'

Looking down his list of written messages, Ron swiftly scrolled down the screen until he got to a confusing collection of symbols, dots and slashes. Decrypting the message before Dirty's eyes, the message soon appeared on the screen.

'No longer in our President's Cabinet. Phone to be returned.'

And so this part of the conspiracy died and was buried in diplomatic myth. The following day a Benefon NMT mobile phone set was delivered to the embassy by courier. In the box was a small handwritten message addressed to Ned Macintosh.

It said, *'Kind regards to you and Herodotus. Via Veritas Vita. P. F.'*

EPILOGUE

2000 LEWKNOR

WHEN THE OXFORD CORONER released the body of Annabel, a funeral was arranged at St Margaret's, the parish church in Lewknor. The Rev Nicholson recommended that it should be kept very low key and strictly for the immediate family.

It was on a rather depressing grey afternoon that she was buried, the grave marked only by a little wooden cross. This meant that it would be some time before a stone would be erected giving details of the deceased's identity.

Sir Arthur and his son James were there, as were Lionel Pergamon and John Kilbey. Norris and Myrtle Cumberpot stayed at home, and waited to welcome their grandson back to Ashford Hill when the funeral was over. There were two other mourners; one was Chief Inspector Michael Lambert from Thames Valley Serious Crime Division, and the other was a rather forlorn looking man in a shabby mackintosh with a noticeable twitch.

None of the Dent family was present, nor was there any sign of Robin Caruthers. After the church service, it seemed that everyone could not wait to leave, and little was said as the mourners swiftly drifted away after the final words were spoken and the coffin covered with the good brown earth of Oxfordshire.

Edwina had asked Arthur if he wanted her to be with him, but he had declined, wishing to put the past behind him with as little publicity and speculation as possible. He did not want her to be dragged into the whole sordid episode, which was something he gladly faced on his own.

As it was, he had to deal with the more practical aspects of his wife's death, which meant selling the house and its contents, winding up their mutual affairs and dealing with the matter of probate. It appeared that his wife did not leave a Will, and so all aspects of her estate would automatically revert to both him and of course James.

'Listen old boy,' Arthur said to his son James, 'I know that this has all been a great shock to you, as it has been for us all, but I want you to know that when this is finally over I would like you to come and stay with Edwina and me in Greece, and for as long as you want.'

'What are you going to do, Dad?'

It was obvious that his career in the diplomatic service was at an end, and it was hard to imagine what he could do, age fifty, especially under the circumstances of his departure.

'Well, they have been very good to me, and they have

retired me early on a full pension. They have also offered me the post of Honorary British Counsel in Alexandropoulis. Edwina has resigned her job, and she will help me there.'

Sir Arthur had always believed that his was a lifelong career at the FO, but now it was all over, he was forced to view his future with an element of insecurity.

'Edwina tells me that she is going to teach English as a second language, so she is presently busy studying for her Cambridge English Proficiency exam. I think we will be OK James, and I have got enough savings to get you through your Leeds degree course, so you will be fine too.'

Mr Griffith took over the sale of Orchard Manor House for the second time, and arranged for the furniture and effects to be sold off at a specialist auction in Lewknor Village Hall. Mr Thwaits of Jones, Jones and Thwaits, had recently retired and so Mr Nigel Jones the Senior Partner took over the reins, and dealt with the settlement of the estate. Arthur kept his fairly new Range Rover, and later that month he drove it back to Greece, packed up with all his mementos and personal possessions, together with a silver framed photograph of Henley Regatta.

This only left the murder case, detective Michael Lambert and the curios figure of Inspector Peter Squinty—Retired. When the firestorm caused by Annabel Cumberpot's untimely death had finally blown over, it was left up to Squinty to put all the toys back in their boxes, and to put the boxes back in the cupboard.

The Police had been baffled from the start, but due to the prominence of Lady Cumberpot, a great many hours of valuable police time was spent interviewing anyone she had known during her life. Very little was said by anyone, especially by Sir Arthur and Lionel Pergamon, and anyone else who had been involved with her in any way had very little to offer the police except watertight alibis.

Inspector Squinty had made double sure that all the boxes remained shut. He had even gone as far as to interview Chief Inspector Lambert himself—on behalf of the Police Gazette—but this time actually using his own name. It was clear that they did not have a single suspect or any evidence which could possibly be used to convict anyone, even at some later date. The Crown Prosecution Service advised the police to stand down, and the Coroner declared an Open Verdict on the death of Lady Annabel Cumberpot.

For his troubles Inspector Peter Squinty—Retired, was given a sizable quantity of cash, which was transferred anonymously to his Panama bank account. It was enough for him to finally retire, and so he and his wife sold their maisonette in the Goldhawk Road in Shepherds Bush, and promptly moved to Spain.

Dirty Macintosh occasionally visits Sofia, but these days he does so wearing a dog collar. The Reverent Ned Macintosh, whose official parish is actually in Bucharest, visits once a month to celebrate Holy

Communion in the bar of the British Embassy, amongst the cans of Newcastle Brown Ale, pickled eggs and packets of pork scratchings. When the service is over, they usually open the bar; British diplomacy finally resumes, and continues to be a light in the world as it always has!

Annabel was guilty of nothing other than being the biological daughter of Jim Kilbey, Britain's most notorious spy. It seems that a jealous God had sought to visit the sins of the father upon her, but so had everyone else. She was the victim of Serendipity, but also of cover-ups and the apocryphal manipulation of very thin evidence, and finally exaggeration.

But she was also heartless, treacherous, self-indulgent and without shame. This was also the character of her true father who was clearly and undeniably a psychopath.